Burn Baby Burn

A Superior Arson Mystery

by Mike Savage

First Edition

Printed in 1999

© Copyright 1999 Michael P. Savage

Cover Illustration ©1999 Diane Matlack

All rights reserved, including the right to reproduce this book or portions thereof, in any form, except for brief quotations embodied in articles and reviews, without written permission from the publisher. The opinions, observations and historical references herein are those of the author alone.

This story is fiction. Places, names, characters, organizations or incidents are products of the author's imagination or are used fictitiously. Any reference or resemblance to "real" people, places, organizations, living or dead, is used merely as artistic license to facilitate the fictional tale.

ISBN 1-886028-39-7

Library of Congress Catalog Card Number: 99-093690

Published by:
Savage Press
P.O. Box 115, Superior, WI 54880
715-394-9513

e-mail: savpress@spacestar.com

Visit us at: www.savpress.com

Printed in the USA

Burn Baby Burn

Other Books by Mike Savage

Dave Davecki Mysteries

Something in the Water
A Superior Murder Mystery

Death by Corvette

Death by Harley Davidson

Death by Poetic License

Death on the Deggerman Road

Mainstream

Totem

Summertime for Russell

The Healing of Peter T. McDonough

Raised by Savages

Short Story Collections

Growing up Wild in Wisconsin

Random Acts of Kindness in Superior-Duluth

Poetry Books

Mystic Bread

Like Horses Dancing

Boobies and Other Prizes

Short Story Books

The Lost Locomotive of the Battle-Axe

Secrets of the Squaw Bay Caves

How to Piss Off an Alien

Acknowledgments

It takes a village to write a book, at least if you're Mike Savage. Thank you Superior for having the charm and good grace to enable these "superior" stories.

Special thanks to Tish Stewart, Judi James, Herb Bergson, Andrea Losiewski, Hazel Sangster, Charlotte Klesman and Jessica Orloski.

Thanks to too: Teddie, Georgie, Mary, Bethie, Elsie, Phoebe, Sadie, Jodi, Molly, Gina and Alpena. Thanks to <u>The Don</u>, Bob, Rod, Bill, Kevin, Tim, Tom, Amorin, Pat and Jehosephat.

Hollis & Dave, thanks for digging deeper on those pesky songs and lyrics.

Thanks too to the anonymous Watts rioter who imprinted the phrase, "Burn baby burn," into America's psyche when his neighborhood was going up in flames.

— Mike

Author's Note

The underlining you will encounter is just for fun.

Dedication

To Patricia Marie Stewart

Burn Baby Burn

Love is a burning thing

and it makes a firey ring.

Bound by wild desire

I fell into a ring of fire

— **Ring of Fire,**
 by Merle Kilgore & June Carter
 Sung by Johnny Cash

Mike Savage

1

All spirits are enslaved which serve things evil.

— Shelley, Prometheus Unbound

Burn Baby Burn

It was an ideal night. The sky was black. No clouds. No moon. No stars. He wondered about that. Back home, during his youth in the country, there were always stars in a cloudless sky. Millions of stars. In this bleak city, this Superior, Wisconsin —a place he'd come to think of as a cesspool, a city of rust and despair— the sky he remembered was denied him. This night, a hard shell, a canopy of impenetrable evil closed him off, isolated him completely from heaven. On nights when the stars shone, the city's buildings were safe. But, on a night like tonight —an ideal night— the city's buildings were ripe for conflagration and mayhem. Something was going to burn. There HAD to be an offering on this night when the stars were denied him.

But first there was other business. The God of Fire was as devoted to order as his Servant. The flames needed their ritual, or the offering would be impure. He didn't know her, didn't want to. But he did know what his dream said. She would be under thirty-years-old. She would be dark haired. She would be singing karoake at Frankie's Bar. And, he knew with a certainty that transcended human reality, she would be intrigued. All his victims were. They smelled the acrid perfume of hellfire in his pheromones. They all resonated to his lust for the inferno. Every one of them —it was thirteen now— were aroused by their deep identification with his smoke infused soul. He knew number fourteen's nipples would harden instantly when he approached her, closed in on her. Got close enough for her to smell his fiery heart. The dream had told him everything. She would be singing *Crazy* by Patsy Cline. They would make eye contact. He would stand too close for comfort and the discomfort would inflame her.

Mike Savage

He locked the door to the apartment and dropped the key into the mailbox nailed crookedly to the door frame. He had no wallet, no keys, no ID of any kind. If caught, he would not exist. In the unlikely event that he would be caught, there wouldn't be a soul on the planet who could identify him. He rehearsed the plan while descending the creaking wooden stairway. If caught, go catatonic, dream of his blazing life to come, dream of his life in Hell and let the fucking cops try to figure out just who in the hell he was, where he was from, WHAT he was.

The walk to Frankie's Bar was only seven and a half minutes. He was attracted to the joint because the owner had made the papers for beating up some poor sap who broke a fixture one night. *The only bad publicity is NO publicity*, he thought, recalling his <u>Weatherman</u> father's advice for a long career in television. The walk was a seven and a half minute stroll amongst the tenth oldest stock of buildings of any city in the nation. His footsteps were virtually silent. He practiced his gliding. It wasn't the pimp roll of the big city, it was the stealthy approach of the black jaguar, the coming of hellfire.

Through a block sized park...he swept. The park used to have giant elms and maples growing in it. Then a big wind blew them down and made it more a field. A stray German Shepherd trotted across the wide expanse of lawn at an oblique angle. Suddenly the dog stopped on stiff legs. It raised its nose and prodded the air like a doctor probing an abdomen for signs of soreness. He glided along silently, all the while watching the dog without breaking off the cold stare. He saw the hair on the dog's back raise. A low growl seemed to come out of the very air in the park. The menacing growl seemed to be completely disas-

Burn Baby Burn

sociated from the mangy Alsatian. He glided through the reverberating sound and smiled, satisfied with his effect on the canine, convinced the extrasensory perception of the four-footed race knew the importance of the man it had encountered. *They always know*, he thought as he exited the north end of the park. Their noses told them clearly what human olfactory abilities only hinted at. He was the future God of Fire serving his apprenticeship in the most unsuspecting town on the planet.

Rounding the corner by the New Jersey Block, he eyed the massive building. He knew it was built in 1889 for fifty thousand dollars and had housed a drug store on the corner since 1897. Eyeing the graceful arches atop the oversized windows of the 102-year-old building, he felt tingling between his legs at the vision of large vigorous tongues of flame licking the night sky from those splendid curves. Maybe, maybe it would be the next to go...

But first... he looked ahead and to his left. His lustful gaze swept along Tower Avenue. The Old Post Office. Maybe someday. The Tower Building! He licked his thin lips. A ghoulish smile spread beneath his long nose. The skin at the corner of his eyes compressed into deep lines, the result of working outdoors for most of his life. He slowed his steps. He didn't want to even HINT at the appearance of being rushed, unsettled. He had to present a perfect patina of serenity. He had to exude ungodly amounts of normalcy to disguise the insidious leakages of evil that always found ways to seep from the souls of the hideously insane.

He shortened his stride by fourteen centimeters, this he did in deference to **Her Highness, Victim Number Fourteen**. He imagined such accuracy possible because

Mike Savage

of his inordinant sense of personal perfection and his obsession with measurement, calculating, planning. He ogled the Tower Building like it was a beauty queen in a bikini. His skin tingled in the fresh July air swooping up Tower from Lake Superior. He turned on the TV screen in his head. He rolled the video tape in his brain's VCR and saw the dark haired **Goddess Elect** taped to her throne in the basement. He saw the tiny Sony camera. It was broadcasting to the remote tape deck in the parked van on Banks Avenue. He saw her thrashing in the green cushioned chair he'd made ready for her by removing the padding. He saw her wide, wild eyes darting. The smoke's density increased. The flicker of yellow flames intensified as the acetylide accelerant spread glorious fire everywhere throughout the large room —except around her throne. He knew her fear, her hatred, her sadness at the tragedy of expected lust turned into human sacrifice. He could read it on her face as she inhaled her last breaths of toxic fumes and slumped into unconsciousness as the smoke obscured the lens. He pondered why she didn't scream. The others had. Her inner strength irritated him. Her defiance aggravated him.

His reverie was broken when he stepped off the curb and looked up to see the old Superior Water, Light and Power building. *God what a town!* he thought. It was an arsonist's wet dream! He shook his head and realized why she didn't scream. He'd been daydreaming. It wasn't real. *YET.*

He shook his head and chastised himself. Such sloppiness couldn't be tolerated. He slapped himself hard across his high cheekbone with his left hand. He was getting too far into the joy of his work. He'd walked right

Burn Baby Burn

past Frankie's. He turned around and promised to impose a greater level of detachment regarding future sacramental rights.

    He pulled the front door of the bar open and let go of his frustration. So what if she didn't scream. What mattered was that, after tonight, he'd be the unrivaled King of Fire on this earth. Even Match Crandal would be humble before him. His nostrils flared upon sniffing the aroma of bar. His black pupils widened. "The better to see you with little girl," he heard his fire-self say. At the ends of his lanky arms, fists formed. The sadistic ritual had begun.

Mike Savage

2

For the third time this year, fire has claimed a major building along an eight-block section of Tower Avenue, searing another gap into Superior's downtown.

"The fire is being investigated as though it were arson," said Superior Police Capt. Richard Pukema.

—Duluth News Tribune
Tuesday, July 28, 1998

Sometimes a man and woman together generate nothing but sparks, sometimes they produce only a warm glow, sometimes —if they work at it— they can generate a loving fire of great intensity.

—Rev. John Gemmill, 1889
Sermon at Lanark, Ontario

Burn Baby Burn

Alphonse "Dave" Davecki stuck a long greasy french fry into his mouth. Unfortunately it wasn't one of Ruthie's from the Anchor Bar. It was a wretched substitute from Hardee's. Davecki was a cop. A Superior Cop. "Detective Dave," some people called him. Right now though, he was just another arson investigator. He was standing on the corner of North Sixteenth and Tower Avenue watching smoke billow from the smouldering remains of the old Roth's Department Store building. Fire fighters dashed about tending their hoses. About two hundred citizens, feasting on the excitement of yet another major blaze in town, crowded the police barriers set up <u>All Around the Watchtower</u>. Davecki chewed and talked at the same time, "I wonder if arson is like murder," he said. His head was tilted back. His deep-set eyes followed the twisting yellow tails of sparks billowing upward.

"What in God's name are you babbling about now?" Andrea "Bubba" Carlstrom asked. A look of puzzlement crossed her oval face. She shook her head. Silky strands of long brown hair tossed forth and back, framing her visage. Of course it was a beautiful face. How could it not be? Carlstrom was five nine, weighed one-thirty-five, wore taupe slacks that matched her running shoes which matched her Land's End jacket. Bubba Carlstrom was so obviously NOT from Superior, that she HAD to have a face that could compete on any super model runway in New York, Paris or London. It was like a law. The law of beautiful faces. If you had one, it got things done for the owner in ways that plain faces couldn't compete with. The face was one reason Carlstrom had managed to become a State Fire Marshal. Of course the face didn't help

Mike Savage

her drag a two hundred pound man thirty yards at a dead run. The face didn't help her put seventeen shots from her pre-ban Baretta inside a three inch circle at twenty yards. At ten yards she was able to knock opponents flat in the fire hose competition. <u>At</u> <u>Close</u> <u>Range</u> she was able to kick the balls and twist the arm of any man at both the Fire Academy and during the ten week Cadet Training in Eau Claire. All that prowess made her a great cop sure, but it was her unwavering devotion to examining evidence that provided the fuel for her rocket ship ride to the top. Carlstrom was the best arson investigator in the state. She had solved hundreds of feeble cases, gotten convictions where there should be none.

However, The Law of Beautiful Faces hadn't "saved" her from being sent to the fairest city in Wisconsin to unravel the mysteries of the numerous fires that had plagued the Jewel Community of the North. She emphatically announced to her new temporary partner, Dave Davecki, that she considered her indefinite assignment a misfortune in the extreme.

That was how the unlikely duo happened to be standing next to one another near the Old Post Office Building in downtown Superior. Never in a million years would they have chosen to socialize. He was Rob Becker's cave man. She was the quintessential feminine warrior. But work has a way of making odd couples and Fred Couples and...

Anyway, as if to confirm the Law of Beautiful Faces, from behind the police barrier, a young male fire spectator hooted at Carlstrom and cat-called, "Sup gorgeous?"

"What's up is your denial level if you think you can even TALK to me loser."

Burn Baby Burn

"I see you're one of those sensitive, nineties-type women," Davecki said.

"You don't see squat Davecki. Now what's this bullshit about arson and murders being alike?"

"You know, Chief Callahan probably THOUGHT he was doing me a favor by putting me on this arson thing. But, after a week of working with you it's clearly a case of..."

"Watch it asshole," Carlstrom seethed.

Davecki sighed. He was sighing more and more as he closed in on his fifth decade. "What I mean, oh profane one, is that, in my experience, strength and hope, murder itself, the act... I mean the actual separate thing. The entity that is murder itself, separate from the person killed, separate from the person doing the killing, separate from all the relatives and friends...MURDER...as a purely abstract concept, requires —no, *demands*— to be solved." He paused for a second and added, "And I was wondering if you'd discovered arson to be the same way."

Carlstrom stared in bewilderment at Davecki. Her mouth opened and words came out. "You hear why Mickey divorced Minnie?"

Looking puzzled himself, Davecki answered, "No."

"Because she was fucking Goofy. Which is exactly what you are," she pronounced.

He shrugged the insult off and rubbed his chin. The persistent stubble that only hinted at his razor anathema scrubbed the soft undersides of his long fingers. He marveled at the brave men and women in heavy coats and funny hats as they rushed around trying to control the massive blaze that roared skyward.

The fire shrieked like an F-16 taking off. In contrast

Mike Savage

to the monstrous tongue of flame that flicked heavenward from the center of the structure, more diminutive flames lashed out of the second story windows. They were shy little accents that balanced the roaring fiend that had "fully involved" the building and claimed fourteen businesses plus the police gym.

Bubba tore her gaze away from the hypnotic conflagration across the street and eyed her temporary partner like he was a bloody five car 10-52 on the Bong Bridge. "They told me you were some kind of mind-tripper," she said and snorted derisively. "If you're right, then why are there so many unsolved murders?" Her voice was Marlboro husky.

Davecki had not lowered his skyward stare. "The stars seem awfully far away tonight," he said dropping his gaze to look into the stars that were Bubba's eyes. "To answer your question. It's because we whose job it is to solve murders don't listen well or closely."

Bubba looked back to the inferno across from them. "Why aren't you bitching about all THIS second hand smoke Davecki?"

"Because it reminds me of a bonfire at Lakeside Beach where we used to roast wienies and torch marshmallows. And because this particular smoke, while unpleasant, hasn't been purposely infused with an overdose of brainstem stimulating toxic chemicals that have been certified to cause mega-cancers in laboratory bison."

Carlstrom snorted.

Davecki grinned. "Good one eh?"

"You're so lame its embarrassing," Bubba said.

The two of them, along with the spectators, stood transfixed by the fluttering flames that lashed at the Ad-

Burn Baby Burn

vanced Data Comm windows. Those windows had either been smashed in by competent firemen or simply gave up fighting the heat and crashed downward in a shattering shower of resignation.

Davecki re-grasped his chin briefly and said, "What I'm getting at is... This is fire number fourteen. It seems to me that we're missing the big picture here, missing the big clue. It's like I can hear some distant music playing, but can't hear the lyrics. Can't understand the words to the song that would explain all the fires at once."

"You getting low on Zantac?"

Davecki snorted this time. "It's Zoloft. And no, I'm all stoked up right now, which is why I'm free associating. It's a side effect, along with decreased libido and increased suicidal ideation."

Bubba Carlstrom scanned the crowd looking for someone who might be smiling or looking pleased.

Davecki sniffed. He looked like a polar bear trying to scent the Churchill, Manitoba dump. He flared his nostrils and tested the vagrant whisps of wind. "He's here. He's watching. I know." The sounds ground out from between his teeth like the Mr. Eat Everything man from France who ate bicycles and glass on European TV.

Carlstrom abandoned her surveillance and glanced at Davecki. She asked, "You sound pissed. And why, might I ask, do you think it is a he and that HE is here?" She returned to scanning the scum gathered for the fireworks display.

"Feminine intuition?" Dave quipped.

"Cute," she snorted.

Davecki scanned the crowd too. He knew, from reading the arson manual, that it was a common practice for

21

Mike Savage

firebugs to stick around and admire their work. He hoped the clandestine video camera currently taping the scene would confirm any suspicious looking characters, if they spotted any. The crowd seemed to reveal nothing. But, still, Davecki sniffed again. If he'd been the owner of a cold, wet nose his floppy ears would have stood erect in anticipation.

"What is WITH you?" Carlstrom asked.

"The bastard's here," Davecki snorted. "I can smell the no-good, dirty, rotten, fire-bug-bastard."

Burn Baby Burn

3

"Hayward, Hurley and Hell"

Back in the 1920s and 30s, Superior was a raucous burgeoning town of unbridled decadence. The Police Chief was written up in the Milwaukee Sentinel as "The Richest Police Chief in the Country." Being a hotbed of bootlegging, drinking, fighting, gambling, prostitution and other degrading corruptions, the seaport town, with it's whores and cheap whiskey took to it's nickname like a sailor to syphilis. How fitting that, in a few short decades, "Hell" would add to its reputation by becoming the arson capitol of the nation.

Burn Baby Burn

Davecki snapped the seat belt of the Caprice unmarked into place and reefed on the shift lever, slamming the car into drive. Since getting a new partner and a "promotion" to the Arson Investigation Department, Chief Callahan also insisted he quit driving his Mustang for work.

In the passenger seat, Carlstrom fished a Marlboro Light from her pack, lit up and blew the smoke towards the slightly open window. The effort to direct the pure tobacco pleasure outside was the only concession she'd made when Davecki asked her not to smoke in the car. "You're really full of shit," she said.

"Thanks," Davecki said and pointed the pregnant whale of a vehicle down Tower Avenue. They were headed toward the North End. In the old days sailors from around the world got off grain ships to vent their claustrophobic compulsions on a cynical Superior populace willing to do anything to make money. This was the infamous red light district where stoic Swedes, numbed Norwegians and frisky Finns held captive too long in the logging camps flocked with their spring pay to raise holy hell with the abundance of hustlers and "window tappers" intent on economic gain.

This section of the city used to be the HELL component of the infamous, Hayward, Hurley and Hell trio of Northern Wisconsin towns that were so wicked, the storied Wild West was tame by comparison.

Davecki was as silent as a tribal chairman at an anti-casino meeting. He was sulking. He absently thumped the steering wheel with the heel of his hand. On the left, the rubble of the old Great Northern Building glided past. Torched on May 16th, 1998 at 6:00 p.m., the City had

Mike Savage

managed to erect a fence around the <u>Remains</u> <u>of</u> <u>the</u> <u>Day</u> building, but the twisted steel beams, rusted thrusts of convoluted stand-pipes and mounds of broken bricks jutted jaggedly toward the sky. Right in the middle of the building was the biggest mound of all, the old GN Railroad Vault, used for storing shipments of money, gold and the cash used for payroll.

"There's more to this case than evidence," Davecki defended.

Carlstrom looked at him, her face laconic, perhaps even bordering on catatonic.

Davecki eyeballed her. Hopeful.

Silence.

The car rolled past the Amsoil Building. Originally known as the Berkshire Block, the handcrafted building was erected in 1892. Built by itinerant Scandinavian craftsmen using Kasota limestone, the fastidious old edifice once had three tall towers overlooking the city that made it look like a castle. Even without the towers, even a casual glance at the building —with its seven and nine arches— revealed instantly the thoughtful consideration and architectural training that went into its design.

The car rolled on. It's gray bumper nosed into the intersection at North Eighth, the site of another unsolved arson. "I heard they're calling this *Arson Avenue*," Davecki said.

Carlstrom took a long drag. She exhaled slowly. She didn't direct the smoke out the window. "Would you shut the fuck up? I'm trying to think."

"Well excuse me all to hell."

Silence.

The buildings rolled past. The Cove, or, as it was more

Burn Baby Burn

commonly known, The Pick Up a Slut Spot, —any and all sexual orientations— went past on the left. On the right was The Gentleman's Club where money hungry hooker wannabes got their start in the business of sex for sale. The sleazy Lamplighter with its C-section strippers was across the street. Across the avenue, cousin to Watergate and distant relative of Jeff Bridges in <u>Starman</u>, was Stargate, the loudest pickup joint in the Twin Ports. Across the parking lot on the same side of Tower, was one of the more beautiful but decrepit structures in town, the old Tyomes Building. The two distinctive oval windows at each corner gave the building a stately look.

All slid past in the semidarkness of street light illuminated gloom. Davecki thought about Officer Kurt Nelson's assertion that, "The only good police work is done <u>After</u> <u>Midnight</u>." *He's probably right*, Davecki thought. *We're sure not making much progress dorking around this way.*

Davecki steered the Caprice into a parking spot next to the Wisconsin Grain Commission offices. He threw the car into park and looked at his partner. She stared straight ahead. Beyond her right shoulder was the corner office of the State Grain Inspector. It's occupant was once the best high school basketball player in the state. Davecki wanted to tell his new partner about the guy, about the big plays and the magic that the guy could do with a basketball. He wanted to be friendly, build rapport. But this chick was all ice and professionalism.

"What?" Carlstrom said too loudly.

"Huh?"

"You're staring."

"Oh. No... I mean..." Davecki turned away, looked at

Mike Savage

the huge cast iron anchor embedded in the grass across the street. Next to the five ton marine artifact was the best bar in seven states.

"Listen Numbnuts. You're being obsequious. Get a life will ya?"

Davecki looked at Carlstrom. "What in the hell are you talking about? What's obsequious?"

"Quit trying to be so buddy-buddy. Don't try to suck up. I'm here to solve these cases and save the city from some pyro-nut, not befriend some hangdog Mulder wannabe."

Davecki looked straight ahead. At the end of Tower, Farmer's Elevator loomed two hundred and some feet straight into the night sky. *At least it used to be Farmer's. Now it's Grain Thieves of America or Harvest States or, whatever the hell... Nothing stays the same.* Recalling the massive grain elevator fire on Duluth's "elevator row" from ten years back, Davecki thought, *Now that would be the Mother of all Fires if Farmer's went up in flames.* Clenching the wheel with both hands he said, "Alright. You want it straight? Here goes. You're better looking than Scully and I'm definitely no Mulder wannabe. I'm just saying that there's more to these fires than simple arson."

"Why's that?" Carlstrom asked. She sagged in her seat a bit. Relaxed her shoulders some.

"If I could answer that, you could go zooming back home to your precious Mad Town. All I can tell you is, this case is too big, too complicated, too out-there to be solved using the purely logical. Using physical evidence only."

"Okay, I'll grant it's big. I'll grant you that it's com-

Burn Baby Burn

plicated and confusing. But, pretending you can smell an arsonist is just going to make it more frustrating."

Silence.

"He was there."

A brown Chevy Celebrity with the vanity plate BURT whizzed past. The Caprice rocked from the pressure wave.

"You could *smell* him?"

Davecki sighed. "I got a James Garner nose."

Silence from the passenger. She drew in the final flows of fantastic filtered fumes and flipped her butt out the window. She shifted around. Got comfortable. "Okay. I'm ready."

"Ready for what?" Davecki said. He didn't look at her, but gripped the wheel steadfastly and glowered at the Farmer's.

"For you to bore me to tears with some cockamamie story," she said raising her hands like a pro wrestler saying, "Come and get me. Come on."

Davecki tore his gaze from what used to be the largest grain handling facility in the world. He sighed. "Okay. You know James Garner?"

She blinked. "Rockford?"

"Yeah. James Garner. From the Rockford Files." He pulled on the steering wheel like a thousand foot ore boat straining on the capstan in a 25-knot offshore wind.

She clapped her hands together lightly. "Jim Rockford. James Garner. Same guy."

"Yeah," Davecki said looking at the Grain Commish's office. He recalled a shot the Commish made in a game against the Mellen Granite Diggers. Could still see the guy bringing the ball up court, getting challenged by the Granite Digger...kid named Boetcher. The Commish was

Mike Savage

hot. They called him *Heater* back then because he had both a hot temper and a hot shot. Boetcher was good, stopped Heater. But Heater just gave the defender an insolent, "ah hell," shrug of his shoulders as if to say, "May as well put it in from here," and he flipped the ball up from the half-court line with a flick of the wrist. Long arch. BANG! Middle of the metal back board. Sounded like some god-awful gong in a Hindu temple. Then nothing but net. The coach, "Measures" Flamang, called time-out. Cool the kid off. Cool the *Heater* down. Davecki wanted to tell Carlstrom the story, wanted to stay connected to the old days.

He shook his head, knew his propensity for distraction. "Anyway," he went on, "James Garner was in Korea."

"A Jarhead?" Carlstrom asked.

"Who knows? Infantry I suppose," Davecki sighed. "Quit interrupting." He focused on her oval face. *Did she pluck those eyebrows?* He released his grip on the steering wheel. Realized his forearms ached from the death grip he'd had on it. "Anyway...Rockford and his squad got pinned down by some Koreans."

"North or South Koreans."

"Okay, okay. NORTH Koreans. They were getting shot at for Christ's sake!" he said.

She waved her hands between them as if stopping traffic. "Details are IMPORTANT," she emphasized.

Slender fingers, Davecki noted, *speaking of details*.

"So, they were pinned down and couldn't tell where the shooters were. They were in these mountains and were being shot at from across a valley."

"And they couldn't see who was shooting at 'em?"

Burn Baby Burn

"Yep," Davecki grinned. *She's interested now.*

"How do you know this?" she asked.

Davecki re-gripped the steering wheel. Sighed. Then he calmly placed his hands palms down on his jean-clad legs. "People Magazine."

"Oh for Christ's sake! Why am I even listening to this?" Carlstrom said, reaching for the door latch.

"You're listening because you can't decide if I'm full of shit or legit," he blurted.

She didn't pull the latch. "Alright. Get it over with will ya?"

"Lighten up Bubba. You're going to have a coronary."

"Just tell the goddamn story." She straightened herself out in her seat.

Davecki remained silent for four seconds and then got out of the car.

"Jesus, Mary and Joseph," She said and jumped out of the car after him.

He was ahead of her crossing the wide Missour...er Tower avenue. A petite Walther .380 in its nylon webbed holster perched on his hip. She darted across Tower, both to catch up and avoid being flattened by a thundering grain truck from North Dakota that was speeding down the street toward Farmer's.

They weaved between a gray Astro van and a two-tone beige and brown Harley FLH circa 1977. This van too had a vanity plate. It said, FEEBS. A man with a huge red beard was mounting the Hog.

"How damn many vanity plates can a small town have?" Bubba bitched.

"My favorite's TEM one zero F eight," the bearded man said.

31

Mike Savage

"What's it mean?" Bubba asked.

The guy grinned and started his Hog. "Figure it out!" he yelled and roared away.

Davecki shrugged and kept walking toward the Anchor Bar. He reached for the silver handle on the off-white door. Davecki said, "Who cares about license plates? It's MY story," and walked through the portal. He grabbed the handle on the second door, this one made from planks, and held it open.

She sauntered past him and mocked, "Lighten up. You're going to have a coronary."

The Anchor enshrouded them with its cloak of clutter. It was the warm greeting of an old friend. Bartender Bean greeted them cheerfully, "Hey Dave...Bubba."

At the bar on the left, John and Mary were studying a pool board. The white cardboard the size of a championship Packers calendar was divided into about fifty squares. Many of the squares were filled with writing. Some were blank.

"You guys want to get on the burn board?" Bean asked.

"Only five bucks," Mary added. She was a dark haired woman with twinkling eyes and a cheerful voice.

"Date and location," John said. His longish blonde hair jostled as he nodded at the board. "Closest one to the actual date of the next fire wins half. Closest one to the actual building takes the other half."

Davecki took the board in his big hands. One square had the word Nottingham and a date. "Elks" and a date were written in another. Scanning the board, Davecki saw that most of the good buildings in town were taken. "How about the old library? Anybody got that?" he asked.

Bubba snorted and bee-lined toward the barber chairs at the back of the room.

Burn Baby Burn

"I don't think so," Mary said. She turned to a man down the counter. "George! Wake up! Anybody got the old library?"

The man on the stool turned from watching figure skating on the TV mounted on the wall above the pay phone. His nose was flat like a boxer's. It looked like the flap of an Air Jordan basketball shoe hung in the middle of his face. Above the flat nose were two beady eyes set in red pools of skin and bloodshot sclera. "Not yet," a gravelly voice echoed from what Davecki figured had to be a cancer ridden larynx. Davecki fished a fiver from his wallet and handed it to Mary. George said, "Old Post Office a better bet," and turned his beady eyes back to Katarina Witt flouncing.

"I'll take the old library on August 15th," Davecki said. Mary handed the money to John and wrote Davecki's name and date into a square with the pen suspended from the side of the board by a string. John handed the Lincoln to Bean who stuffed the bill in a bottle. "See you all later," Davecki said, leaving the scene of yet another victimless crime.

Seated at the barber chairs, Davecki adjusted the height of his with the pump handle on the right. Bean brought the root beer.

Carlstrom sipped.

Davecki gulped.

"You now have my complete and undivided attention, Detective Dave," Carlstrom said.

"Right," he said sourly.

"Finish the story will ya? Pouting's unbecoming for an officer of the law."

"Geeze, a four syllable word. How unbecoming."

Mike Savage

"Cute," she said.

Root beer sips both. Stares at all the nautical crap on the walls and ceilings. After a few calming moments he said, "Okay, here's <u>The</u> <u>Rest</u> <u>of</u> <u>the</u> <u>Story</u>. Garner's pinned down in Korea. They can't locate the shooters. All day. They're trapped."

Root beer sips both.

Davecki rotated his chair, clanged the foot rest against the steel post holding up the table. "All night. Trapped. They move even a little bit. WHAM! Shots fired."

Root beer sip.

Carlstrom asked, "Why didn't they get away in the dark?"

"It was a full moon and clear sky I suppose. How the hell should I know? Night scopes maybe."

"They didn't have night scopes in Korea," Carlstrom said.

"Okay. Okay, just forget all that stuff," his hands started weaving the air. "What's important is, the next morning, Rockford..."

"Garner," she interrupted.

"Yeah, right...Jim. Jim wakes up. He wasn't really sleeping I suppose. I mean... who could sleep that well being outside and all... being shot at and all."

She sighs. Looks up. Then says, "Stay on task will yah? He wakes up. What next?"

Before Davecki could answer, a blonde haired studman with a tight T-shirt and the look of Mark McGwire —complete with all the signs of an androstenedione stoked body— stalked by. He smiled at Carlstrom. He had braces on his teeth.

"Hi," Carlstrom said waving her slender fingers.

Burn Baby Burn

"Hi," he said and walked past the baggage cart, destined for the john to try and find his steroid shrunken manhood to tap a permanently damaged kidney.

Davecki sighed. *If I flirted like that I'd get chewed out.* He shook his head. Resisted the urge to complain. *Focus Alphonse*, he thought.

Carlstrom helped, saying, "Okay. Garner's awake. Now what?"

"Okay. So. He starts waking up. He comes to and suddenly starts sniffing. 'I smell garlic,' he says. 'Huh?' someone says. Jim says, 'I smell garlic. They're cooking breakfast.' And he sniffs and sniffs and looks around and says 'Smoke.' He points to a spot across the valley and says, 'They're right there.' They radio in for an air strike and WHAM! They're saved!" He chugged a gulp of sarsaparilla.

Carlstrom picked up her soda. "The point?" She sipped.

"The point is, even if we didn't see anyone at the fire who was looking orgasmic, I could still smell him. Smell the presence of evil, of him."

"What about all the smoke? You smell that? And I smelled beer on that drunk kid who wanted my ass in his hands. Just exactly what did the arsonist smell like?"

Davecki squirmed. "I'm not sure what to call it. The smell of Evil, capital 'E' probably. Lilies too."

"Lilies?" Carlstrom scoffed.

"Yeah. It reminded me of years ago, going to church at St. Slobodan. It smelled like Mass at Easter. Incense. Only Evil."

"You are so full of shit Davecki."

"Thanks." He picked up his glass. They both drank

and retreated to the solace of studying the Anchor walls for new and interesting artifacts.

After a few minutes of trucing, Davecki said, "Okay. Other than the Smell of Evil, what HAVE we got?"

"We've got shit really," Carlstrom said. "Eleven suspicious fires in eighteen months. Pretty much all of them occurring on a Tuesday or Sunday night. There's the crackpot theory that the City Fathers..."

"And Mothers..." Davecki interjected.

Carlstrom scowled at the interruption. "...are conducting an innovative urban-renewal-by-fire plan to rid the city of unwanted, untaxable buildings."

His face took on a devious look. He said, "And, of course, we can't forget the infamous bad bagel boy lead," Davecki said laughing.

"EVERYone gets investigated when they publicly comment on a fire. Can I help it if the kid was joking around? Can I help it if his co-worker overheard and called the tip in? Can I help it that the kid must have been starved for attention and would say anything, even confess to arson, to make his co-workers laugh? Can I help it that it was the Peak of silliness? It COULD have been true," Carlstrom said sounding defensive.

"Hey, don't take it out on me. I couldn't agree more. But, it was kind of funny. Kids these days," Davecki said shaking his head ruefully. "It's no better than the theory that the Superior Fire Department is setting the fires to emphasize their need for new equipment and more manpower."

There was a pause long enough to allow them to stare at one another like idiot savants calculating the probability factors of solving even one of these cases.

Burn Baby Burn

"The long and the short of it is, we haven't got ONE solid lead. Am I right? It would appear to me that we are screwed without intercourse. Isn't that about right?" Davecki pontificated. He sighed and sipped his drink.

Carlstrom sighed too, took a deep pull from the longneck, gulped and said glumly, "For the time being anyway."

Mike Savage

4

When He had said this, He spat on the ground, and made clay of the spittle, and applied the clay to his eyes, and said to him, "Go, wash in the pool of Siloam" (which is translated, Sent). And so he went away and washed, and came back seeing.

— John 9:6

The dreamer is the greatest warrior of all.

— Oronhyatekha,
   Lower Ontario Mohawk Chieftan
   and Oxford trained M. D.

Burn Baby Burn

High above the land an eagle soared. It wheeled and turned rushing ever eastward, pushed on the updrafts of the hot soil below. To the west, a sight only the eagle, from its lofty vantage point, could see.

Thunder heads building over the Dakotas. Caressing the drafts like a mother bathing her baby, the eagle massaged the air down and up, forth and back; wheeling, wheeling, wheeling.

Looking, looking looking, the eagle scanned the land, searching for provender for its family. Below, Cloverland, Wisconsin, thirty-six square miles of woods and hay fields. Most fields old and fallow. Some still used. In the northeast quarter of the southwest section the eagle spied a woman in her garden. She raised her head from the task at hand; eradicating the weeds of the rich humus soil. There was no such soil within a hundred and thirty-three miles. From it sprang the lushest crop of string beans on the planet.

The ground all around the garden was nothing but Lake Superior red clay. Lake Superior red clay, suitable for growing only hay, or, at best, if the farmer was energetic, oats. But this soil had been transformed. It was fecund. Better by far than even the rich soil of the White River valley around Mason and Marengo. This one hundred and five by fifty-five foot plot of ground had been composted for eighteen years. Every day for six thousand five hundred and seventy days, in some way or another, she'd spit something into the clay to make it miraculous.

It could not NOT grow things. Weeds, corn, potatoes, tomatoes, pumpkins. Sweet, succulent watermelon if it didn't freeze after June third or before October eleventh.

Mike Savage

Acorn squash. Camomile. This five thousand seven hundred and seventy-five square feet exuded produce the way its caretaker emanated psychic power.

She was a slender woman. Willowy. Legs from here to Heaven. She turned her sculpted face skyward and blinked her green eyes. To look at her, none would discern her half-Mohawk lineage. Few knew her great great grandfather was taken from his tribe in lower Canada to be Oxford trained, a personal educational experiment of The Prince of Wales, the future King Edward the Seventh. The young Oronhyatekha was ripped from the bosom of his tribe to become a royal object lesson. <u>The Once and Future King</u> needed proof that the savages of North America could be civilized.

Despite the "higher" education, the great great grandfather passed on the gift. It came to her in the fashion of all spiritual gifts, mystically, through the generations. An elusive inheritance, she knew little of it except that she dreamed vaguely of epic conspiracies involving mass hysteria, mass happiness, the communal consciousness and events in the news that involved the culture's subconscious decisions to do whatever it took to survive.

Even if it meant human sacrifice.

She looked west. A dark veil of clouds approached. Above the tree line a vast sheet of purple bore down across the land from the west, its trailing edge raining on the just and the unjust alike.

It didn't occur to her that the rain gods had been appeased. Molified by her own humble actions. But deep in her Mohawk jeans she realized the arid summer was over and the rush to a rain-filled fall was on. Some dim part of the woman knew that the heat, the fire, the inferno was in

Burn Baby Burn

remission and the water signs were gaining power.

The Iroquois had done it openly. So too the Aztecs, the Mayans. Every culture. Some tribes forced virgin girls to leap into volcanoes. Some fathers simply had the charisma to talk their sons into lying on a stone altar to be sliced open at the neck like an unblemished lamb. Some forced little children to climb sacred mountains until they froze to death. If the tikes survived the climb, well, no matter, there was always a caring adult around with a handy sacred club, the better to bash in the left side of their skulls. All managed to "force" these sacrificial lambs into cooperation by inculcating the belief that their sacrifice would be greatly rewarded in heaven.

The Beans of the world knew differently. The weeds and small grasses she pulled decisively from the ground knew the truth. The string beans lived on prettily. The weeds died. Beans are nurtured. Weeds get sacrificed.

To whom? What?

The God of Survival? The God of Life? The One God? The Many? The God of Night? Selfishness? Love? Selflessness?

The woman's white blood tried to figure it out on occasion. At the conscious level, these sacrifices could not make sense. Unconsciously it worked a little bit better. Subconsciously the puzzle pieces all fit. At the quantum level the morphic field was such a magnificent dance of non-local communication, not one soul on the planet doubted its authenticity. But that deep level was virtually unplumbable by all but dogs and select human Beings; the youngest, the purest, the lithium-laced and the nearest to death.

Take for instance, the fires. They HAD to happen.

Mike Savage

Purge. Purgatory instead of Hell. Cleansing fire. Cauterize. Sure there was collateral damage. Always was. Always will be. Ghengis Khan? Collateral damage. Vietnam? Friendly fire. Death, the great propitiation. One weed dies so the many Beans may live.

The woman's white side knew that her great great grandfather was "sacrificed" to higher education. Her Indian side knew, but only in dreams, that HIS father had been captured by the Huron and beheaded to insure a bountiful fall hunt.

On the surface, all she was doing was raising a garden, living a life of quiet contemplation in pursuit of the Bible admonition, "Godliness with contentment is great gain." She pulled a weed. Looked at the roots. For some inexplicable reason she spat on the tangled mass of intertwining threads and threw the "problem" on the pile destined for the compost pile. For an equally inexplicable reason, the god of fire was appeased.

Who knew the extent of her power?

Burn Baby Burn

Mike Savage

5

Will the Lord reject forever? And will He never be favorable again? Has his loving kindness ceased forever? Has His promise come to an end forever? Has God forgotten to be gracious? Or has He in anger withdrawn His compassion?

— Psalm 77:7-9

"THE ANSWER IS MOST CERTAINLY NO!"

Text and lesson of First Covenant pastor Stephen Staurseth the day after the congregation's church burned to the ground in a total loss.

Burn Baby Burn

Police Chief Richard "B.D." Callahan was a barrel chested man whose personal grooming habits were obviously impeccable. The moustache was trimmed so precisely, it was the standard by which the department's accident reconstruction experts held themselves when laying out right angles on their FIRs (Field Incident Reports).

The term FI has undergone an interesting evolution in the field of police work. At one time, long ago and far away, FI referred to Fucking Indian. As in, "Yeah dispatch, we've got a highly intoxicated FI here at the laundromat. Tried to steal a dollar thirty-five from one of the dryers and dropped it on his head."

Then the First Nations got the casino franchise and, along with the commensurate integration into mainstream society that much money brings with it, the term became inappropriate. FI next evolved into Fucking Idiot and its derivative, FA for Fucking Asshole. As in, "Yeah dispatch, we've got an FI here that was trying to drive his F-150 into the neighbor's living room. And, dispatch, call the jail and let them know we're transporting the FI's FA passenger who puked in the back of the squad." As with all good and accurate terms, FI got watered down to official language and became, simply, Field Incident.

At the moment Callahan was staring at Davecki who sat in the blue vinyl chair to the left of the Chief's big desk. On the right, holding her head in her hands, was Bubba Carlstrom.

"You know, it's bad e-fucking-nuff that the bastard burned down Roth's Department Store. Noooo, that wasn't good enough for this prick. He had to murder some barfly karaoke singer to boot."

Mike Savage

Davecki looked straight through the Chief. Carlstrom shook her head in her hands and huffed like a dog snorting into the crotch of a newcomer to the farm.

Callahan looked at the huffing Fire Marshal and said, "What's the matter with you? Hung over?"

"I wish," Carlstom responded.

"Oh well," Callahan shrugged verbally. He turned to Davecki and said, "You ever go to Roth Brothers Dave?"

Davecki snapped out of the "thousand-yard-stare" made famous by WWII GIs fighting in the South Pacific and replied, "When I was a little kid, a couple of times. Christmas shopping."

"We went in there all the time," Callahan said. He tipped his high-backed leather swivel chair and added, "Mr. Quinn was the funnest thing about going there. He was balder than Kojak. He seemed about eight feet tall. Sold shoes there forever. We'd walk by. Ma on her way to the beauty shop on the second floor. He always smiled at me. Never said a word. Just smiled."

Davecki steepled his fingers. Looked at Carlstrom. She, noting the pause in the Chief's stream of consciousness, looked up, eyeballed Davecki and nodded toward the <u>Leader</u> <u>of</u> <u>the</u> <u>Pack</u>. "Uh, B.D. Uh, Sir. We'd like..." he stammered.

Callahan interrupted, "Well goddamit this is the last straw." He stood and walked over to his windows. Looked west. "All those other buildings I could take. But losing Roth Brothers. It's just too much. I mean. I mean. I used to go there with my MOTHER for Christ's sake! What's next? The Androy? The Capitol Tea Rooms? Is nothing sacred anymore? You have GOT to catch this guy!"

Davecki said, "Actually, we've been wondering about that."

Burn Baby Burn

"Huh?" Callahan turned and looked at the dynamic duo seated on their cushy asses.

"Speak for yourself on this one," Carlstrom said looking at Davecki.

"What the hell are you babbling about?" Callahan crabbed.

Davecki looked at both parties of the second parts and said, "Well... your comment about nothing being sacred. After what happened to me this morning on the way to work, I'm wondering if this is some sort of ritual thing."

Carlstrom put her face back into her hands.

"What in God's name are you talking about Dave?" Callahan barked.

"What I'm talking about is the dream I had this morning about the fire that burned down First Covenant Church."

"You're losing me," Callahan said, "losing us," he added, nodding toward Carlstrom who was breathing noisily through her fingers.

"Remember when First Covenant Church burned to the ground?"

"Yeah I do. Vaguely," the Chief said getting up and walking toward his westward facing windows. His was a husky frame, made the more toned and toughened by his thrice weekly Tai Chi hours at the Waist of Mekong— Exercise, Yoga and Meditation Center that Andy Kathrenson had set up in the basement of the Old City Hall Building on Broadway and Hammond.

"This morning I dreamt about that fire. I woke up right in the middle of the scene where the steeple fell over and crashed into the church. The dream was so vivid it woke me up. It was early and I was hungry, so I went to Big

Mike Savage

Apple Bagels. I was having my customary Cheese Twist bagel with Lemon Lift tea..."

"Alright already with the menu!" Callahan said waving a dismissive hand at his detective.

"Couldn't agree more," Carlstrom said through the heels of her hands.

"You hung over Carlstrom?" Callahan asked again.

"Un-fucking-believable," she said.

Davecki cleared his throat, "Ahem. Anyway. Okay. So you don't care about my healthy eating habits. What you might care about is the conversation, unprompted I must add, with this guy about the former church that used to stand on the very spot where we stood." Davecki looked at the other two. He beamed like a ten-year-old who'd discovered his Old Man's porno stash in the back of the garage. There was silence as he grinned.

"So, go on Dave," Callahan finally said.

"Thought you'd never ask. Anyway, there I was in Big Apple Bagels and this guy I'd never seen walked up to me. Said, 'You the Dick on the Arson Squad?' I said, 'Yes sir, I am now officially a man with AIDs.'"

"Huh?" Both Carlstrom and Callahan said.

"You know," Davecki said looking innocently forth and back between his two dumbfounded co-workers. Arson Investigation Department? AIDs?"

"You're weird Dave," Callahan said.

Carlstrom put her face back into her hands.

Davecki laughed at his own joke and went on, "Anyway, this guy, he just sat down. Didn't even ask. Just plunked down and started talking. Talk about weird! Right away he started in on the church that used to be on the corner, right where we sat..."

Burn Baby Burn

"What'd he look like?" Carlstrom asked pulling a small, blue covered spiral notebook from her hip pocket.

"How d'you get that thing in there?" Callahan asked.

"Up your's Callahan. You want a lawsuit, just keep on with the funny comments."

"Excuse me all to hell."

Davecki laughed again. "She's got no sense of humor this early in the morning boss," he tossed out.

"And how would you know?" Callahan asked.

"Another one of his frigging wet dreams," Carlstrom volunteered. "What'd the suspect look like?"

"Suspect?" Davecki questioned.

"Yes suspect. Anyone who even mentions the fires or talks publicly about arson in this town is a suspect, you know that."

Davecki looked at Callahan.

The Chief simply grinned.

"Like the bagel boy from Peak?" Davecki asked.

Carlstrom glared at Davecki. "Yes as a matter of fact. Just like him. Just like anyone who jokes around about the loss of millions of dollars of real estate, the threat to human life and the loss of a tax base from which your grossly overpaid salary is taken," she said forcefully. "Now what'd the guy look like."

Davecki's shoulders slumped. "Being a cop just isn't as much fun as it used to be. Used to be you could go to the Saratoga Hotel, bust some drunk's head and then mosey on over to Indian Sadie's for a quick piece of hooker hindquarter before picking up the graft money from the rum runners. Remember those good old days B.D.?"

Callahan coughed and laughed a little. "Come on Dave. What'd the guy look like?"

Mike Savage

"For Christ's sake. What a couple of humorless blobs," he announced. "If you must know, he looked just like the Unabomber."

"Ted Kaczynski?" Bubba blurted.

"No, not Terrible Ted. He looked like the artist's renditions of the Unabomber before they caught Kaczynski. Remember those drawings in the papers? Sunglasses, hood, beard stubble?"

"Yeah," Callahan answered.

"Well, my guy looked like that. 'Mr. Unabomber Look-A-Like, Elean the bagel Queen called him."

"Bagel Queen?" Carlstrom choked out. She'd stopped jotting in the notebook.

"You know. Elean! The woman, er, person... The person of equal worth and dignity who works the early shift at Big Apple."

"What a loser," Carlstrom advised.

"Quit goofing around," Callahan ordered.

"I'm not goofing around. The guy looked just like the Unabomber. He was five nine, weighed one-sixty-five, one-seventy. Caucasian. Wore a nylon Packers windbreaker and had a three day growth on his face."

Carlstrom wrote.

"Go on Dave," Callahan cajoled.

Davecki looked at his boss who was propping his head up with both hands jammed under the square jaw and both elbows stuck into the armrests of his mauve executive chair at thirty-seven degree angles.

"He told me the fire happened on November 27th, 1994. 'That was the last day of hunting season. A SUNDAY night,' he said. He emphasized the word Sunday. He said that the fire started in the women's bathroom.

Burn Baby Burn

That the bathroom window was hidden from view between the buildings. It was broken inward. A can of Heet gasoline deicer was discovered under the fire debris indicating that the Heet was there before the fire debris came down. Mr. Unabomber-Look-A-Like informed me that the Heet was used as the accelerant."

"So?" Carlstrom said.

"Well, the guy sounded convincing. So, when I got to the office I looked at the report. He knew the damn thing like it was his obituary. He knew it word for frigging word practically."

"So?" Callahan said.

"Well, that's not the important part. He told me not to focus on the report. Told me to keep in mind that the fire was started in the women's bathroom."

"So, big deal?" Callahan quipped.

"Mr. Unabomber-Look-A-Like grinned at me and said, 'They get extra-special big hard-ons when a woman is sacrificed to the god of fire in the blaze.'"

"What?" Carlstrom yelped.

"How's that?" Callahan queried.

"That's what he said. I couldn't believe my ears either," Davecki related.

"Jesus I gotta talk to this guy," Calrstrom announced. "Where is he?"

"Wish I could help you there," Davecki said looking at the floor.

"WHAT!?!"

"WHAT?!?"

"I knew you'd both flip-out over this, but it's true. I told him the same thing. Asked him really. Asked him if he'd mind going the two blocks to the office to be interviewed. He said, 'Sure. I'll help. I just gotta take a pee. You mind waiting a minute?'

"Well, I knew there was no way out of the Big Apple bathroom, so I said okay and he went in and shut the door and never came out."

"You're overdosing on Zantac aren't you Dave," Callahan said.

"No I am not. In fact it's Zoloft and I'm out of pills right now. Have to get Dr. Larry to write another prescription," Davecki answered.

Carsltrom announced, "Chief Callahan, I've got to get you to assign another detective to this detail. I've had it with this mind tripping bullshit."

"You can piss and moan all you want, both of you, but the truth is, the guy never came out of the bathroom. I opened the door myself and looked inside. Nothing. Nada. Nope. Not one molecule of Mr. Unabomber-look-a-like." Davecki folded his hands into his lap and looked out Callahan's windows. <u>Seven Spanish Seagulls</u> flew down from the sky and landed in the far corner of the parking lot.

"I can't do it Carlstrom. Davecki's got the job until further notice. Everyone else is trying to figure out where in the world Carmen San Diego is."

"My rotten luck," Bubba boo-hooed.

Davecki groused, "Listen. Like I WANTED to tell you that stuff. I gotta say though, it makes some sort of sense."

"To who? Some New Age Anarchist?"

"To whom," Davecki corrected. "And yes. Why not? The guy's obviously some sort of angel or something. Maybe he's like that TV show on Sunday nights."

"Oh God," Callahan said. He stood up. "This is crapola

Burn Baby Burn

Davecki. Now shut the fuck up and get this straight. No more of this angel shit. Nada. Nothing. No more! You and Carlstrom are to go out there and find the SOB who burned down my department store! Now get the hell out of here!"

They both jumped up from their seats and fled the Chief's sanctuary.

In the blue hallway Carlstrom walked on the far side of the passageway. "Don't even get close to me you frigging lunatic," she assailed.

"Don't get your Victoria's Secrets in a bundle," Davecki answered and inched closer.

"I mean it Davecki! Don't come a step closer."

At just that moment, Grover Gronsby, the elder statesman of the Gronsby family of fine policemen popped out of the next office down the hall and looked them both over. "Lover's quarrel?"

"Up yours Gronsby," they both said simultaneously.

Once past Gronsby, Carlstrom said, "B.D. seems more concerned about the loss of an old department store than the fact that a murder's been committed. What's B.D. stand for anyway?"

Davecki looked over his shoulder. "Lots of things," he answered in a stage whisper. "Big Desk. Big Dick. Butt Dimple. Some people call him P.D. for Pencil Dick. But my personal favorite, one I thought of my own personal self is, Bewil Derred," Davecki said chuckling as they walked across the hallway toward the exit.

"I wish I could find someone around here with at least a high school or higher sense of humor," Carlstrom quipped.

They walked in silence into the high August sunlight.

Mike Savage

Standing on the steps before descending to the parking lot below, Davecki said, "All joking aside, you know, it ain't so farfetched."

"It ISN'T," Carlstrom corrected.

"Touche' but get a life. It could be some sort of really close knit gang or something. Maybe some sort of Shiite group. You know the Humorus or something."

"Oh God!, Carlstrom choked, "It's Hamas!" she said loudly and took off down the steps.

"Huh. That's how you say it. And all this time I thought their secret leader was the former Bishop of Superior," Davecki quipped. He laughed loudly at his own joke and followed her down the steps. He went on undaunted, "After all, just last summer there were Iraqi terrorists in town looking for creative new ways to blow up New York City." He followed Carlstrom across the parking lot, enjoying the view. "We're talking murder now and if the angel is right, ritual killings of women in church bathrooms."

"There was no body in the First Covenant fire."

They approached the bloated boat of a car GM called a Caprice. "True. But, it ISN'T something I want to disregard. After all, I did dream about it just this morning," Davecki said getting in.

Carlstrom slammed the rider's side door and looked at Alphonse "Dave" Davecki. "Could we talk about some of the facts of this case please? I'd like to leave paranoid schizophrenia behind us for a while, okay?"

"Be my guest," Davecki said. Starting the engine, he backed the <u>Titanic</u> of a car away from its moorage like the ship of state that it was.

Burn Baby Burn

Mike Savage

6

We all live in a house on fire, no fire department to call; no way out, just the upstairs window to look out of while the fire burns the house down with us trapped, locked in it.

—Tennessee Williams, 1936
The Milk Train Doesn't Stop Here Anymore

Burn Baby Burn

The apartment was lit with thirty candles. The flickering of the yellow flames melded with the 60-cycle flickering of the TV screen to cast a light of ominous portent. Illuminated by this shifty, beady eyed light was a man. He was slouched on a tattered couch of murky fabric. The man's pants were pulled open and down. He held a flaccid penis with his right palm. In his left hand, the remote control.

"God DAMN her," he growled.

He thumbed the remote. The scene on the screen rewound. The hyper-movements caused him to jiggle his right hand.

"Harumph," he said and thumbed the control again.

The TV showed a smoke filled room. In the center of the room, tied to a chair, a woman. She writhed in fear. Agony was to come.

The scene evolved before the man. His body became rigid. He jerked himself off wildly. There was no response from the lifeless member in his hand.

"Son of a bitch!" he yelled. He punched the remote. The TV went to network, a Seinfield re-run. He punched the remote and threw it violently on the floor. He stood and buckled himself up. Striding over to the VCR, he shut off the TV, took out the tape and went to the kitchen table. It was bare. There wasn't a salt shaker, a spoon or a crumb on the surface. He threw the tape on the table and went to the counter near the avocado colored refrigerator. As he walked the flames of the nearest candles wavered. Fear?

He pulled open a drawer and removed a Sharpie permanent marker and a Priority Mail box. He stomped back

Mike Savage

to the table, grabbed the tape and stuffed it in. He scrawled an address hastily into the white rectangle on the patriotic colored box and went back to the drawer. He threw the marker in, pulled out a roll of strapping tape and sealed the box with seven wraps of tape. He threw the tape in the drawer and pulled out a book of stamps. Affixing postage, he grunted grossly at the taste of the paste.

He went to the middle of the combination dining/living room. On the uneven hardwood flooring was a painted yellow circle. In the middle of the circle a cluster of dancing flames was painted in red. In the center of this flame he stood. He steadied himself in the middle of the circle of flame. He looked straight ahead. He stared at the far wall. There, a poster sized photograph of a thousand foot ore boat passing under the aerial lift bridge hung. Across the bottom of the poster, large block letters spelled the name of the boat, V. Bernie LaFlamer. Below the framed in plastic picture were the words WELCOME TO THE HALL OF FLAME scrawled in yellow paint with broad, messy brush strokes.

He slowed his breathing. "Fucking bitch," he cursed softly. "You should'a screamed," he said. His voice was a whisper.

He concentrated on breathing deeply. *Everything here is a problem. It's all evidence*, he thought.

He counted to one hundred. *So what? Nobody in the world suspects me. The benefit of Minnesota politics. Above suspicion.*

He breathed even more slowly. His eyes closed. His forehead furrowed. The candle on the TV flickered more violently. It was like the flame was being strangled. The flame snuffed out. Smoke rose in tiny curls from the wick.

Burn Baby Burn

The man turned to his right, rotating within the circle of flame. As he moved, a wave of darkness moved across the room as his dark visage panned right. As he spun, each candle, in its turn, struggled, fighting against the strangulation. But, each candle lost the battle.

In three point three minutes every candle in the room was dead. Total blackness engulfed the man. Then, all that could be heard was a dead bolt lock being opened. The door opened and Hellfire went to the mailbox.

Mike Savage

7

Trapped on the tundra with Neanderthals.

Burn Baby Burn

Davecki piloted the prairie schooner of a car out of the cop shop parking lot, turned right in the alley behind Ross Furniture and left between the Elks and Letsos Realty. He looked at the big bold building that was the Elks Club. "We should get all the names off that burn board at the Anchor. If any of the buildings go up on or near the date, we should do an interview." He turned right on Belknap.

"That makes you a suspect," Carlstrom said.

"But I didn't do it officer. Honest!" Davecki grinned.

"What we should do is quit farting around and get some hard evidence. Sift through the rubble. Look for suspicious stuff. Study the forensics report on our corpse," Carlstrom said.

"All in good time my impatient little chickadee," he said with a smile. Why were you holding your head in your hands in there?" Davecki asked.

"Because I'm trapped on the tundra with Neanderthals."

"What have you got against Superior?" He turned left on Tower. They cruised south in silence.

Bubba fidgeted in her seat. Finally she said, "It's a well known fact in Madison that the further north of Eau Claire you venture, the more bizarre everything gets."

"Such as?"

"Well, take Washburn County for instance..."

Davecki pounded the steering wheel. "I KNEW you were going to bring that up."

"You asked."

"Well forget it."

"No I'm not going to forget it. It's a perfect example of why this is the tundra and it is populated by cave men."

Mike Savage

"Great. Another sermon."

"Live with it," Bubba gouged Davecki. She started in, "Where else in all the world would a court of law allow a teenage boy to continue sexually abusing his half-sister AND get the guardian ad litem disbarred for challenging the powers that be?"

"As if shit like that doesn't happen in Madison."

Carlstrom sighed. "Yeah, well there's abuse everywhere, but at least in Madison the courts TRY to stop it and lawyers are complemented for doing what's right."

"Cry me a river," Davecki said. He looked straight ahead. Wouldn't turn his head. Could feel her glare burning a hole in his right cheek. "And another thing..."

"Shut up," she drew in a long breath. "You know what's the worst thing about this assignment?"

"Haven't the foggiest. But I'm sure you're going to tell me."

"Damn right. It's the whole culture up here. It's so damn male oriented."

"What are you talking about?"

"What I'm talking about is this. Take the restaurants around here. Every single time we go into a restaurant, the waitress always talks to you first. Always asks you what you want first."

"Who wouldn't? I'm such a handsome devil."

"That's exactly my point! The men up here are from the Dark Ages. I haven't had an intelligent conversation in the twelve weeks I've been here."

"If I'm such an asshole why don't you trade me in for a lesbian who listens?" Davecki blurted out.

"I rest my case," Carlstrom answered. "Now, on a more cheery note, can we talk about some facts? I don't

Burn Baby Burn

think the Tower Building fire and the Flea Market fire are connected."

"Flea Market fire?"

"You know, across from Kari Toyota."

"Oh. You mean the old Great Northern building."

"No. I mean the Flea Market building. That's what the paper called it."

"What the hell do those young whelps at the Snooze Tribune know anyway? Pups just out of J-School. Been in town all of a few months. Most of them anyway. Guaranteed they don't know The Great Northern existed."

On the right was the vacant lot that once was a 12-unit apartment building. "That one was burned on a Tuesday too," Davecki said, nodding to the right.

Silence.

On the left stood one of Superior's grandest old buildings. The Nottingham was designed by architect John O. Bach to resemble the fine old brownstone apartments of Manhattan. The grand opening of the building was July 27th 1926. "I saw the Nottingham on the burn board at the Anchor," Davecki volunteered. "Do you know that the chick who owns the coffee shop there is a dead ringer for Pamela Lee Anderson?"

"Chick?" Silence and brooding from Carlstrom.

The car sailed on like a Carnival Cruise ship heading for the next island. On the right, Super America and Peak Bagels, home of cheap but good hot dogs and one former suspect in the Superior arson investigation.

"Why don't you think the Tower Building and the Great Northern fire are connected?"

"I thought you'd never ask," Carlstrom snipped. "Because the owner of the Flea Market was from Iran and, according to the real estate agent..."

Mike Savage

"That lady that was a dead ringer for Pamela ANDERSON Lee?"

"Quit interrupting. The report said the building was purchased because it had a super-safe bank type vault built into the center of the building. That the Iranian was going to store a portion of his gold hoard in the vault. The Iranian never used it to anyone's knowledge. The flea market got started on a shoestring..."

"Insurance job?"

"Quit interrupting. But, yes. I think it's a copycat crime. The "mad arsonist" hoopla is the perfect cover for any building owner going through a divorce or in financial trouble."

"One in the same," Davecki interjected.

Carlstrom cast him a withering glance. "Up yours. In this case the motive is the salvation of a bad investment by the rich son-of-a-Shah."

"Could be," Davecki said. He hauled the Caprice hard-a-port full rudder into the Dairy Queen parking lot and docked next to the DQ drive-in board. He rolled down his window and said to Carlstrom, "You want anything?"

Before Carlstrom could answer a piercing squeal shot out of the speaker beside the menu board. Dogs in a six block radius covered their ears with their paws and whined in pain. Apparently someone was asking for their order.

"Not after that," Carlstrom said rubbing her dainty ear lobe.

"I'll have a chocolate dip cone, medium," Davecki bellered back.

More utterly unintelligible but highly intense squawking. Davecki drove ahead around the corner of the building. At the drive-in window the DQ queen opened her bi-

Burn Baby Burn

fold windows and said, "That'll be four twenty four,"

"For a cone?"

"You ordered two all beef patties, special sauce, lettuce, cheese and pickles all on a sesame seed bun with fries," the queen said.

"Forget it. All I wanted was a cone," Davecki said. He rolled up his window and drove away.

"That was rude," Carlstrom commented.

"So's their sound system."

Captain Dave gave the ship's wheel another series of left full rudders and the boat of a car was soon on a due-south heading again.

"Where we going?"

"You'll find out. What were you saying about the facts of this case?"

Carlstrom sighed. "Well, the Flea Market Fire, or as you old guys call it, the GN Building Fire, happened on a Tuesday. Started at 6:00 p.m. on Tuesday, May sixteenth. The Tower Building burned on Monday night, Tuesday morning. I think the Flea Market Fire was a professional arsonist who came to town to pick up a little weekend gambling money."

"Or a whole lot," Davecki muttered.

"What did you say?" she asked.

"I said, did a whole lot of scientific evaluation go into this conclusion Carlstrom? Or did you dream this up over a breakfast of Marlboros and Miller Lite? Or is it just because YOU think it's a professional arsonist that this supposition is now raised to the level of fact?"

"Give me a break Davecki," Carlstrom said, sounding like she was tired, tired, tired.

"Well which is it? Do you want to have an intelligent

Mike Savage

conversation or not? Do you want to be talking about REAL facts or do you really want to just bitch about being trapped with Neanderthals so you don't have to act like a human, have some manners."

"Its just as viable as being <u>Touched</u> <u>by</u> <u>an</u> <u>Angel</u>."

"Well, as long as we're both making up the facts and building cases out of thin air, we'll just merrily go along questioning teenaged bagel shop boys who joke around about their pyromania."

"Give it a rest will you? You know we follow-up on every lead, no matter how ludicrous," Carlstrom asserted.

"Ludicrous? No wonder you can't have an intelligent conversation around here. Isn't that three syllables? You're going to have to dumb it down considerably to communicate with us riff-raff north of Highway Eight."

"Up yours"

"Now that's ludicrous," Davecki snorted. He called for right full rudder and the ship of state responded by careening around the corner of Tower Avenue and Highway 105.

Carlstrom opened her purse, a Gucci, light brown, to fetch a fag.

"Must you?" Davecki whined.

"Alright already. I won't. Now where the hell are we going?" She put the cigs back into the purse.

"To visit Hjelmer Hjarvis."

"Who?"

"Hjelmer Hjarvis. You'll see." Davecki looked at the old bank building on the corner. Sulking behind the gaudy Video Vision awnings was a majestic building. Built over 100 years ago, the last vestiges of its grandeur were still standing proud, magnificent carved sandstone pillars with

Burn Baby Burn

ornate carvings on the capstans. Lions roaring emerged from the stone declaring that the age of decency and decent architecture was only a generation or two gone. "Be a shame if he burned that nifty old building."

Carlstrom looked over her left shoulder. "Who? Hjarvis?"

Davecki laughed. "Noooo. Tommy the Torch. It'd be sad to lose such a nice building."

"What are you talking about? Who is Tommy the Torch?"

"Tommy the Torch isn't Hjarvis. Hjarvis is an old friend. Tommy the Torch is my pet name for whoever's Burning Down the House, so to speak."

"God you're weird."

"Thank you." Davecki smiled. He piloted the Caprice Ship of State... err, City, across the Burlington Northern tracks. "I found out long ago that people need to have things named. When my sister was sick, she told me the worst part was not knowing. She said she actually felt better when she found out it was cancer. She hated the cancer, but she said she hated it even more when she didn't know what she had."

"So you come from a family of weirdos."

"Thank you officer Carlstrom. What I'm doing is calling our unknown arsonist Tommy the Torch just to give him..."

"Or her..."

"A name," Davecki completed.

"So," Carlstrom asked, "Who the hell is Hjelmer Hjarvis?"

Davecki grinned and hauled the Caprice left off 105 onto the road that leads to the building materials landfill

Mike Savage

owned by one of Superior's most innovative movers and shakers, Joe Kimmes. It was also the road to the Riverside and Hebrew Cemeteries. How nice of the Jews and Gentiles to get together in death.

"He's the least Neanderthal man you'll ever meet, though I doubt you'll be able to see through his disguise," Davecki said with a guffaw.

Burn Baby Burn

8

In Vietnam, inexperienced overnight patrols established "fields of fire" where the platoon could shoot in the direction of any approaching VC. What quickly became evident was, specific fields of fire didn't exist because the enemy surrounded you at all times.

Some LTs would rouse the squad in the middle of the night and order commence firing on full-auto in 360 degrees for two uninterrupted minutes. Known as "maniac minutes," the futile exercise was little more than a comforting expression of mass hysteria, though the surrounding foliage was slaughtered effectively.

The Elysian Fields of Vietnam also slaughtered a great many vulnerable psyches. Woe to the wounded soul who came home and refused to forget or eschewed their daily dosage of lithium.

Burn Baby Burn

As the Caprice nosed down into the dip in the road for Pokegema Creek, Davecki said to Bubba, "Who would do such a thing? Burn down a building? It's such an act of destruction. It's got to take a lot of depravity to strike that match Don't you think? I mean, you'd have to be unconscious to be not thinking about the destruction. Don't you think?"

"Beats me," she said.

"I think of all the work, all the money and effort to create any building," he said.

"It gives me the shivers to think someone would burn it down for money," Bubba added.

"Or revenge," he added.

They rode along in silence. Carlstrom started to pull her cigarettes out, but closed her purse. "Whatcha thinking?"

"About Shiva."

"What?"

Davecki answered, "You said you got shivers. I was thinking of destruction and that made me think of Shiva."

"You have some suspect I don't know about?"

Davecki turned the boat right into the Hebrew Cemetery. "No I don't. But, thanks to my bank teller Laavanya, I do have a tiny bit of knowledge about the Hindu God Shiva."

Carlstrom looked at the driver. "Un-fucking-believable. Your bank teller is teaching you Hinduism?"

"Hey, God works in mysterious ways, His wonders to perform."

Carlstrom grunted and looked out at the acres of headstones. "What are we doing here? This some sort of rendezvous?"

Mike Savage

Davecki parked the car next to a big gravestone with the name Malkovich on it. "Well it is a meeting, but really, it's more of a prayer."

"God help me," Carlstrom said.

"Since you asked, She will," Davecki said. He grabbed the under-seat latch, yanked and slid the seat backwards. He slumped down.

"It looks like you're settling in," Carlstrom said.

"Naw, I'm just giving him a chance to check you out."

"WHAT? WHERE?" Carlstrom said jerking her head around.

Davecki chuckled. "Relax. See, nobody really knows much about Hjarvis. Where he lives. How he gets around. I figure he must have a shack built from scrap lumber stolen from Kimmes' dump across the road. All we're doing now is acting like we're trying to catch horses that have been out to pasture all summer."

"What?"

"You know, like horses or deer that are curious but wary."

"I am truly in the sticks."

"Right. Sure you are. I forgot you're a city girl. All we gotta do is go slow. Sit here a while. Give him a chance to come up from the river bottom, get a look at the car, see who's visiting the boneyard. Once he knows it's me and sees I've got company, IF he approves of you, he'll come out."

She was still fidgety, glancing around. "This is nuts. It's like being on another planet. What's Shiva got to do with anything?"

Davecki looked his partner over. His face was devoid of demeanor. He spoke, "It's Hjarvis' nickname. So, be-

Burn Baby Burn

cause we don't have any solid leads and because I'm not willing to rule out ANY help we can get, we've come to this. We will talk to Shiva."

"Talk English will ya?"

"Hjarvis is a Vietnam vet. A psycho. He thinks he's Shiva The Destroyer. Thinks he can control reality through dreaming. Very antisocial. At least on the surface. About fifteen years ago one of the local slum lords paid a scrote bag Vietnam vet twelve hundred dollars to burn down an apartment building. Trouble was, a couple of woman tenants were burned to death." Davecki rubbed his eyes. Sighed.

"And..."

"Well, there were, as always with arson, no leads. No leads, that is, until I was driving to Oliver one evening. This wild man jumped out of the swamp grass, ran in front of my car. Nearly got himself killed."

"Hjarvis?"

"The same. Damndest thing. I squealed to a halt and jumped out ready to rip him a new orifice. Before I could say word one, he yelled, 'Donnie McClelland!' Then he took off like a panicked deer into the tall grass and alders."

"And you looked up this Donnie McClelland..."

"Exactomundo. He was a Vet and very flaked out."

"They run in packs," Carlstrom interrupted.

Davecki continued, "I knocked on the door to his room at the Saratoga Hotel. Which burned down, by the way. Room 214. It swung open from my knocking and there was Donnie sitting on the floor stoned three ways from Herbster. Before the door stopped opening all the way, Donnie Mac confessed to the crime. Named the building's owner and the amount." Davecki sighed, "There were never any charges against the owner. Donnie did time, got out and got a job working for the state in Madison."

"How charming. What's all this got to do with Superior's urban-renewal-by-fire-program?"

Davecki stared straight ahead. "Well, in regards to Shiva. What Hjarvis doesn't know that Laavanya my bank teller does, is that Shiva changes roles depending on how he holds his hands." He looked at Carlstrom.

She stared like a shock victim. "I'm speechless," was all she managed to utter.

"Lavvy says Nadarajah is a phase of Shiva that is The Creator. I'm hoping Hjarvis will create some leads."

"You are so fucking weird."

"Thanks. Anyway, I'm hoping Hjarvis will Donnie McClelland us. If he decides to let you see him."

Carlstrom opened her purse and pulled out a smoke. "What's that mean?"

"You'll see. Now we have to go to the Cohen Headstone and wait."

"I'm not hanging out in no graveyard," she said, flicking her Bic.

"It's the only way."

She sighed. "Been here less than a month and not only is my grammar going to hell, I'm reduced to getting help from Herman's Hermit. How's this going to help?"

"I have no idea, but it'll be something...IF he comes out." He sighed. "You ever hear of Proverbs 10:1?"

Carlstrom stared. "Like in the Bible?"

"Yeah. It says, 'In a multitude of words there is great folly.'" He jerked the door latch and shoved the door open. "I've been talking way too much."

Burn Baby Burn

He started walking toward the back side of the graveyard. Behind him the car door opened and slammed. He leaned against a massive polished red rhyolite and scanned the woods a hundred yards away. Carlstrom joined him. They stood in silence while gathered all around them were the many headstones of the Hebrews.

"Now what?" she asked.

"We wait."

"For what?"

"To see if Shiva or Nadarajah shows."

Carlstrom grunted and sucked in a long drag of nicotine delight.

"This reminds me of Stonehenge," Davecki said.

"How can it. I bet you've never been there."

"Good point. This reminds me of pictures of Stonehenge I've seen."

"Easter Island too," she volunteered.

Without making so much as a subtle shift in his posture, Davecki suddenly called out, "WELL, IF IT ISN'T THE HERMIT OF POKEGEMA!"

Carlstrom flinched and looked straight west.

Coming out of the bushes was an apparition.

"Oh my GOD! What the hell is that?" she added.

"Be polite," he said. "He rarely comes out for strangers."

"What could be stranger than that?" she asked. Her mouth hung open in a gape of amazement.

"Don't be a jerk," Davecki said. "This is a great man you're meeting."

The air was August warm and Lake Superior fresh. The wind was off the water and pregnant with the purity of four quadrillion gallons of mostly pristine H_2O, now that Jimmy Hoffa's body and the pile of plutonium in the barrels had been pulled from Mother Superior's bottom.

"Hjelmer," Davecki said sticking out his right hand.

Leaning forward, stretching out a left hand that was black with dirt, a man —no, more of a gnome— grabbed the back of Davecki's outstretched mitt. Hjarvis had only one arm.

"Great, another frigging Fugitive," Carlstrom cawed gutturally, like a crow constructing a nest. She scrunched up her nose and sniffed.

"Who you got dere," Hjarvis shrugged in Carlstrom's direction. "Sumpin' wrong wit' her nose?"

He had hair. He WAS hair. It was all hair from whence the gravelly words emerged. Wild. It was gray and dirty hair. Stringy. On top of the head, the hair sprouted like string bean plants. On the face, the beard encircled dark eyes. Smokey black eyes. Deeply wrinkled skin radiated away from the sunken eye sockets. The deepest wrinkles looked like ravines filled with black dirt. A great drooping moustache veiled the lips that had just spoken. A green worm of snot twisted from a bulbous nose that was hirsute as well.

"My new TEMPORARY partner Bubba Carlstrom from Madison," Davecki said as the one armed man reached awkwardly inside his filthy Army field jacket. He extracted a small box. Printed on the outside of the package, a picture of a Pentax IQ Zoom camera. He handed the package to Davecki. The gnome then turned toward Carlstrom. The upright bipedal bag of stench stuck his arm out toward the stiffened Fire Marshal. The filthy shoulder of the green jacket shed flakes of dirt like snow from a Christmas cloudburst.

Burn Baby Burn

"Pleased," emanated from beneath the moustache.

"I'm sure," Carlstrom said holding out her hand.

The gnome patted the back of the hand before him with his hairy paw. "You know what Madison women put behind their ears to attract men?" he asked and turned to Davecki.

Carlstrom looked at her temporary partner. He was grinning but he didn't say anything.

"Their ankles," the gnome said.

"Cute," Carlstrom said.

There was a moment of silence as Hjarvis studied Carlstrom. His whiskers moved. A smile? "She passes. So... now what?" the gnome said.

Davecki nodded to Carlstrom and said, "Congratulations." To the gnome he said, "Hjelmer, what have you been dreaming?"

The gnome tilted his head back and emitted a sound that could only be decoded as a laugh. It could easily have been a death rattle, but the creature was still upright and breathing. "Dreams've been busier than a one legged man at an ass kicking contest, what with the Thirty Seventh Order of Freemasons fucking everything up. Then there's the Great Whore continuing to fuck every religious zealot into submission. I'm thinking of contacting Spencer's in New Jersey to try and sell 'em a T-shirt that says *My Pope can kick your Governor's ass*. Anyway, it's been hell. I hardly had the energy to come meet youse guys. If it weren't for the calling card," he jerked his head toward Carlstrom, "I'da stayed home. Great ass I bet."

"Hey!" Carlstrom shouted.

Davecki laughed. "Seen Smoke Signals? Anything fiery?"

Mike Savage

"I hated that movie," Hjarvis burped.

Carlstrom interrupted, "Now wait just a goddammed minute."

Hjarvis sniffed the green booger back into his great gray nose. Utterly ignoring the Fire Marshal's complaint he said, "Term legwork mean anything to you asshole?"

"Now listen Dickhead..."

"No YOU listen Buttwipe..."

"BOYS!" Carlstrom shouted.

Davecki hooted. Hjarvis guffawed. Bubba boiled. Davecki leaned his own nice ass off the gravestone and stretched the small of his back. "It's all being done Hjelmer. Debris sifting. Accelerant analysis. Physical evidence comparisons. Fingerprinting. Spectator video surveillance and analysis. Interviews. Trouble is, by the time it gets figured, the whole town's gonna be nothing but ashes."

Hjarvis stared at Carlstrom first. Then Davecki. Then his whiskers moved. Actual words wove their way through the bush on his face, "Tell you what. I'll share my dreams if you get her to haul MY ashes." He snorted loudly and the greenie flew out of his nose. The booger landed on the bottom part of his beard. "Cocksucker!" Hjarvis ejaculated. He swatted at the booger, dislodged it and the snot landed on the black toe of his jungle boot. "And I SO hoped to make a good impression."

"No fucking way dirtbag," Carlstrom screeched. "Besides, he's got SHIT to say about it anyway," she added jerking her head at Davecki.

The beard shifted around the moustache which twitched. Something akin to a chortle emerged from the gnome's whiskers. "She DEFINITELY passes."

Burn Baby Burn

The frown that had erupted on Davecki's face when Carlstrom called the Prophet of Pokegema a dirtbag vanished at Hjarvis' favorable reaction.

She reached for her purse. Relaxed visibly. The gnome leaned toward her. The nose of a million blackheads wrinkled. The hair thereupon danced like a leafless dogwood bush with a coating of ice swaying in a lively breeze. "Could use a couple-a-doze," the thing said eyeing the cigarettes.

Carlstrom finished pulling her Marlboro's from her Gucci and flicked a stack up from the opening.

The gnome's gnarled fingers plucked four cigarettes by their filters and elevated them from the pack tenderly. Like a magician doing card tricks, he stuck two of them filter first into the hair at the top of his head. The other two he deftly de-filtered by bending the pure smoking pleasure in half. He flicked the decapitated filters at the red marble headstone with a quick flick of his wrist. The remaining two white cylinders he stuffed into his mouth. All with one hand.

A mat of moustache hairs bent into the gnome's mouth as it chewed. A single piece of cigarette paper clung wetly to the beard about four inches below the animal's feeding orifice. The wind sighed through the tall pines as the troll arranged the tobacco in its mouth. "Not as good as Copenhagen, butt," he laughed at his own pun, "it'll do."

Carlstrom lit up.

Gnome masticated.

Davecki folded his arms.

Headstones waited.

A robin sang. Perhaps the song was a recitation of the crimes Hjarvis had committed in Vietnam. Perhaps the lyrics of the pure animal melody wanted to <u>Tell</u> <u>the</u> <u>Old</u> <u>Old</u> <u>Story</u> of man's crimes against the Gods.

Gnome spat. "Ahhhh." Filthy sleeve whipped up, wiped whiskers. His eyes glazed over and he went into a trance. His voice went monotone. "Dem Freemasons could fuck up an anvil with a rubber mallet," the voice chanted. The eyes clouded over further. The voice smoothed somewhat, leaving the sandpaper quality forgotten. "Purification by fire. They thinks it's pay back time when it's really just cauterization. Punks. Power. Think there's power in pyre. Any one of 'em had a REAL dream...be a puddle of puke for the dog to lick up like vomit. Fuckin' twerps. Fuckin' weekend warriors. They knew who their Masta was dey'd quit playing 'round and start going back to church. Least de great whore'll suck cock. Dese ones dough, dey'd rather do demselves den let pussy get near 'em. Dey have no idea 'bout Orpheus...Orpheus'll get em."

The one armed man clomped his jaw twice and turned away. He walked west. Davecki didn't twitch. Carlstrom said, "Hey!"

Davecki laughed and walked toward the long suffering Caprice.

"Fucking tub," Davecki insulted the car as he got in.

"What the hell's going on?" Carlstrom asked as she caught up to Davecki. She jumped into the car just as he was putting the package under the seat.

"What's that?"

"How the hell should I know? A brick of hash I suppose."

"Aren't you going to open it?"

"No."

"That's it? No? You're just going to put it under the seat?"

Burn Baby Burn

"That's about right," Davecki answered.

"Well, aren't you curious? Why'd he give it to you? What if it's evidence or something? If it's evidence you've got to bring it to headquarters."

"Would you get off it? It isn't evidence. It isn't even for me goddammit!"

"Well... WHO is it for?"

"None of your goddamned business," Davecki said as he sat and watched the green jacketed man merge back into the foliage of northern Wisconsin. He looked over his shoulder and started backing away. He mumbled, "I should'a known."

"What?" Carlstrom asked.

Davecki looked over his shoulder and backed the vehicle out of the Hebrew Elysian Field muttering again, "I should'a known."

Mike Savage

9

Hell hath no fury like a CITY spurned or a prophet unheard.

Burn Baby Burn

Kent's Korner is one of the most misunderstood restaurants in Superior. Looking at it, people expect the place to be dreary and depressed. Kent West, the owner, wanted to name the place RICHES because he wanted to get rich in the restaurant business. But he discovered it cost money to remodel, money he wanted to spend fixing the best food in town. The place has never looked exactly appetizing from the outside. So the Yuppie wannabes from Duluth stay away. They go to Porter's and Bennett's and Lake Avenue Cafe, pay twenty bucks for big plates with too little food on them.

But, inside Kent's there's gawd-awesome food served to gawd-awful customers by goddamned good waitresses. There's good old fashioned meat and potatoes. Pancakes with a three tablespoon gob of butter on 'em. A Friday all-you-can-eat fish fry that can fill the gullet of any six-foot-four blonde Nordic eating machine that stops in. There's Luxurious Laura, the most voluptuous and pleasant waitress in the Twin Ports, serving flirters and welfare moms with the even temperament that keeps her on her Harley trike all the way to Sturgis every August.

Kent's Korner is a straight forward, no nonsense eatery. A perfect place for cops digesting a difficult case.

"Should have known what?" Carlstrom asked, sliding into the booth between the kitchen and the johns. She took the seat with her back to the wall.

"That's my spot," Davecki said. On his face hung a pouty look. The only thing missing to make him look like a five-year-old was the protuberant lower lip.

"Grow up," Carlstrom sneered.

Davecki reshuffled his face into a tough-guy look and

sat down. The look, had Carlstrom been able to decode it, would have warned her of the mental tortures to come. "Hjelmer's dreams and the Angel. They were right."

"Who? What?"

"What Hjelmer said makes sense of the Angel."

"How so?"

"Well, the angel said there's a sacrifice going on. Hjelmer talked about punks and purification."

"Just shut up," Carlstrom said. Angry.

Davecki nodded a greeting to a local contractor. He was a tall man with intelligent eyes and the angular weather-beaten face of someone who eats lightly and spends much time outdoors. The builder frequented Kent's and knew it as a four-star joint.

"Why doesn't he get arrested?"

"Who? That guy?" Davecki asked nodding toward the contractor. "What's he done?"

"No dimbulb. Not him. Hjarvis."

"Oh he get's pinched sometimes. When he wants to," Davecki explained.

"And when's that?"

"Sometimes in the fall, late fall. November. If it's too cold or he doesn't want to head south for the winter."

Laura walked up. "Can I get'cha?"

"Tea..." Davecki started.

"With lemon and honey," Laura interjected.

"Right." Davecki smiled.

"And you sweetheart?"

"Coffee and more creamers," Carlstrom said lifting the small bowl that held only half a dozen tiny plastic buckets of Half and Half.

"Sure thing," Laura said smiling.

Burn Baby Burn

"She's got the prettiest smile," Carlstrom said as Laura sauntered away.

"Really?" Davecki said.

"Yeah, people who aren't fixated notice things like that," Carlstrom chided.

"Huh?"

"Duh...What?" Carlstrom rechided.

"What the hell are you talking about?"

Carlstrom snorted. "You're not THAT dense. Laura, stupid."

Davecki snorted too. He sighed and looked across the room. In a booth against the far wall was a black haired, round eyed busty woman. Two kids sat opposite her. The littlest child was a doll-like blonde girl with a visibly dirty face framed by huge curls in her silken hair. The child was shoeless. The next "Jo" Jackson? The woman leaned out of the booth to pick up the shoe. Davecki saw that her bra was the same color as her hair. As she sat up their eyes met. The woman smiled. "Jesus," Davecki cursed.

Carlstrom said, "NOW what's your problem?"

"If women don't want to be looked at why don't they wear turtle necks," Davecki gruffed.

"Huh?"

"You're not THAT dense are you?"

"Up yours. What's gotten into you?"

Davecki hacked up a good gob of phlegm, sniffed and swallowed. "Nothing that I can't handle. Nothing but a bunch of your second hand smoke which I have to cough up every half hour or so. Nothing but a constant stream of intriguing and beautiful women to distract me. Nothing but a god-awful spiritual war that's localizing in my jurisdiction."

Mike Savage

"You've completely lost me," Carlstrom complained. She raised her hands as if stopping traffic and shook her head slowly forth and back.

Davecki sighed again. He nodded toward the doe-eyed woman across the room. The twenty-something lady was jamming the plastic sandal onto the dainty foot of the doll-like daughter. "See that lady? Stripper from the Lamplighter."

"And how would we know that?" Carlstrom said smirking.

"I'm a cop. I'm paid to know these things."

"Right."

"Well, forget about all that. What makes sense is what Hjelmer told us," Davecki said drumming the blue table top with four fingers.

"What? He didn't say a goddamned thing. He just babbled and stared at me with those stoned looking eyes.

Laura brought the fixings for a good break. She set the tea service, coffee and creamers (piled high in a soup bowl) on the table. "Anything else?"

"Not for me," Davecki said.

"Me neither," Carlstrom added.

Laura waddled westward toward the wayward mother. At the table she bent down to pick up the same sandal that had been kicked off the little foot again. Davecki looked away, back to his partner. "Well? What do YOU think Hjarvis was talking about?"

"I don't know. Some crap about purification and caught eyes or something." Carlstrom said, ripping the top off a creamer.

Davecki watched as she ripped the top off three more creamers and dumped them into the coffee cup. The slush

Burn Baby Burn

colored fluid brimmed to the top, capillary action and surface tension the only thing holding the two physical states in cohesion. In other words, it didn't spill. One tiny bump of the table and Whamo! Disunity! Instead of exploring the theory of chaos and its relativity to coffee cups and fluid capacity, Davecki said one word and one word only, "Cauterization."

Carlstrom rolled her eyes and went down to slurp the cafe latte from her cup. Davecki marveled at the quantum beauty of a woman bending over.

Laura returned. "It's never a new building you know."

"Huh?" Davecki said.

"He always burns down an old building on Tower Avenue. Never something new or something like Sundquist Hall on campus," Laura said. She stood there with her arms folded.

Both cops looked at her, speechless. Puzzled for a second. "What?" Carlstrom asked.

Laura answered, "It's so obvious. When you two came in, I smelled smoke so I assumed you're working the arsonist thing."

"There's a Force somewhere with a detective's desk that has your name on it, Laura," Carlstrom said.

"Not me. I love waitressing. No stress, some mess, never have to wear a dress," she chanted.

The silver teacher's bell on the ledge between the kitchen and the front counter dinged and Laura took off to fetch plates of steaming food for the lecherous old men lined up along the counter who kept ordering dinner rolls and half an order of french fries so Laura couldn't sit down for a smoke and would have to keep stretching up to the service window for their pitiful orders.

Mike Savage

"Who's on first?" Carlstrom asked. She opened another creamer and poured.

"What's on first. Who's on second," Davecki said.

She shook her head. "Let me put it to you in words you'll understand. Details man! DETAILS!!" She opened another creamer. Poured.

"You're like a mayfly Bubba."

"Gee thanks," she said, slurping her concoction. She sucked and said, "You know, having a conversation with you is like talking to thirteen different people at a time."

"Just call me Sybil," he said, squeezing the lemon slice above his empty cup.

Carlstrom fetched three packets of sugar from the stainless steel condiment carrier at the back edge of the table. She aligned the paper packages and whapped them against the fingers of her left hand like she was fanning a deck of cards.

"But what?" Davecki said squeezing honey from the plastic Sue Bee honey packet retrieved from the saucer beside his cup.

Carlstrom, having dumped the load of sugar in her white looking coffee, grabbed three more sugars. "Would you quit hedging?" She spoke with an edge of anger in her voice.

"Touchy! Touchy!" Davecki said. He was stirring his empty cup, looking at her. Smiling. Grinning.

"What are you doing? Are you enjoying this?" Carlstrom asked. She stared at the vacant stirring. The spoon clanked repeatedly against the cup's sides. A hollow clinking echoed from the ceramic deeps.

"Mixing my honey and lemon while the tea steeps."

"You're so weird."

Burn Baby Burn

"Thank you."

Silence.

Clink-clink, clink-clink, went the spoon. Restaurant noises insinuated themselves into their bubble between the furnace and the flusher. The cash register chimed as Laura took an old geezer's money. "I love you too Bergy," the waitress said.

"Oh oh," Carlstrom said.

"What?" Davecki resisted the urge to turn around. Instead he looked directly into Carlstrom's eyes. Her pupils were constricting, a sure sign that something was going wrong in her line of sight.

"What?"

"The waitress is directing that old guy over here."

"That's a relief."

"Why's that?"

"Because I was thinking it might be some Unsolicited Advice Lords or Jiminey Cripes gang members coming in for a shooting spree."

"You notice too much. Focus Dave. I thought we were going to talk about the case."

Davecki pulled his tea bag from the stainless steel pot, cradled the sodden mass in the bowl of his spoon, wrapped the string from the tab around the brown bulge and garroted the bastard. "We are talking about the case, but you're not listening and all these people are interrupting."

Little rivulets of tea streamed from the bag back into his cup where all good things belonged, in his cup which ranneth over. He looked up and saw that Carlstrom was watching the ritual lynching of the tea bag. "I'm trying to connect things that don't seem connectable. I'm trying to

Mike Savage

explain to you the intricate nature of spiritual warfare." He was about to go on, but the old guy walked up.

The man had to be at least eighty. He moved right up close to the table. He had white hair and a red baseball type cap with BORN TO BE WILD embroidered by Jersey City in white letters across the front. He wore a blue zipper jacket. On the left breast, a yellow emblem, the symbol of the United Steelworker's of America, stood out above the white embroidered name, **Bergamo**.

"What can I do for you Bergamo?" Davecki asked while putting down the spoon and hung bag.

"Just wanted to say thanks for saving the lake last summer and to tell you what I've been hearing over in Duluth," the old guy said. His voice was strong and younger by thirty-eight years than his posture. His face was handsome, with full shining skin.

Healthy old bugger, Davecki thought as he smiled up at the smiling down gentleman. "You're welcome. And, what do you hear over in Duluth, Bergy?"

"Well," the old guy said, taking off his hat, "I'd be happy to tell you but I can't be as rude as you," he said nodding toward Carlstrom. "You should never be rude to a beautiful woman," the old guy said grinning.

"Couldn't agree more," Carlstrom said. "I'm Bubba Carlstrom and pleased to meet you," she said extending her hand.

"Pleasure," Bergamo said taking the extended fingers lightly in his hand. It was a practiced gesture of grace and aplomb. Davecki stared at the exchange wide eyed.

"I'm sure," Carlstrom said.

Davecki looked at her. He saw genuine pleasure in her eyes. He looked at Bergamo. He was grinning and

Burn Baby Burn

looking at Carlstrom with unaffected admiration. *What's he got that I don't?* Davecki thought.

Bergamo held the hand longer than he should have, but not so long as to be....what? rude? It was more of a "forgivably impish" delay. Something on the order of sassy, for an old guy. He grinned like the cat that ate the custard pie with the blackbirds in it...or was it plumbs? Or was it a canary?

Regardless, Bergamo finished with his worship of the Beauty of Bubba and let go of the by-now-trembling hand. The old Italian turned to Davecki and said, "What I hear over in Duluth is that the Superior Fire Department is burning all the old buildings in town to dramatize their need for more firefighters, more equipment and more money."

Carlstrom raised her immaculately plucked eyebrows.

Davecki took a sip of tea. "Is that so?" Davecki said. "And just where do you hear this information Bergamo?"

"Well, you know. Around. Coffee shop talk."

"And we can quote you on these allegations. We can interview you later this week once we do some checking into this accusation?" Carlstrom asked.

"Well...er. Well, sure. You can interview me all you want. But I'm just telling you what I heard at coffee with the boys. You know donut shop talk."

"Which donut shop?" Davecki asked.

"The Flying off the Handle Pantry," Bergamo answered. He put his hat back on.

"Where's that located?" Carlstrom asked pulling a note pad from her Gucci.

"Well," Bergamo fidgeted. "Ahem, it's up by UMD. In the Mount Uniroyal Plaza."

91

Mike Savage

"We'll check it out," Davecki said. "When do you guys get together?"

"Seven thirty," Bergamo said.

"A.M.?" Carlstrom asked. She jotted on the pad.

"That's right," Bergamo answered. He fidgeted some more.

"We'll check it out. Thanks for the lead," Carlstrom said.

Bergamo leaned toward the exit. But before he could escape, Davecki asked, "Uh, Bergamo. I was wondering if I could ask one more question. It isn't exactly related."

"Sure thing."

"I was wondering. Why would anyone live in Duluth?"

"Huh?" Bergamo stuttered.

"Who would want to live in a city that passes a law that says you have to move your empty garbage can within twenty-four hours?"

"Duluth did that?"

"Sure enough," Davecki answered.

"Glad I live in a condo," Bergamo answered. He started leaning toward Duluth again. But, again, before he could fall away from the table and the condescending questions, Davecki said, "Bergamo? I was wondering. Didn't Duluth pass an ordinance that said home owners had to shovel their snow within twenty-four hours or get fined?"

"Yes I believe they did," he replied.

"Uh, before you go Bergamo. I'd like to say that I think Duluth's a pretty bad placc to be from. I mean, what they going to pass a law on next? Going to the bathroom before going to bed or not swimming off Park Point for an hour after you eat?"

Burn Baby Burn

Bergamo laughed. "You got yourself some pretty good points there officer. The fact is, we've got some City Councilors that think they can pass laws just to keep their little dream-world alive and well according to their own private interpretation." With that comment, Bergamo bolted quickly for the exit.

Davecki called after the retreating form, "Hey Bergamo? You know what Duluth women put behind their ears to attract men?" The retreating Italian never looked back. "You ever want to live free again Bergamo, you and the Missus are always welcome to move to the City of Rust and Despair," Davecki said. "See yah," he added.

"Nice talking," the man called over his shoulder.

"How do you know he's married?"

"Ring," Davecki said.

"He's old. Could be his wife is gone."

"Where? Michigan? No. He's still got a loving wife at home."

"And how do we know that Mister Smarty Pants? All I know is he's seen <u>Backdraft</u> a few too many times."

"You see how nice and smooth his skin is? How well fed he looks? See that shirt? Not one glob of spaghetti sauce on it anywhere. Those khaki Dockers? Not one stain where an Italian meatball bombed off a fork and landed in his lap. No. He's married. If I was his age and single I wouldn't change my shirt for two weeks. I'd never change my socks and I sure as hell wouldn't brush my hair and wash up so clean."

"This from a man who chokes his tea bags?"

Laura walked up. "More coffee?"

"Sure," Bubba bubbled.

"What DO those Duluth chicks put behind their ears Dave?"

Mike Savage

Davecki blushed. "Ah nothing Laura. I was just toying with the old guy."

"Um hmmm. I see. More hot water?" Laura asked.

"No thanks," Dave answered grinning.

When she'd left, Bubba asked, "What's so funny?"

"I was just thinking about crime and tea bags. That's all."

"Jesus," Carlstrom sighed. She ripped the throats out of a couple more Half and Half creamers and squeezed their guts into her coffee.

"I was thinking about how crime...any crime is like a tea bag."

"Lord help me."

"He will," Davecki said smiling. He continued, "It, crime, keeps getting tighter and tighter around itself until something pops." He picked up his spoon. The tea bag was still in the bowl, securely garroted. He pulled on the string. He looked up. Carlstrom was looking at the spoon. He looked down. The string had cut into the swollen tea bag so tightly that the leaf-guts were spilling out.

"Sorta reminds me of the hermit's nose," Carlstrom volunteered.

"You gotta see past his looks. Gotta listen to the little words not the big ones or you'll miss the whole point of what he's saying." Davecki shook his head slowly forth and back.

"What?" Carlstrom asked. "I know you're thinking something. You're looking sad."

"Not sad. Chagrined."

"What the hell is that?"

"You don't know what chagrined means?" he asked setting down the spoon and picking up his cup. Slurp.

Burn Baby Burn

Carlstrom slurped herself. "Ummmmm, perfect. I know what I think it means, but I want you to say what you think it means so I can see if it's the same."

"Liar," Davecki said. Slurp. Slurp.

"Whatever." No slurp at all. But a stare, a glare, a bare look of contempt.

Silence.

"It means I'm nonplussed."

"Bastard."

Davecki laughed. He shrugged his shoulders. A loud cracking sound echoed from his clavicles. "Actually, to be accurate, I'm more embarrassed than anything," Davecki said.

"Why?" Carlstrom slurped more of her slurry.

"Because I'm from a little town in northern Wisconsin and you're from the big city of Mad Town where everyone is always pissed off for some reason or another."

"I hope you're enjoying yourself," she snipped.

"A girl once said that to me in a hay mow."

"I'm thrilled."

He sipped his tea. "Ahhhh, perfect."

"Okay," she said.

"Okay what?"

"Okay, I give up."

"Give up? Give up what?"

"You win."

"Huh?"

"You win. You're smart and I'm dumb. You're a home boy and I'm from the big city. You win. I'm ready."

"Ready? For what?"

"For whatever you've been dying to tell me since we sat down."

"Oh. You mean my revelation?"

"Whatever," she answered slowly. She glared.

"Okay," he said. He took another tea hit. Set his cup down. Leaned forward. Elbows on table. Cupless hands clasped. "He practically solved the whole fucking case."

"Bergamo?"

"NO! Dammit. Hjelmer!" Davecki shouted.

People in the restaurant stopped eating. Looked.

Carlstrom sat expressionless. "You don't have to yell at me."

"I'm not yelling AT you. I'm just speaking with assertivness."

"Christ I hate the nineties," she said, taking a sip of coffee. "How so?" she asked.

"How so what?"

"How has he solved the whole case? Practically speaking of course."

"Hjelmer said, 'They.' He spoke in the plural. He spoke... all the time he was speaking, he spoke in the plural. 'Weekend WarriORS,' he said."

"Now we're talking about the National Guard?" Bubba asked. Cynicism dripped from every word as if she were a too intelligent high school girl.

"Very funny," he said.

"Humor me," she said.

"It's a cult or something," he said.

She stopped her cup midway to her luscious lips. Silence.

"Ahem," clearing his throat, he leaned back. Tried to look around the room. "I hate it when you get your back to the wall all the time. It's not fair."

"Life's unfair. What the hell are you getting at?"

Burn Baby Burn

"Aces and eights," Davecki said.

Carlstrom put her cup down and started to leave the booth. "You are driving me nuts. Talk like a normal person will you?"

Silence from Davecki..

She slid back under the table. "Cult?"

Davecki's shoulders slumped. He hadn't realized how tense he was. He knew he wasn't making sense, but his best work had always been in the free association arena. He put his hands under the table for the first time and lowered his shoulders slowly. "Every fire's been on a weekend..."

"Or Tuesday," she interrupted.

"Different accelerants. Obvious inconsistencies in M.O. either designed to look like different perps or..."

"Actually different people," Carlstrom said.

Davecki grinned. "Say for instance, different people in a group who have to pass some sort of strange initiation rite..."

"Or a cleansing ritual," Carlstrom chimed in.

"Like what Hjelmer was hinting at. So, maybe the leader's got something against Superior?"

"Like you've got something against Duluth?"

"No. I love Duluth. It's just that some of the people there are dorks. This is different. Maybe it's a bigger challenge to set the fires all in one town."

"Or maybe Superior's at the crossroads of some of those harmonic convergencies or whatever."

"Or maybe Hjelmer's seeing an even bigger picture," Davecki said.

"And that would be..."

"Who knows? He's the lithium laced dreamer. But he

was talking trash about weekend warriors. Like they were puppets or something."

"I don't get it," Carlstrom said. She picked up her cup. Sipped. "Yuck! Too cold!" she blurted out.

"Neither do I. That Higher Power stuff. You can't incarcerate God. All I want to do is catch the bastard..."

"Or bastards," she corrected.

"...using your favorite word, who are actually striking the match."

"It's gotta be somebody smart," Carlstrom said.

It was Davecki's turn to question, "How so?"

"Well, somebody educated. Somebody with an attitude about white trash or something."

Davecki didn't want to admit to Carlstrom that he was confused, that he often thought himself into a state of utter confusion. His quick cure was always confession which was always good for the soul. "I don't get it," he said.

"Laura's right. He, or they, aren't burning down the National Bank of Commerce or the new ice rink."

Davecki downed the last of his tea. Plunking the cup into the saucer he said, "You saying it's someone who doesn't like old buildings?

"It could be a yuppie scum thing. You know, someone who doesn't think there's much virtue in maturity. Some demented soul who's got something against OLD itself."

"Much like you?"

"Very funny Dave. However, I happen to be very respectful of people your age. I just don't want to date 'em."

"Too bad."

"For whom?" she said and stood up.

Burn Baby Burn

"For you," he said getting himself up.

Together, exercising one of the time honored perks of police work, they, like Elvis, left the building without paying for their goodies.

Mike Savage

10

DISCO INFERNO

Satisfaction
came in a chain reaction
I couldn't get enough
so I had to self destruct.
The heat was on, yeah
rising to the top
everybody going strong
that is when my spot got hot
I heard somebody say...
Burn baby burn
disco inferno
burn baby burn
burn the mother down

— The Tramps, 1977
Written by: Leroy Green &
Ron "Have Mercy" Kersey

— Also released by Tina Turner, 1993

Burn Baby Burn

Star Woman struck the match. Her long brown hair reflected the soft glow of flame's flair. Included in the mix of soft light was the setting sun's last rays. The match-burst settled into a steady burn. She dropped the flaming stick manufactured in Cloquet, Minnesota into the burning barrel. Soon black smoke would curl skyward. Solved was the problem of increased dump fees at country landfills. Country folk always remedied their problems in the simplest ways possible.

If the busy bodies who called themselves bureaucrats, but were nothing more than mild mannered Nazis, knew the effect of their regulations... If they knew the true amount of PCBs, chlorofluorocarbons, mercury and miscellaneous toxins their regulations effectively put into the atmosphere... If they knew the full extent of their do-gooding they would be so guilt-laden they would have to vote themselves another pay raise just to afford the additional therapy and salve the psychic wound they'd inflicted on their own unsuspecting soul.

As it was, life went on as usual. *Nobody* knew what the hell they were doing in the overall sense. The country folk burned every possible fleck of refuse to save on exorbitant dump fees. The city folk paid their garbage tax thus making the City and not themselves responsible for contaminating vast acres of Wisconsin Point. The politicians thought they were leading. The followers felt they were free, and the match in the barrel went out.

"Rats," the woman said, and shook the red, white and blue box in her hands. No sound came from inside the cardboard container. "Matchless," she said. The sky above Cloverland was safe for at least another week. There

Mike Savage

would be no <u>Smoke</u> <u>Signals</u> and there would be no buildings burned in Superior. All for the want of a single match.

She had no idea her power.

This was good.

* * * * *

Davecki drove the Mustang hard into the sweeping left hand corner. Was there any other way to drive a Mustang with the power of three hundred and fifty horses cranking the drive shaft like a burly baker torquing a twist-tie on a loaf of Wonder Bread?

On the right, a big, old windmill stood on the bluff of the Amnicon River. The white and green refugee from Holland had been built by Jacob Davidson. An unlikely surname for a Finnish man. But, nonetheless, tis true, the man was a Finlander. Completed in 1906, the mill ground the grain of local farmers into flour until 1926. Davecki smiled. He imagined the industriousness of the hardy Finlander who'd built the contraption. It was ironic to him that the building had been constructed for practical purposes and here it was, only a few decades later, sitting like a meditating monk, useful only as eye candy for the thousands of tourists on their way to the newly gentrified Bayfield and its gelatinous Twin Cities Yuppie refugees.

So much had changed since the old days, when Davecki was a kid riding with his Old Man in the rattling Ford truck hauling scrap iron to the junk yards in Duluth to sell for good old fashioned money that was worth a good deal more than today's illusory dollar.

Back then the mill and the surrounding farms were roiling with activity. Everyone was paying their dues.

Burn Baby Burn

Contributing to their own livelihood. They were making hay, milking cows, calf birthing, corn planting, pumpkin harvesting, pulp peeling, herring harvesting, smelt seining, and the other one hundred and one commonplace activities people pursued to keep their families fed.

Not since the Beverly Hillbillies moved to California had Davecki seen the kind of industry that made families out of individuals, communities out of individual families and nations out of separate nationalities all gathered together to find life, liberty and happiness.

That was all gone. Gone were the days when a kid like Davecki could walk up to the screen door at the neighbor's farmhouse and ask for some bread and butter with sugar on it. Now it was all paranoia. These days it was his job to protect those farmers and their offspring that had moved to town to work or get an education.

Protect them from what? Screwball prophets who live in swamps? Angry firebugs who get their thrills burning down buildings? Speeders like himself?

He looked at the speedometer. One hundred and twenty-four miles an hour. He looked back at the roadway. Lakeside Baptist Church flicked past on the left like an outtake from a John Woo movie. Before he stopped trying to tickle the injection system with the toes of his right foot, he'd swooped down into the bottom of the dip that cradled the Poplar River and back up past County Highway D.

Soon the rocks and dust of Bardon Creek Road bounced off the bottom of his beloved Bomber like hail hitting a machine-shed roof. He knew he shouldn't be driving eighty on the dirt road, but he liked the way the car lofted over the hillocks and drifted left and right on

Mike Savage

the loose gravel like it was floating. That's exactly what the "Stang" was doing, floating. Not on the water, but on the loosely piled gravel that Ursula's husband had graded up with the town's big yellow John Deere grader. The pleasant floating sensation was only vaguely offset by the anxiety Davecki felt about Officer Jim. In nine years of driving to Cloverland, Deputy Jim had only nailed Davecki once. One hundred twenty two dollars and ninety cents for "Blowing through" (Jim said) the stop sign at the corner of Bardon and Hay Bale Lane. Davecki hadn't stopped for that particular stop sign in thirty years. He didn't even think of complaining when he saw the red lights of Officer Jim's cruiser behind him. Jim asked for his D.L. Davecki spent the time waiting for the ticket calculating what all the "rite of passages" at this particular crossroads had cost him. Figuring conservatively, Davecki knew he'd rolled the stop sign at least four thousand times. In reality it came out to considerably less than three cents per passage. It was a price he was willing to pay, for, there was one thing Davecki had learned in his <u>Short Happy Life of Frances Macomber</u>, everyone paid their dues. One way or another, everyone paid.

* * * * *

"Hello Starr," Davecki said. He squatted and patted the black cocker spaniel that was snuffing its nose in the crotch of his black blue jeans. "And hello to you too Molly." He rubbed the dog's ears between his hands and looked up at the willowy woman looming above him. The dog yelped in pain at the ear rub and scampered away.

Starr's father had been a special prosecutor in a land

Burn Baby Burn

and time far away. Willow Woman smiled and said, "Hello Dave." She looked down at her feet as Davecki stood.

"You know how to tell when you're talking to an assertive Finlander?" Dave asked.

"No."

"When he talks he looks at your feet not his own," Davecki answered.

Starr chuckled politely.

Davecki looked at the two towering Balm-of-Gilead trees behind Starr. They were magnificent. One hundred and thirty feet tall, they stood as two enormous sentinels that guarded the estate of Starr McKenneth. *Those trees were growing tall and strong before we were born*, Davecki thought.

"Eagles sometimes roost in the tippy tops," Starr said, seeing Davecki was admiring her trees.

"You don't say," Davecki said. He turned away from the trees and looked at the garden. It was huge. It was rife with life. Corn rose in the center aisles. Four rows, straight and wide. Pumpkins on the right. Potatoes left. Tomatoes marched across one end. Strawberries balanced the opposite end. "I stopped by the cemetery yesterday."

"Why else would you come by?" She said. "How is Shiva anyway?"

Davecki let the insult pass. She had always been jealous of her brother. Instead he said, "He's a pain in the ass as usual."

"He solve your crime for you?"

"Not really. But he did widen my paradigm."

"Paradigm? Talk English."

"He expanded the options. Made me see a wider view."

Mike Savage

"He's like that. Want some tea?"

Davecki said that tea would be just about precisely what he wanted, taking the opportunity to be more wordy than people liked. They walked up the steps of the porch. Starr went inside. Davecki hung back, leaned on the railing of the porch and looked across the lawn, the garden and the fields beyond sloping across the valley to the Big Lake. Fifty feet away, near the tall grass border of the mown hay field, the cocker spaniel stalked. It looked for all the world like a cat hunting mice.

Starr came out. "It'll take a while to heat the water." She sat on a bench abutting the porch rail. "So, how much change did Shiva give you?"

"Huh?" Davecki said, hopping into the swinging chair suspended from the ceiling of the open veranda.

"You said he gave you a pair of dimes." She grinned and looked down.

Now it was Davecki's turn to laugh politely, "Very funny," he said.

Molly trotted up the steps. Her claws clacked on the wooden planks that made up the deck of the porch.

"So?" Starr asked.

"He opened up the suspect list quite a bit," Davecki said, watching the dog lay down at its master's feet. The pooch opened its mouth. A dead mouse flopped off the flap of pink tongue.

"Good dog," Starr said reaching down to pat the puppy's pate. "You're such a good dog, even though you stink."

The dog panted, drooled and looked at Davecki through cloudy eyes. "Mostly we think it's businessmen and landlords who need to make large withdrawals from

Burn Baby Burn

their insurance company's bank accounts," Davecki answered.

The dog blinked. "Call Tri-pod," Starr said, stopping her head patting. At the same time she waved her hand in front of the dog's eyes and made a go-fetch gesture. Looking at Davecki the dog emitted a sound that was sort of a growl but more of a deep throated meow.

"Other than greedy landowners, demented teenage pranksters and certified nut-case firebugs, what is there?" Starr asked.

A three legged cat climbed the stairs and hopped past Davecki. The cat was tiger stripped with a stub of a tail like a Manx. It had no ears to speak of. The feline fiasco limped up to the dead mouse. It meowed softly. The two humans and the dog watched as the cat bit the mouse in half, left the rear end for the dog and went to lie down under the bench, behind Starr's feet.

The two animals ate as Starr explained, "Two winters ago I found the cat half dead on the side of the road. She was smashed into the snowbank but breathing. There were swervy snowmobile tracks leading up to her. Some damn berserker snowmobiler drunk with power. Brought her home. Her left front leg was mangled to a pulp. Looked like hamburger with fur blended in. Had to cut it off. Ears and tail were frozen. They eventually fell off. During her recuperation, Molly licked her about a million times. They bonded."

Crunching sounds came from under the bench.

"Very weird," Davecki said. Listening to the crunching, he scrunched up his face.

"Not really," Starr countered. "After she got better, the cat would stand in the middle of the kitchen table balancing on three legs. It was clear that her name was Tri-pod. By the time she got used to three legs, it was spring and Molly showed her all around the acreage. With only three legs, the cat couldn't hunt very well so she taught Molly how to be a mouser."

"That explains..."

Starr interrupted the interrupter, "I started calling Molly Meowly when she came up with that funny growl to announce that dinner was being served."

Davecki scanned the trio. Woman, dog, cat. "Whenever I come here I realize what a Neanderthal I am."

The dog stared. The cat blinked. Starr smiled and said, "That's a new awareness?"

"Cute," Davecki swatted the insult-ball back.

Starr smiled warmly and said, "Seriously, Shiva gave you a new awareness?"

"Huh?"

"The suspect shift. The wider vision?"

The cat retched up its dinner.

"Oh. That. As usual Shiva was going on and on about the Free Masons..."

"Thirty-seventh order?"

"Something like that. Anyway, he also chanted on about punks and pyre and purification. Made me think of a cult."

The dog farted.

"Ugh!" Davecki groaned. He got up.

"Leaving before tea?" Starr asked.

"Naw, I just forgot the package Hjelmer sent for you."

"I'll take care of the tea," Starr said.

He walked to the Stang and wondered at the weirdness of life. He wished he was less meat and potatoes and

Burn Baby Burn

more incense and aroma. Returning to the porch he waited for Starr to appear. He handed the package to the woman and said, "Listen. I need to know something."

"Why else would you drive all the way out here?"

He wanted to say, "To see you," but passed on the complication. Instead he said, "Because driving around visiting old friends and beautiful women is way better than work."

"Which category do I fit in?"

"Beautiful," he said brusquely. "Now. This question. It's not easy to ask."

"Fire away."

Davecki groaned.

Starr looked at him a second and then giggled. "Oh. No pun intended."

He sighed. Looked across the valley to the mighty Gitchee Gumee sitting bluely in its cauldron of green. "You think your brother is setting any of these fires?"

She looked down at the four by four package in her hand. It was now wrapped in what appeared to be a white plastic grocery bag from Jubilee foods. She rolled the container around between her slender fingers. "I don't think so."

Davecki ignored how pretty she looked and how he felt when she expressed indecision. Coming to the rescue had always been a turn-on for him. "Was he ever much of a firebug when he was a kid?"

The package stopped moving. "Every kid plays with matches."

"Well, that doesn't exactly answer the question does it?" He didn't like this part of himself. This part that could be hard, or, when necessary, cruel.

Mike Savage

She looked right at him and didn't look away. "He's not burning down Superior." Her fingers started tearing at the plastic wrapping.

"What do you mean, 'every kid plays with matches'?"

Her eyes tightened down. "Every kid plays with matches."

He looked away. He was angry, hated her evasiveness. He looked down. He saw she was opening the gift. He looked up. She was still holding him in her fixed gaze. She was opening the gift without so much as looking at it. Her hazel eyes were unflinching.

He let go of the anger and said, "Sure. We all played with matches. But I've gotta ask you if he was ever, you know, if he ever had a problem, er, a fascination with fire?"

Her look was still directly at him. *Or was it through him*, he thought. Heavy sigh. Resigned tone, "Okay. He WAS into it. Long after the rest of us stopped. But he isn't torching buildings. He and his friend Ray fooled around with gasoline making Molotov cocktails and making Moses Bushes, but they never burned any buildings down or anything."

"Moses Bushes?"

"They'd soak a dogwood bush or a lilac bush and light 'er up...pretend it was God talking to them the way God talked to Moses in the desert."

"Hmmm. Sounds like he's had a spiritual bent all his life."

"You could say that," Starr said. She pulled the plastic away from the package and dropped it on the bench seat next to her. The Pentax logo was now clearly visible. Brown paper wrapping. Unconsciously, she plucked at

Burn Baby Burn

the tape on the box. It sounded like someone flicking their fingernails on a balloon. She glanced down and pulled at a tape piece. "I don't know... I guess I remember a few other things."

"Like?"

"Like, well... Once they poured gasoline in a line across Highway 13 and lit it just as a car was coming."

"Really?"

"Yeah. Damndest luck. The one car they choose to flame turned out to be Dad coming from St. Paul to visit us. Dad stopped and searched around the ditch and found Shiva and Ray hiding in the cattails."

Davecki looked at the box. The end flap was open.

"They said it was a 'Wall of Fire' thing they'd seen Joey Chitwood do at the Bayfield County Fair. They wanted to see a car go through it in real life."

A crow cawed in the distance. "What else?" Davecki asked.

She pulled at the guts of the package. Out slid a bundle of tissue. "Fire bombs, campfires, once they started the Chequamegon National Forest on fire."

He looked at her sharply, "You're kidding."

"You asked," she said plucking at the tissue.

"A forest fire?"

"They said they were camping. It was July. Dry. They were, 'encamped under the shelter of a great Jack Pine,' he said."

"He talked like that back then too?"

"Nam made it worse."

"I don't remember any forest fires in the Chequamegon forest, none big enough to mention that I recall."

Mike Savage

"The volunteer fire department put it out right away."

"No buildings?" Davecki asked.

The tissue fell away. Davecki couldn't discern what was in her hands. She lifted the strange looking thing. It seemed extraordinarily heavy in her hands. It looked like a bag or some pouch-thing made from? What?

She smiled. Looked down for the first time since talking about Hjelmer's fire fascination.

"They did burn down Uncle Perlee's cabin," she said, lifting the object.

"What?"

"He said they were all in Uncle Perlee's shack smoking straws of grass and a couple of cigarettes they'd stolen from Ruben's garage. A match caught the mattress on fire and they all ran away. It burned right down to the concrete blocks it was sitting on and murdered the large white pine the cabin was under."

"Murdered?"

"Anyone who kills a white pine is a murderer," she said, pulling some strings on her brother's gift.

Davecki squirmed at the sight of the bag in her hands. "What the hell is that?"

"It's a medicine pouch."

"A what? What's it made from? It looks funny."

"It's a heart sack from a deer."

"A what?"

"It's a medicine bag made from the heart of a deer," she said smiling. She got up and said, "Tea's going to be really strong."

Burn Baby Burn

Mike Savage

11

For some people, evil is a religion. For some, an obsession. For others, its a profession. Then there are those who play the "game" of evil like they were playing Monopoly. These "players" always have a way of bumping into the board or breaking the rules or playing so stupidly that the game is ruined for the more serious minded folk. God <u>does</u> work in mysterious ways, His wonders to perform.

Burn Baby Burn

It was too volatile. According to Match Crandal's manual, modulating the explosiveness of acetone as an accelerant could be accomplished easily by, "misting with 409 from a spray bottle." It was all supposed to burn, "hot, fast and without a trace."

Looking at the tall wall of electrical meters, he wondered how Crandal and the mystery videotaper from Duluth could start so many fires that didn't appear to be arson. He'd done his research. The building had almost burned down once. On January 11, 1954, a Sunday, fire swept through the Mauke's apartment causing $10,000 damage. There were two Maukes. They had to be rescued from the third floor by firemen using an extension ladder. The blaze was contained to the apartment and all the other residents escaped unharmed in any way. *A botch job*, he thought.

That was forty-five years ago. Back then the Nottingham was unwilling to be a victim. Now it was ripe. He'd snooped around long enough, asked enough innocent sounding questions to learn about the building's weaknesses. Now it was a perfect victim. "Why's that light flickering?" he joked with the Pamela Lee look alike who was working in the coffee shop.

"The wiring in this building sucks," the beauty said.

Hot Diggity. If he could pull this thing off, he knew, he'd be certain to make it to at least the high twenties, maybe even break into the thirties. Such a high ranking would mean that chicks like the coffee shop babe would sit on his lap at parties. They always flocked around the high ranking guys.

He thought about the women he wanted. It wasn't just

Mike Savage

A woman. It was women. Tall ones. Short ones. Blondes, brunettes, fat and funny, skinny and shy, he wanted them all. Just like those fucking cops. *They always get ALL the girls.*

Fumbling with his bottle of fingernail polish remover, he wondered why they just didn't label it acetone. He wondered why anyone would bottle a liquid that would wipe out an entire ethnic group. *Do they sell this stuff in Poland?*

Splashing liquid all around the wall of electric meters, he considered why he didn't try for the fortieth level...*Victim With Fire.* Everyone lusted for the high rankings. But that was too high for him. Sure he'd never get to go out with supermodels as a lowly thirty, but murder? That was just not his style. He was less aggressive. Even though he was butt-ugly, the better chicks still had to like him if he was a thirty or higher. After all they wanted to ascend the ranks as well.

He sloshed acetone around like he was watering a boisterous bloom of marigolds instead of a group of electrical meters. There had to be a hundred of the round glass bulbs bulging off the east wall like an orderly squadron of upturned Mason jars. Sticking the nearly empty bottle in the pocket of his "Live to Ride/Ride to Live" denim jacket, he wondered why the alley door was open when he'd tried it. He couldn't fathom such lax security. Being from South Saint Paul, it was a given that every door was locked and every window secured in someway. The Dragon was smart to select Superior as the battleground. Full of people too stupid to move to the Twin Cities, it was also replete with worthless old buildings that burned, burned, burned.

Burn Baby Burn

The acetone dripped from the meter faces. He listened to the silence of the old building's bowels. Unhealthy. Such silence was unhealthy. Before flunking out of medical school he'd learned that a healthy bowel transmitted the rumblings of peristalsis. *Why didn't they just call them bowel sounds?* he wondered as he swooshed 409 mist everywhere. A healthy building this big would transmit some sort of sounds. Air ducts opening. Mercury switches switching. Something. But not this building, this Naughtyham. It was too old, too tired, too weary to even burp or grunt in pleasure or pain. He sniffed. The slightly musty air was tinged with the acrid hint of volatility. Fire skulked nearby. "Ah, sublimation," he whispered. The fastest way to a flammable gas and a flammable lass at the next convocation. He felt a stirring in his groin.

Maybe I should have accepted the Roofies, he thought. It wouldn't have been too hard to knock out some desperate-for-a-man Welfare Mom from Catlin Courts. Courage grew within his chest at the potential aroma of flame. Knowing he was summoning fire where only air and dust and storage rooms existed thrilled him. The knowledge gave him a boldness that replaced the timidness bestowed by thirty-three years of ugliness. He looked at the timbers, the pipe, the concrete...all safe and ignorant of the rage that was coming. He smiled. He may not be able to lure a woman to sacrifice. He may not have the balls to use Roofies to drug a bitch... But there were other paths to the highest orders. It was appalling how easy it was to reach level twenty-two. *Thank you Milwaukee*, he thought. There he'd managed three buildings and one innocent victim. The stiffness in his pants grew, *this building could yield some innocents*, he hoped. It wasn't as good as pre-

Mike Savage

meditated murder, but it was good enough for the mid to high thirties. His walking was seriously altered now.

Returning to the big steel door, he hooked the 409 bottle into the pocket of his blue jeans by the pump handle. He pulled out the baggie and matches. "Damn!" he whispered. The baggie had broken. The kerosene soaked rag, the rag with the Dragon's image sketched on it, had soaked Crandal's match book. This glitch caused his stance to return to normal. He scrunched up the baggie and put it into the inside pocket of his Harley Eagle jacket. With trembling hands he opened the match book. He didn't want to show up at the convocation/seance as a failure. The Dragon likened failure to masturbation. Plus, failures were severely frowned upon. How would he explain to his boss, the sudden need for two weeks off? He couldn't afford even a day or two in the RFP camp. He'd seen what "Reprogramming" did to people. *Ugh!* he thought. It made the Scientologist's reprogramming camps seem like a couple of weeks at a Girl Scout Jamboree.

He switched off the basement lights. He opened the door slowly. He stood in the portal. Peered out the opening into the darkness. No headlights. He listened. No sounds of walking or traffic. A cricket cricketed in the back yard of the yellow house across the alley. He waited for his eyes to adjust. The match heads, he hoped, weren't completely soaked. The more matches missing, the lower his rung of ordination. He *HAD* to make at least the high twenties.

The match pulled away easily. Too easily? He stroked the head across the strike bar. The kerosene soaked match head crumbled and the shaft bent over like a limp dick. The matches were useless.

Burn Baby Burn

Staring at the match, he realized something else was wrong. He raised his head to listen. There was no sound. But something was wrong. There was an interior alarm, a silent inner warning going off in his head. It was something he could and could not hear. It was like staring at the Northern Lights and swearing he could hear music playing in the far off distance. *Someone's coming!* He balled up the rag and jammed it into his pocket.

The sound of a door opening across the basement made him stuff the matches and both hands deep into his pockets. The lights sprang on. Across the basement, a blonde haired man appeared. If it wasn't Matt Damon, it was his twin brother. "Anybody here?" the man called.

Before the blondie saw him, he stepped out of the doorway and headed down the alley. Before he'd taken ten steps the headlight beam of a car appeared on 19th street ahead of him. He felt the bump of the 409 bottle against his leg. In an instant he grabbed the bottle and stuffed it hastily inside the half open flap of his jacket.

Play it like you're a tenant leaving the building, he thought as he stuffed his hand back into his jacket pocket. He hustled down the alley's pockmarked surface. Hoofing it toward the Quickprint parking lot across nineteenth, he saw his shadow loom large. Another wash of headlight beam settled on him from behind. The intensity of the light grew. Then a car rolled alongside and his shadow vanished. A white fender. Red numbers. Fifty-four. *Shit!* he thought. A spotlight, door, red and blue lettering, TO PROTECT AND SERVE.

Fucking A! A cop!

Rider's side window powering down. "You okay?" A man's voice resonated from inside the car. Smell of ciga-

Mike Savage

rette smoke wafted out. *There's gotta be a law against smoking in a City vehicle.*

"Fine," he said. Sweating. His palm squeezed the oily rag. He hoped it wasn't dangling out. His other hand groped the pocket for Match Crandal's match book. It wasn't there. "Late night," he said, trying to put an airy lilt to his answer. *Change in plan*, he thought. *Play it like I hooked into a one night stand. Like I'm leaving for home after a night of shagging. Cops understand sport fucking.*

The squad rolled along at the same pace his watery legs were propelling him. It seemed like he was walking in gumbo mud in April. Gravel. Crunching from beneath the tires and his shoes. *Say something dammit!*

"You live here?" the cop's voice called out.

At last. "Naw. I'm from," *FUCK!* "Wilmer." *God damn. Don't panic.*

There was a squawk from the police car's radio. The cop called out, "What? From where?"

F - U - C - K M - E ----- BUSTED! RUN? Stay Calm. Finesse 'em. He's just a jerkwater testosterone freak from a jerkwater town. "Wilmer." he answered. *Not too loud asshole!* "I'm up here working for the BN doing maintenance of way."

More radio chatter. "Squad Fifty-four. Where are you?"

"Roger on the ten-eighty," the cop's voice came out the window.

What the fuck's a ten eighty?

"It's awful late," the cop's voice came out the window as they approached the end of the building and the sidewalk. "Besides, isn't it the BNSF now?" he added.

His voice sounds harder. The edge of the building's

120

Burn Baby Burn

coming up. The sidewalk. The street. This fucker's going to follow me until I get to the parking lot and my car isn't there and...

"Yeah. I was at the Lamplighter and scored a hot cunt. She was all greased up and ready for some righteous trouser trout," he said.

Half hearted laughter from within the squad.

Continuing his slow ambling walk, he looked down into the car's open window. The passenger seat was empty. A brushed aluminum ticket book reflected muted light. *In the Cities they'd never let a guy patrol alone.*

The cop's voice echoed, "The Lamplighter? A stripper? Lives here? At the Nottingham?"

"I don't know if she was a stripper or not. All's I know was her pussy was dripping to get fucked and she took me here to get nailed."

The sidewalk.

Look right.

FUCK! The blonde Matt Damon guy was hustling down the sidewalk toward a second squad that was parked near the entrance of the apartment building.

"That's him!" Damon man yelled.

There was no real decision made. It was all instinct that made the arsonist turn on his heel instantly and bolt down the alley in the opposite direction.

"SON OF A BITCH!" bellowed from the interior of squad fifty-four.

This would never happen to Match, he thought as he heard tires squeal. He sprinted. He flailed his arms for the utmost speed. There were two squads and a civilian pursuing him now. There'd be two more squads in two more minutes. He dashed left. Heard the sound of howl-

Mike Savage

ing rubber in the distance. *That's the squad on the street. Backing up to Tower? Can't outrun radio frequency.*

Sprinting blindly down the dark alley, his path was suddenly illuminated. Headlight beams from the squad. Two shadows loom large in front of him again. *The squad got turned around. Why two? Blondie? I'm toast!* He darts right toward a backyard. Suddenly, WHAMO! He gets tackled from behind. He turns to fight. *God Almighty! This fucker's strong!* He wrestles with the figure on his back.

"You're not going anywhere," Blondie's voice growls. Incredibly strong fingers squeeze his throat. *Can't breathe.* He claws at the strong guy's arms. His feet are flailing. Breath is failing. Bright lights oscillate around the edges of his vision. *Don't black out!* He spasms his back into an arch like he used to do during football practice. It has been twenty years at least since his last neck bridge. However, this is life and death, or at least twenty years to life in prison for attempted arson, so the lack of practice and disappearance of muscle tone are replaced by adrenaline enhancement. Who needs steroids?

The blonde attacker is caught off balance. Flies forward. Releases the choke hold. *Breathe asshole!* With Blondie bouncing into the neighbor's swing set, Arsonist Man jumps up and starts running. This time he dashes behind an old car up on blocks. It's an old green Dodge Dart with rusting fenders and no wheels. Bustrak is spray painted in white letters on the trunk. "Stop in the Name of the Law or I'll shoot!" he hears behind him.

RUN BABY RUN!!!

Shots are fired.

He hears another sound in the distant foreground. It

Burn Baby Burn

is unmistakable. A Harley. It's coming closer. He dodges between another house and zips down the sidewalk. He turns left and sprints toward the sound of the cycle. *THERE!* Ahead is a tall man astride a rumbling Harley Sportster. A passenger is getting off the back of the bike. They are stopped and at idle in front of a house on the alley behind the video store that used to be 7-11.

Somehow he runs even faster. *Knock the fucker off!* he thinks and runs up at full speed. Without breaking stride he launches himself at the tall man. As he is flying through the air Tall Man turns away from the babe getting off the bike. The ruggedly handsome face of Tall Man erupts in surprise. "WHAT THE HELL?!?" Tall Man yells.

As is always the case in crisis, time does everyone a favor by slowing down. As he approaches the collision with the man, he is granted a long languorous look at the woman who has just dismounted the Sportster. *I'm in love!* the arsonist asserts instantly. A perfect face, round lovely cheeks and a beautiful smile with lips like Bernadette Peters.

THUD! the sound of two bodies colliding without the benefit of football gear or being surrounded by a few thousand pounds of automobile.

"ARGGGHHH!" the beefy biker bellows.

"EEEEK!" the beautiful biker's babe babbles.

"Uggggh!" arsonist asserts.

The Sportster falls on its owner's leg. The bad guy leaps up and grabs the handlebars. He lifts the bike as if he were Jesse Ventura body slamming Norm Coleman and Skip Humphrey simultaneously.

"NOT MY BIKE!" Tall Man hollers. He starts kicking Arsonist in the hip with strong sure strokes as if he

Mike Savage

were Scottie trying to make the Enterprise do something it wasn't designed for.

Arsonist twists the Sportster's throttle. It had been on its side for only a couple of seconds and the S&S carb was only moderately choked up from the overflow of gas.

"VAROOM VAROOM VAROOM!!!" The mighty engine roars through Flying Eagle slash-cut straight pipes. *This machine is stroked and toked and will haul my ass to freedom*, Arsonist Man realizes. He looks up. He looks ahead. The guy on the ground kicking him is starting to be irritating. But, what he sees ahead is even more aggravating. Blondie is coming at him in the same flying tackle type of maneuver he'd just executed on Tall Biker Man.

Arsonist Fellow is luckier by a little. Tall Biker Man had an excellent reason to be distracted. *If I had such a babe on the back of my bike, I wouldn't be looking anywhere else either*, he reasons. But he concludes that that isn't his problem right now, his problem is this: *There is this guy who is solid muscle and looks like Matt Damon flying through the air at me. He is going approximately the speed of a runaway Mack truck coming down Mesaba Avenue. What's a mother to do? Calgon take me away!*

Arsonist man doesn't really answer the question. He simply reacts. He leans way back. He lets go of the handlebars and leans so far back he is actually lying flat out on the seat of the motorcycle.

This done, Flying Matt (Wallenda) Damon-look-a-like whizzes past and crashes directly into Tall Biker Man who had just then managed to erect himself into the formidable fighting machine he obviously was. It could happen to even the most evil biker. After all, being struck full in the chest by a one hundred and eighty five pound

Burn Baby Burn

projectile of flying muscle-bound boy toy is no small thing. Tall Biker Man and Mr. Good Looking Civilian To The Rescue Man both tumbled into a heap.

Arsonist Fellow thinks, *"Free at last, free at last, thank God Almighty I'm free at last.*

Not so fast there Mr. Arsonist A-Hole. There's another player in this scene. Her name is Beautiful Biker Babe. Seeing her man go down, besides making her grin, forces her to realize that her ride will soon be vanishing down the street.

"NOT MY BIKE!!!" she yells. Whereupon she whips her specially licensed Harley Davidson mini-purse in a wide arc at the end of its extra long straps (the better to span her ample bosom with).

The mini-purse is small for sure, but it does contain four dollars and thirty cents in change, three credit cards, a dispenser of birth control pills and the remains of a half pound brick of hash.

This object, traveling at the leather-purse-equivalent of the speed of light, is a credible weapon.

Utilizing the uncanny ability most women have for finding small objects in the dark, Biker Babe manages to whack Arsonist Fellow full in the face. Besides instantly breaking his nose, the blow causes him to ball up into a fetal position making noises much akin to several feral pigs devouring a stray cat. At this sound everything in the surreal scene seems to halt. *What the hell is that noise?* crosses all four minds at the same time.

Arsonist Fellow, having the most to lose, realizes the strange squeal is his own face trying to scream through a quart of gushing blood containing the unappetizing bone fragments of what was once the rather striking nose.

Mike Savage

Thusly motivated, Arsonist Man falls off the once-again-falling-motorcycle and, clutching <u>The Remains of His Face</u>, dashes down the alley toward Louis' Cafe. Everyone thinks it's a restaurant, but the sign says CAFE.

RUN! is all that goes through his mind.

This he does.

With each step, another semblance of coherence returns to his pain enshrouded mind. After several steps, several more coherences congeal in his muddled cranium. Arsonist Arsehole manages to string together something resembling actual thought. These synaptic occurrences seem to be screeching: <u>*RUN SPOT RUN*</u>!

This he does.

And he does it some more. Hold nose. Bleeding. Spitting blood. Spitting bone. Sprinting home. *Mama! I want my Mama!!* He's in a blind rage. He's incoherent for the most part. All he knows is his face was smashed in by a beautiful woman and it was by her purse and not another part of her anatomy. *Damn the luck!*

But he knows a couple of other things as he runs at full speed past two diners exiting the rear entrance of Louis' Cafe. There doesn't seem to be anyone chasing him. There doesn't seem to be any red flashing lights flirting around the corners of the buildings. This indicates that Superior's Finest is nowhere near. He runs across the parking lot of the Library, dashes between the Social Security Building and the Minnesota Block.

Into the Keyport parking lot he humps. There a sleek new T-80 Volvo awaits. He stops. Panting like a dog, he pinches what's left of his nose and listens. Nothing. He reaches into his jacket pocket. *Oh Fuck!*

He pulls out keys only. *Where's the oily rag? The*

Burn Baby Burn

match book? He pushes the keyless entry and the car chirps. He gets in, starts the car and exits stage left from the parking lot and turns right onto Banks Avenue. *Don't look like you're fleeing the scene. Drive slow. Drive toward the action. They'll never suspect a Volvo heading right back toward the crime scene. Don't act unnatural. Don't attract attention. God I wish I didn't have to hold my nose!*

He keeps rolling sedately down Banks Ave. No flashing lights behind him, in front of him. *I'm going to make it!*

"JESUS!" he screeches through his hand. A wild man is running right down the middle of the street at him. *GO!* Arsonist Fellow's mind shrieks. He steps on the gas and steers the car directly at the wild hairy beast charging like a water buffalo straight at him. At the last second, the water buffalo dives to the side and the Volvo doesn't run down an innocent man.

At Twenty-first Street the Volvo turns right and vanishes up the bridge into the night. It doesn't stop until it gets into Minnesota. At the Thompson Hill Tourist Information Center, he gets out. His nosebleed is stanched. He pops the trunk. He hurries around to the back of the car and lifts the lid. He pulls out a small yellow cotton rag. A Johnny Cash CD flies away from the cloth and clatters noisily to the pavement. He pulls the bottle of acetone from his pocket and douses the licence plate. In his rage he scrubs the plate vigorously removing the still soft lacquer he'd applied only hours earlier. The Minnesota plate, HCL 800 vanishes. In it's place is the real license plate. It says HOT SHOT.

It should say DUMB FUCK, he thinks, rushing to get in and go, leaving the CD behind.

Mike Savage

12

Knowest thou not this of old, since man was placed upon the earth, that the triumph of the wicked is short, and the joy of the hypocrite but for a moment?

— Job 20: 4-5

Burn Baby Burn

Davecki hated being called out at four thirty in the morning. Hated it when some criminal wouldn't, as dispatch explained, talk to anyone but him. He was not going to leave his ore dock aerie, was planning on hanging up on dispatch. But then Connie said, "It's some nut-case calling himself Shiva."

So, instead of being rude and staying warm and cozy, Davecki got up, dressed and left his favorite spot in all the world, his bed. Then he had to leave his second favorite spot, the storied and enviable "Ore Dock Home" of Detective Dave. Ten years earlier he was sick of being a cop. He thought of running for mayor, but decided to pursue his other lifelong dream, owning and operating a restaurant. Of course it had to be a unique and one of a kind restaurant because Davecki ALWAYS did things unconventionally. He would never have thought of buying the old Great Northern ore dock next to the Nemadji River, but his friend Lucy who was unfairly fired from the Assessor's Office happened to mention one day that the structure was for sale.

He paid $48,000 dollars after fibbing about his plans for the monstrosity. Said he was buying it for the demolition value. But, when the two Dan's of the Building Inspector's office started getting applications for permits, Davecki's real intentions became known.

It was a good plan in some ways. Instead of spending hours and hours in his squad thinking about how much he'd come to hate police work, he mused about the menu. Ore Dock Appetizers. Timber Taters. Great Northern Goulash. Taconite Tacos. Pier One pastries.

If you're just dreaming, why not dream BIG, Davecki

Mike Savage

had rationalized. He liked the thought of diners looking out over Allouez Bay while they devoured fresh lake trout, hot apple cider and good steaks. He'd saved his pay for years and had a sizeable cash stash. The kind that made financial planners get teary eyed. He swung the buy-out easily and used the equity and his still hefty balance as leverage for start up loans.

He fought like mad with government agencies in the City County Complex, the capital building Madison and even a few in Washington D.C. (Something about the national defense and the country's possible need to start shipping wartime amounts of taconite pellets in the event of an Armageddon with Saddam Hussein). Luckily his nephew Brian was an engineer for the entire country of the United Arab Emirates. The plans were flawless and had to be approved.

When all was said and done, the strain of the preliminary permit work was about enough to dampen his desire to be a restaurant owner. However, Davecki, sometimes short on smarts, but always long when it came to stubbornness, persisted. He saw himself as a combination of Nash Bridges and Don Johnson in real life. Then came building the grades and approaches, the highly engineered on-and-off-ramps and the ADA approved emergency exits. It was a nightmare. Just the thing to cure his professional malaise and his taste for entrepreneurship. *Besides, there's only one Nash Bridges*, he thought.

It was the biggest flop since Remo Gallagucia ran for governor of Minnesota against Jesse Ventura.

But, there were several good results. Number one: He was the proud owner of the most expensive driveway in North America. Number two: He could park the motor

Burn Baby Burn

home he bought after selling his house at the end of the dock. Number three: Having discovered the convenience of living full time in a wee motor home, he could stand in said dwelling and wonder if the fierce nor'westers screeching in off the lake from Canada were actually going to blow him and his tin-can-home into the bay. Some of those blows were exhilarating to say the least.

Not as exhilarating as stepping out of the used Honey Bee motor home and seeing the exquisite pink of an early sunrise in August. Across the swamp (er, excuse me, "wetlands") to the east, the old BN dock stood in dark silhouette. Ten planks away waited the Mustang. He stood still and breathed. He raised his hands and spread his fingers to receive all the air and sun and dark and light and spirit the world and God had to offer. He turned around three hundred and sixty degrees and was glad there were no neighbors to see him acting like such a fool. Then he smiled and got into the Mustang and contributed to the ozone problem by starting the infernal combustion engine.

He drove south across the planking. It rattled under the tires. He wondered what the hell Shiva was doing in jail in August. December he could understand. Solace from the cold. But now when the mosquitoes were at their best in the Pokegema River bottom? Strange indeed. A third of the way along the pier, the car plunged down the access ramp his nephew had designed. The huge pillars and mighty pine timbers of the structure eased past like stoic columns in a European cathedral. He rolled down the wooden ramp and onto the blacktop approach. He punched the electronic garage door opener on the dash that triggered the power-gate he had to put up to keep the curious and bold at bay. Once all the hoopla died down and people came to accept the fact that some nut was living atop an abandoned ore dock, the gate was less needed. But, still, he liked the sense of security the barricade provided. Even if it was flimsy. The headlights illuminated the gate retracting. He zipped past the moving metal as close as he could get without hitting it and punched the button again as he drove onto the parking lot of the Spur station. He groped for the cell phone on the passenger seat and punched the hot key for dispatch.

"Hey Connie, tell Jerry I'm going to be a little late. I'm going to stop and pick up a chicken burrito for Hjelmer," he said into the phone.

* * * * *

"Hey Jerry," Davecki said, entering interview room two.

The squadman with the silvery locks and rugged good looks rolled his eyes and said, "He's all yours. I've got a report to file," and left the room.

The second squadman in the room was black haired and intense looking. "Caught him running away from the Nottingham. Found this stuff too."

"Thanks Brad," Davecki said. He tossed the Taco Bell bag on the table. The wild prophet of Pokegama glanced at Davecki with the disdainful look Starr Woman had used on him when he left her farm.

Hjarvis grabbed the burrito. "Wasn't running AWAY," he said as he ripped open the bag like a six-year-old opening a Christmas present.

"Those are the first words he's said since telling Jerry

Burn Baby Burn

he was Shiva and wouldn't talk to anyone but you," the young blue said.

"Figures," Davecki said. He yawned and sat in a chair across the green table from Shiva. Davecki yawned again, scratched his jaw. "Nice medicine pouch," he said.

Hjarvis was devouring the burrito. His bushy eyebrows raised. "Mmmmmm," he said. "Chicken. You know chicken tastes a lot like skunk?"

"Cough. Cough," from Bradley Blue.

"Yeah...I've heard," Davecki said.

Hjarvis looked at the young officer leaning against the one way mirror. He swallowed and said, "Hey Jerry! Thanks for not cuffing me."

There was a tapping at the window glass.

Hjarvis looked at Brad. "You'll never see road kill between Kimmes' and Diamond Jills."

"Really?" Brad said.

Davecki coughed and said to the blue, "Hjelmer here is the Hermit of Pokegema. Ever hear of him?"

"Can't say I have."

"Not many know about this guy," Davecki said. "In fact, it's probably the most remarkable thing I've ever seen, you being in town on a Sunday morning," Davecki said addressing the still munching hermit. Davecki reached over to a tape recorder on the table and pushed two buttons at once. "You want to tell us who you are Hjelmer?"

The great beard fluttered. The two pieces of chicken parts that had fallen from the burrito and lodged in the tangle of whiskers, tumbled down the beard front and vanished beneath the table. The drooping mustache tweaked around like it was a mouse curling up for a nap.

Mike Savage

His eyes focused first on the recorder, then on Brad. "I'm Shiva the Destroyer," he said in a booming gravel voice.

"Humph," Bradley said.

Davecki scratched his head. He adjusted the chair. "For the record, I'm talking to Hjelmer Hjarvis, AKA the Prophet of Pokegema, AKA Shiva God of Destruction. Am I right?" Davecki asked.

"The power to destroy is resident in us all. This dark side is what makes us godlike. You are correct sir," Hjarvis answered.

"Ed McMahon may also be present," Davecki laughed and looked at the Blue standing behind him. "Also present is Officer Bradley Donald Trump. We're conducting this interview at 4:55 a.m.," Davecki said looking at the green and brown waterproof Timex on his right wrist. It is Sunday..."

"Ahem," Trump interrupted.

"Oh yeah. It's Monday already isn't it? Reminds me of the old saying, 'Time's fun when you're having flies.' This interview is taking place on Monday morning August thirty-first, nineteen ninety eight," Davecki said and reached for the crumpled up bag between himself and Shiva. He started straightening out the balled-up rectangle of off-white wrapping tissue. Without looking at the man across from him, he asked, "Why were you running from the police Hjelmer?"

The munching gnome swallowed hard. Tears leapt to his sparkling eyes. "Was running TO 'em," he said through a straining neck. "Got any root beer?"

Davecki waved his hand slightly toward the one way mirror. "TO them?" he asked.

Hjarvis stretched his chin and swallowed again. "Yeah.

Burn Baby Burn

I smelt him going past. He used the Oliver Bridge and I smelt him and saw a bunch of fried people being carried out of the Nottingham," he coughed.

The door opened. Jerry came in with a can in his hand. "Sprite's the best we could do."

"Gimme!" Hjarvis said reaching for the beverage.

"Saw them?" Davecki asked.

Hjarvis swigged wholesale gulps. The cops waited. He gasped for air after drinking and said, "Dream."

Davecki could see out of the corner of his eye that the blues were shaking their heads in disbelief at each other. He was glad Hjelmer was focused on the soda. The cranky soothsayer didn't suffer fools lightly.

Silence.

Hjarvis burped.

Brad Blue snuffed down a laugh.

Jerry left the room chuckling.

"What's this?" Davecki asked lifting a yellow wash cloth.

"Wash rag dummie," Hjarvis said.

Davecki transferred the rag to his left hand and rubbed the thumb and forefingers of his right together. He raised the digits to his nose and said, "Smells like fuel oil."

"Kerosene dummy," Hjarvis said. The tramp reached across the table for the match book that was still on the table top.

"That's evidence," Brad Blue growled.

Hjarvis snatched the matches up before Davecki could stop him. The dirty fingers held up the yellow match book. "So's this!" the troll said as he gleefully flipped the blue the bird. He grinned wider, but the only evidence of the expression was the widening of the great grey beard. His hair bush parted enough to reveal long yellow teeth. He leaned toward the tape recorder and read loudly from the match book cover, "THE HOT PLACE!" He flipped the match book over and read again, "HOTTEST PUSSY IN TOWN!"

"Give me that," Davecki said.

Hjarvis tossed the matches across the table.

"Quit fooling around Hjelmer. This is serious. Your sister told me about the Wall of Fire and the Moses Bushes and Uncle Perlee's Cabin. This is serious shit you're in."

"You don't know serious shit from Shinola ALPHONSE. You live up dere in the clouds on your fancy dock and drive around in your fancy smancy car and play at copper man while all the power of the people is being sacrificed to greed. Serious Shit is an island in the Bad River Slough, look it up. Serious shit is a man who will shoot his best friend in the face because the legs of that friend are hanging off a rubber tree limb thirty feet away having just been blown there by a Sapper's Claymore stolen from that friend's very own fire base probably by the poor grunt's house boy. Serious shit is leaving a perfectly good pine martin frying in a pan, running on railroad ballast for four miles to get busted and fed chicken flesh from Jacko Hell. Serious shit is not accidentally burning down a cabin, serious shit is burning down an apartment building leaving thirty-two dead and fifty-one critically burned. Serious shit..."

"I get your point," Davecki said.

But Hjarvis was on a roll, "You can eat shit, get your shit together, be shit out of luck, have shit for brains, wade around in a tub of bull shit, have a shit fit, be up shit creek without a paddle, look like shit, be a lucky shit,

Burn Baby Burn

dumb shit or be just plain shitty. And that's saying absolutely nothing about..."

"I GET YOUR POINT," Davecki yelled.

But Hjarvis wasn't done. "You can shit or get off the pot and get your shit headed self and your chicken shit partner to Saint Paul and catch these bastards who think their shit doesn't stink," he bellered.

"This is weird shit," Brad Blue Trump added.

Davecki sighed. He looked at Trump. "I understand Hjelmer."

Hjarvis pounded the table violently with both fists. "The hell you do! Here's some serious shit," he said, reaching into the front pocket of his army field jacket. He threw a slip of crumpled paper across the table. It landed next to the wash cloth. "Serious shit is a woman who has no idea her power, her gift. Serious shit is an asshole in Washington D.C. who'll send fifty eight thousand to death and end up being called an American hero."

Picking up the smudged paper, Davecki asked, "What's this?"

Hjarvis' whiskers moved. No sound came out. Then, as if the vocal chords suddenly decided to begin operating, he said, "This is some serious shit." He clomped his jaw several times. The lips smacked beneath the grubby facial hair.

"What's so serious about this?" Davecki asked as he examined the paper.

"What's serious is, you don't know what you got there."

"It's a receipt for a fish special at Fuller's Restaurant," Davecki said.

Hjarvis shook his shaggy head. He looked like a

Mike Savage

spavined old lion whose teeth had gone and was slowly starving to death. "The other side asshole."

Davecki snorted and turned the paper over. "HCL 800," he said. "This is a Minnesota plate."

"It would appear that you get to visit your daughter again," Hjarvis said.

"Where'd you get this Hjelmer?"

The hermit laughed. "I got it just after the asshole tried to turn me into road kill. I got it from the squirrel's eye view as that fucking blue Volvo tried to tag my behind with its five-mile-an-hour bumper that was doing fifty down Banks Ave.

"Huh?" Davecki said.

Hjarvis shook his head. "Davey, Davey, Davey. What are we going to do with you?"

"Amuse me. Tell me everything. Spell it out. Spoon feed me. Serve it to me on a silver platter..."

"I GET YOUR POINT!" Hjarvis said holding up a hand. "Here's what happened. I was dreaming. Saw two bodies fried to crispy critters being carried out of the Nottingham. Saw the headlines on the front page of the Daily Smelly Gram about all the dead and wounded. That woke me up. Then I caught the scent of hellfire going past on 105 and I lit out for town. By the time I got to the Nottingham, all the action was over. All the red flashing lights were down on 18th. I found the rag and the match book and had a hunch the asshole would backtrack. So I ran over to Banks Avenue and this jerk-off holding his nose tried to run me down."

"Jerry said that Peggy broke the guy's nose with her purse," Trump said.

Dave leaned back, looked at the Blue. "Who's Peggy?"

Burn Baby Burn

"Guy tried to car-jack a couple's bike for a getaway vehicle. He tackled the old man. Knocked him down. But the woman on the back of the bike, her name's Peggy. She whacked him good with her purse and he ran off bleeding like Manitou Falls," Trump explained.

"Wouldn't that be a bike-jacking then?" Hjarvis asked.

Trump looked irritated. "Well geeze. I wouldn't know for sure and I wouldn't really care, jack off."

"Touchy. Touchy," Hjarvis said.

Davecki looked away from Trump and said, "Knock it off you two. What makes you think it's a Twin Cities vehicle Hjelmer?"

Hjarvis snorted this time. The moustache hair rustled. "Show me one T-80 Volvo in Duluth and I'll show you a suspect. Besides, even if there is one in Duluth, the owner's not going to be driving around Superior in a $250,000 dollar car holding his nose and trying to run down innocent residents," he said.

"You got that right. Only the filthy rich, spoiled young and insecure powerful drive that rig," Davecki said. He reached over to the tape recorder and punched the off button. "Take 'em back Brad."

"We're letting him go?"

Hjarvis stood quickly. He glared at the mirror. Triumph exuded from his face. "First motorcycle in the Bible," he crowed.

"What?" Brad said.

"What?" Davecki said.

"It's in Exodus. The sound of Joshua's TRUIMPH was heard throughout the land. I always feel so good when I'm not going to jail." The Prophet of Pokegema laughed and raised his hands. He started doing a small dance. He spun around weaving his hands in the air like tall sunflower heads swaying in a strong wind. "Do a little dance. Get a little romance."

"You want to book him. Feel free," Davecki said rising.

"Let's go," Trump said reaching for Hjarvis.

"DON'T TOUCH ME INFIDEL!" Hjarvis yelped.

"Settle down Hjelmer," Davecki said.

"Shiva to you oh Dim Bulb," Hjarvis snipped. He lowered his hands and lunged for the recorder. "I want that tape!" he shrieked.

Officer Brad Trump, despite the fact that his Old Man had millions in a trust account with Brad and Roxy's name on it, dove to protect a thirty dollar tape machine.

"NO!" Hjarvis yelled.

"Knock it off you two," Davecki yelled louder. He snatched the recorder to his chest before either of them could reach it. They knocked heads.

"Tape!" Hjarvis said less loudly. He rubbed his head.

"Assaulting an officer," Trump said rubbing his noggin. "You're a suspect. You're not getting the tape."

"Why do you want the tape Hjelmer?" Davecki asked. He opened the cassette gate and pulled the TDK 90-minute out.

Hjarvis looked at Davecki. The gnome scrunched up his face, slouched his shoulders and sighed forlornly.

"Doing pitiful won't get you the tape Hjelmer. Just tell me why you want the tape."

Hjarvis let his visage return to its normal scary status. He said. "I was on a roll. Preaching good. It's on tape. That's an opportunity. I was thinking I'd make a dupe. Send it out to my sister's lengthy mailing list. You know,

Burn Baby Burn

raise some easy capitol. Only fifteen dollars. Free will offering. That kind of thing."

"Get him outta here," Davecki said tossing the tape into the hermit's clutching hands. "I want that back in two days."

Trump said, "Un-fucking-believable." and opened the door.

Hjarvis cackled. He shuffled toward the exit and said, "Anything you say Detective. You know I'm a law abiding citizen."

"Right," Davecki said setting the tape recorder down.

"Have a nice trip," Hjarvis said. And he left the room with a flourish.

Mike Savage

13

Men Aren't from Mars

Women Aren't from Venus

They're from EACH OTHER

Burn Baby Burn

The Caprice hulked down I-35 like a professional wrestler heaving himself toward the Twin Cities in search of meaning for his life. For the umpteenth time Davecki hated driving the car. But, it was on Callahan's orders that the General Motors behemoth be used on ALL official business. Besides, it was a more comfortable vehicle for passengers. At this point in the trip, the car was passing the Sturgeon Lake exit. Davecki had once seen an actual sturgeon in shallows of the spring-water clear lake while fishing for bass. It swam by the boat looking like an eight foot long prehistoric monster. The sight scared him to his bones and he shivered every time the vision came to his mind.

His shiver subsided and the vision of Bubba wearing a baseball cap played across the detective's mind screen. He was wondering why a woman of beauty would wear a baseball cap. Across the bench seat sat State Fire Marshal Bubba Carlstrom. Her eyes were closed. She looked relaxed. She wore a black sweat shirt with the words BUM EQUIPMENT embroidered across the front. A pair of mottled black jeans and Adidas running shoes completed the sporty ensemble. On her dainty head was a long billed baseball cap, light green. "Is there some reason we can't listen to the radio?" Carlstrom asked without opening her eyes.

"The better to hear you with my dear."

Her eyes opened. She turned to look at the driver. "You are so lame."

"Thank you," he said and smiled.

"What do you want to talk about?"

Davecki did an internal shrug. *Usually all she wants*

Mike Savage

to talk about is the case. "I was wondering why you're such a ball buster," Davecki asked.

"Get a life Davecki. I'm not going to spend the next two and a half hours airing my dirty laundry. Either act like a professional and discuss the case or just shut up and drive."

Choosing the latter, Davecki thought, *you have SUCH a way with words you charming devil.*

The miles rolled by swiftly, as swiftly as a beached whale disguised as an automobile can roll. <u>By</u> <u>the</u> <u>Time</u> <u>They</u> <u>got</u> <u>to</u> <u>Hinckley</u>, it was raining. Davecki thumped the steering wheel lightly. He coughed softly. "Hey Bubba," he said. "I'm sorry. I'm just used to speaking my mind. I apologize for being a prick."

Heavy sigh from across the car. "Don't let it happen again jerk-off."

For a split second there was a silence that weighed the future. Fate? Or just some indescribable cosmic infiltration of truth? In that split second the nature of the relationship between a man and a woman, a detective and an investigator, a partner and a friend was determined.

They both exploded in laughter.

The Caprice sailed on for a mile. Then Bubba spoke. "I'm a ball buster because its more fun than typing."

"Oh?"

"Yeah. When I was in high school I could type faster than anyone in Madison. Then I entered a statewide contest and won. Eventually I even went to San Francisco for the national typing finals. They were held at the IBM Selectric Towers Hotel."

"No shit? There's a hotel named..."

"You are so gullible Davecki."

Burn Baby Burn

Davecki grunted. He said, "And what happened? Not that I'll believe anything you say from now on."

"I got second place. Some guy from Louisiana beat me! Can you imagine that? A guy?"

"Oh the nature of roll reversals," Davecki said.

"Huh?"

"Oh nothing."

"Don't say nothing to me if you want to talk, dammit. You've been itching to get inside my head ever since we met. Well here's your opportunity and you won't give me even one little crumb."

"What the hell are you talking about?"

Carlstrom, instead of reaching for her smokes, reached for her knee and intertwined the fingers of both hands there. "I'm talking about all the goof-ball intellectualism, the sassy humor, the forgivably impish insults."

Silence. Outside, a monster billboard seemed to glide by on its way to Duluth. On the panel, a busty babe advised viewers to listen to turn Howard on.

"So?" Davecki asked.

"So. What?"

"So, what are you getting at?"

Carlstrom unhooked her fingers. She hooked one thumb in the seat belt. She took her gaze off the highway and looked at Davecki. "I'm talking about the incredible defense you have. It's better than Bill Clinton's."

Davecki glanced at the woman beside him. "Get real."

"I am real," the woman beside him answered. "All this head tripping. All the jokes. All the maleness is an avoidance response."

"That's bull."

"Prove it."

Mike Savage

Davecki sighed. He moved his hands to the bottom of the steering wheel. "I CAN prove it. You know that book? <u>Men</u> <u>Aren't</u> <u>From</u> <u>Mars</u> <u>and</u> <u>Women</u> <u>Aren't</u> <u>From</u> <u>Venus</u>? As a metaphor that sucks. It's too divisive. Men are from cultural reality and women are from cultural reality. The reason you don't like Superior, or The North, or men who aren't ninetyized is that you're spoiled."

"Ninetyized?"

Davecki sighed. This time it was a bigger, longer sigh that signified, well, nothing. "You know what? It's just too much work to try and explain it again."

"Suit yourself," Carlstrom said and quit looking at the driver.

A few more miles passed beneath the seats of the combatants. Outside the landscape changed from True North where the brush was thick and had an unmanageable look, to the Faux North where big oak trees camped alongside cornfields that were next to car dealerships that dealt in concrete pumps as well.

"What makes you think I want to get in your head? Usually women think I want in their pants."

Carlstrom smirked. "Because my head is way more interesting to you than your own. What do you mean I'm spoiled?"

"I mean you seem to be the type of person who expects a lot."

Carlstrom fidgeted. "That's the farthest thing from the truth."

"How so?"

"I USED to expect a lot. Now I don't expect anything."

"So you're disappointed in love."

Burn Baby Burn

She laughed. "Do you HAVE to read into everything? Can't you just accept a statement for what it is?"

"I thought cops were supposed to be suspicious of everything."

Carlstrom sighed. She refolded her hands. "We're not being cops right now."

"We're not?"

"Jesus, Mary and Joseph," Carlstrom whispered.

"What?" Davecki asked.

"Nothing," Carlstrom said.

Silence.

"Gotcha didn't I?" She grinned.

Davecki chuckled. He breathed out long saying, "Well yes Andrea, you did. It just comes as a surprise to me that you're willing to turn off the high powered investigator persona for a while."

"You started it."

"Yes I did. So what makes you think I'm defensive?" Davecki asked.

"All the verbal crapola. All the mental jousting. All the complicated talking. It's your way of avoiding talking about feelings."

Davecki laughed softly again and moved his hands back up to the top of the steering wheel. "You know Bubba, I've always FELT that feelings were just indicators, were just the starting point for the truth."

"How's that?"

"Well for instance. I feel nervous right now."

"Why?"

He snickered. "Well, because we're actually talking. We're not doing business. We're not sparring. We're not joking."

Mike Savage

"Pardon my interruption, but, isn't the nervousness a sign that you'd rather NOT be talking?"

"It could be. But, in my experience, it's more a sign of being happy and engaged. Excited. I'm feeling like I caught my first fish. Kind of like a breakthrough."

"What is it with you and these rural metaphors?"

"Actually it's a simile."

"THERE YOU GO AGAIN!"

"What? What?"

"You go on the attack and change the subject and effectively avoid discussing anything that makes you nervous!"

"I'm not doing that! I'm just talking about my feelings."

"No you're not. You're telling me I'm stupid because I don't know the difference between a metaphor and a simile. Every man I've ever known has done that."

"What?" Davecki said raising his hands. A desperate look was on his face.

"Made me feel stupid."

He sighed. He thumped the steering wheel. He stole a glance at the woman across the seat from him. "Listen," he ventured. "Listen. I don't think you're stupid. I KNOW you're smart. You're tough. You're hard working. You're dedicated. You know how to have fun. You know how to work hard."

She laughed. "<u>You Don't Know Jack</u>!!"

"Do too."

"Do not."

"Do too."

"Prove it, she demanded."

"You're here aren't you?" Davecki asked.

Burn Baby Burn

"What?" she answered.

"You heard me," he said.

"Of course I heard you. But you are making absolutely NO sense at all," she maintained.

"That's because you're not listening," he said.

"No. It's because you're not talking, you're hinting around," she explained.

Silence.

Outside, the Snake River coiled near the roadway. Those river bends lead away to the west for twenty miles and then reached north for another thirty to the swamps above McGrath, Minnesota, so named after McGrath logging of the early 1900s. The river undulated to the east a few miles to join the St. Croix in Grantsburg, Wisconsin.

"Okay. I'll stop hinting, he said. "I know all these things about you because of what the Bible says."

"Right."

"You interested or you want to scoff?"

"Oh pardon moi," she said. She smiled and waved a hand in a welcoming gesture as if to say, slide right across the seat here mister and just hand me your stupid ideas.

"Thank you," Davecki said. He pulled on the steering wheel enough to bend it back and forth. "The Bible says, 'By their works you shall know them.' You've accomplished so much. You're staying in Superior, a place you don't like, to finish your assignment. You're showing up for work every day. You're putting in your hours. You've PUT in your hours, paid your dues."

Silence.

She took off her cap. "Seems too simple."

"Now who's hiding behind complication?"

"All right already. Don't get snippy with me."

Mike Savage

Silence.

"I'm not spoiled," she said.

"Sure you are."

"Are you trying to piss me off?"

He grinned. "No, no I'm not. I'm just trying to share my FEELINGS."

"No you're not. You're sharing your opinion and you're sharing it with someone who hasn't asked for it."

"So it's like, 'When I want your opinion I'll GIVE it to you?"

"Hey it works for me," she said. She was toying with the hat in her lap like it was a <u>Cat</u> <u>In</u> <u>The Hat</u>. She snickered again.

"What?"

"I was just thinking of how you remind me of my Dad."

"Oh?"

"Yeah. He was the Denali Fire Chief. Now THERE were some expectations."

"Like?"

"Like wanting a boy and getting a girl and teaching me how to make a fist and..."

"Make a fist?"

"Yeah. I remember it like it was yesterday. Tommy Ludak was teasing me and Mom told me to just ignore it, that to get mad or try to get back at him was, 'Just giving him power.' Dad was standing by the door. He was going to go back to work after lunch. He silently motioned with his head for me to come into the garage. When I got out there he said, 'Next time he teases you punch him in the nose. Now make a fist.' I made a fist and he said, 'Don't do it that way. Don't tuck your thumb in.' And he grabbed

Burn Baby Burn

my fist and remade it with the thumb on the outside." Bubba held up her hand and made a fist with the thumb. Jabbed it at the air between her and Davecki.

"Well?" Davecki asked.

"Well what?" Carlstrom re-asked.

"Did you pop Tommy?"

"You see Detective. We now have a classic example of why men ARE from Mars."

"How's that?"

"You want to know if I hit him and I want to tell you that what I remember most about that whole thing was how my Dad's rough fingers felt when they were touching mine."

"Huh?"

"Dad hardly ever touched me and when he did it in the garage, it was like being molded by God. I went to the playground after doing the dishes and walked right up to Tommy and socked him so hard he fell down. It didn't hurt or anything because I was still remembering how good my Dad's hands felt on mine."

"And you call ME lame," Davecki said.

He looked quickly at the person in the car with him. She eyed him. *Please think that was funny*, he thought.

She smiled.

Then they both laughed.

"You know," he said, "this is kinda fun. When we get back I'm going to actually have to try and be nice to you."

"Don't outdo yourself. I might have a heart attack."

"No really. Seriously. I'm going to do something nice for you."

"Like what?" The cap in her lap stopped being toyed with.

Mike Savage

"Well, I don't know. It's gotta be something YOU'D like. Something I'm sure you would want to do and not something I'd like. Hmmmm. Let's see...."

The car rolled onward.

He pounded the steering wheel. "I'll take you to the nicest restaurant in Duluth. It'll be like going to a classy place, a place like you'd go to in Madison or Chicago."

"What if I don't want to be seen in public with you?"

"Well, of course. It goes without saying. WITH YOUR PERMISSION of course, I would like to take you out to dinner at the Lake Avenue Cafe. It will be haute mode."

"Haute mode?"

"Yes mode. It's French for fashion."

Carlstrom threw a glance at Davecki. "I wouldn't have thought you knew French."

"I don't. I just have a big dictionary. So how about it?"

"Awwww. Ummmm. I don't think that would be such a good idea."

"Why not?" Davecki asked. "What's wrong? It would be the perfect way to brighten up your dreary Superior existence. A night out at a culturally elite restaurant."

"Well. You know. It... Well..."

"Oh come on. What's the problem. You just got done whipping me for being indirect. What's the problem?"

"Well. It would be too much like a date."

"Oh for Christ's sake! And you call me lame."

The car rolled on in silence, Davecki lightly bumping the steering wheel. Finally he spoke, "Okay. I know what to do. I can fix this. I promise not to show you how to make a fist and we'll skip the fancy stuff. I'm hungry. I'm hungry now and I'm not going to take you anywhere. I'm

Burn Baby Burn

not going to do anything FOR you. I'm just going to zip into Rush City and stop at the Grant House for some grub. You hungry? You want to help yourself to some good hot food?"

"Fine," she said. "Fine. I'm hungry. I can always eat. But you know what I'd like? What I'd really like?"

"Fill me in."

"I'd like to tell you what I want from a man."

"Knock yourself out Bubba."

"I want him to listen and not try to fix everything. I want him to just sit there and listen and not say anything critical."

"That doesn't seem like too much to ask."

"Trust me. It's mon-u-fucking-mental."

"Hey, it's just a guy thing to want to fix stuff."

"Hey, it's just a Bubba thing to want to fix stuff herself. That's what Dad taught me to do. That's why my marriage fell apart."

"You were married?"

"Surprised?"

"Absolutely."

"Well, I'll give Gregg one thing. He taught me to quit sending mixed messages."

"Huh?"

"I drove him crazy. I figured it was the womanly thing to do. Pretend like I wanted help. I'd even ask him. But then when he came up with a solution or fixed something his way, I wouldn't be happy or it wasn't good enough for me."

"So he stopped asking."

"Exactly."

"Why fight a battle you know you're going to lose?"

"Exactly," she said again. This time with more emphasis, like she was pumped that somebody understood.

"Hey, makes sense to me."

"Well it didn't make sense to me back then. Now I'm better. I don't ask if I don't want help. And if I do ask, I'm ready to accept the offering without complaining."

"It makes so much sense that all I'm going to do now is go to the Grant House and eat. Then I'm going to go catch bad guys. Want to come along?"

"Lead on McDuff."

Davecki looked at Carlstrom. He was grinning. "WHAT was that?"

"My Old Man used to say it all the time. I think some sorta famous writer coined the phrase back when."

Davecki took the Rush City exit. "Have you ever heard of the Grant House? It was first built in 1880. A grand Victorian hotel. It burned down in 1895 and was rebuilt in 1896. It's a really cool building and has been in continuous operation ever since. The restaurant there is...

"Would you shut up and drive! I'm hungry for chow not your inane details."

Davecki laughed.

"What's so funny?"

"Oh nothing."

"What dammit."

"Oh it's just that not long ago you were badgering the hell out of me for details."

"Up yours scrote bag. Let's eat and get going. I'm feeling the urge to kick some ass."

Burn Baby Burn

Mike Savage

14

"Scorching, flaming, raging, blazing."

Burn Baby Burn

After the Minnesota state legislature decided not to change the name of Summit Avenue to Ventura Highway, things settled down in St. Paul. The once sedate state got used to government with a flair and the Twin Cities grew in stature and favor with Hollywood. After Jack and Sean visited, it was even hip to be a Minnesotan. Davecki had always liked Pig Town and Murderapolis. He liked the culture, the business, the ease with which large volumes of traffic could move about the Metro area. What he didn't like was the fact that the same attraction kept his daughter from living closer to her father.

This single anathema made Davecki always adopt a facade of dislike for Twin Towns. "Why anyone would want to live down here is beyond me," Davecki said.

"It's called a career, Dad," Bethany said.

The two of them sat across a small square table covered with a cheap vinyl checkered table cloth, red and white. The cafe was French Meadow Cafe and Bakery on Lyndale in the Uptown neighborhood of Minneapolis. The ambiance was lost somewhere between early sixties Greenwich Village and New Age Gay Boy Entrepreneur land. It would find itself eventually and the clientele would then settle into predictability. For the here and now though, Bethany thought it offered the most diverse dining experience in the metropolis.

Across the aisle two young girls sat around their microscopic table with a slick young man that was a blend between Robert Downey Jr. and Paul Reiser. One of the girls had short hair and clothes that said St. Vincent DePaul in big bold letters. The other young woman had long pink hair with the matte finish of a poorly dipped Easter egg.

Mike Savage

The hair clashed with bright red lips that drooped sadly beneath high cheek bones and eyes with false lashes longer than the Viking's Superbowl losing streak. One of those eyes was purple and puffy from being struck soundly by a solid object. "Scary. Positively unnerving," Davecki said eyeing the odd trio. *Why am I thinking of the Star Wars cafe scene?*

"What?" Bethany asked.

"Oh. Nothing. I was looking at the goof balls behind you and wondering how diverse our culture has to get before it's acceptable to the societal designers from the Trilateral Commission."

"Daaaaad. Would you quit joking around."

Davecki smiled and said, "Sure thing honey. Anything for you."

They munched in silence for a minute or so. Davecki pulled apart large tangles of hash browns, stirred the trailing mass of wormlike spuds in the pools of yellow egg yolk congealing on the edge of his plate and stuffed the sodden mass in his strangely silent mouth. Bethany ripped little chunks of raspberry scone off with dainty fingers. At the end of those fingers were long black false nails. She self-consciously slipped the bits of carbohydrates between her magenta colored lips.

"You could move to Duluth and write for the Tribune."

"Daaaaad. We've had this conversation before. "People don't WRITE for the Tribune they WORK for it."

"And your point is?"

Bethany Johnson, long lost daughter of Dave Davecki sighed. "Just because you think it's a cesspool down here, doesn't mean I have to hate it. The Star has a huge news

Burn Baby Burn

hole that makes it possible for me to actually get some decent play on the stories I write. At least it isn't like those Knight-Ridder rags that are little more than shoppers. You should see their pages! Mostly ads with a little editorial copy perched on top of the page like those little green leaves and the stem on top of a tomato."

"Being fired from the Pioneer-Mess wasn't easy for you, I take it." Davecki picked up his water glass, empty save the ice, and rattled it at the passing black haired, white faced waitress. The Goth Chick ignored him.

"Dad! GOD! Couldn't you be a little more from the sticks?"

"What?" Davecki defended. "I was just trying to get her attention."

"You're such a...."

"Neanderthal?"

Bethany eyed her dad. "That new partner been setting you straight?"

"How perceptive."

"Where is she now?"

Davecki tipped several ice cubes into his mouth and chewed. Before swallowing he said through the ice field, "Dropped her off at the Mall of America to give me some quality time with my daughter before we go disco dancing tonight. Plus, she's got my Visa Gold card to get us some appropriate threads."

"Threads?" Bethany grinned. "Quality time doesn't mean I have to accept unacceptable behavior. Is it too much to ask that you simply ask Little Miss Death Chick to get you some more water?"

"That would be better than, 'Excuse me bitch, more water NOW and this time don't spit in it.'"

Mike Savage

"Incredible," was all Bethany said.

They ate quietly for two minutes and twenty-two seconds before Bethany asked, "Can I go with?"

"Where?" Davecki asked looking up from the righteous toast he was slathering strawberry jam on.

"Dancing. I want to check her out. I didn't realize this was a social trip. I kinda thought the only reason you came down here was for work."

"I come here to visit you."

"But only when you can do some work too."

"I love you too daughter of mine," he said. He stuffed the toast in his mouth and chewed.

"Don't pout," Bethany said.

Davecki swallowed his toast and pride in one gulp and said, "We got a Minnesota plate number from a witness. Ran it. Nothing. Nada. It was registered to a Dodge Caravan that had been junked three years ago. The Duluth police called in a tip on a Johnny Cash CD found in the parking lot of the visitor's information center on Thompson Hill. Got some prints off that. Three different sets, one was the officer's. The other was the woman who found it. The third, unknown. Perhaps our arsonist. Then there's this." He pulled the match book from his shirt pocket and tossed it on the table.

Bethany picked it up. "The Hot Place. I've always wanted to go there," she said.

Davecki's face hardened. He looked at this daughter. "Because it has the hottest pussy in town?"

Bethany eyed her dad back with much the same steely stare. Testimony to DNA, they both grimaced simultaneously. Bethany looked away first. She looked down at her tea cup and picked it up. "No," she said quietly. "I'd

Burn Baby Burn

like to do a story on it. They say it's a pretty rough place and I'd feel safer going there with my father and another police officer."

Davecki looked down. "Awww Bethie. I'm sorry. I am a Neanderthal from the tundra. I'm really sorry. You can come along if you still want." He looked up, hopeful.

"Of course I do, you goof! I just wish you'd figure out a way to stop saying everything that comes into your mind."

"That doesn't sound too hard," he said.

"Mon-u-mental," his daughter said.

Davecki's face fell. His shoulders lowered. He looked stricken.

Bethany broke into peals of body shaking laughter. "Oh Daddy, you are so cute when you're repentant!"

"You'll come then?"

"Sure," she said. "But the big problem isn't going. It's getting in."

"Oh? What's that mean?"

"Well The Hot Place is hot. Everyone wants to go dancing there. There's always this big line and they have these big bouncers who won't let just anyone in. There's some sort of code or some sort of test about getting in that nobody can figure out," Bethany explained.

"Oh I have a feeling we'll be getting in," Davecki said grinning.

"What's that mean?"

"Well, you haven't met Bubba yet and I have a feeling my credit card is experiencing tremors off the Richter Scale about now. I suspect, based on what I know about her, she's about ready to make some pretty radical fashion statements tonight."

Mike Savage

"WHAT in the world are you babbling about?"

"Well, let's just say Bubba has been trapped on the tundra with Neanderthals for six weeks and, well, I think she's about ready to bust out in style tonight."

Bethany looked at her dad. His eyes were twinkling. "She's that hot huh?"

"Scorching, flaming, raging, blazing."

"Oh my God," she gasped.

Burn Baby Burn

Mike Savage

15

...each man's work will become evident; for the day will show it, because it is to be revealed with fire; and the fire itself will test the quality of each man's work.

- First Corinthinans 3:13

Burn Baby Burn

The Important Man sat in the third pew up from the pastor's back. He was seated in the choir nave of the Fifteenth Lutheran Church of Duluth. He listened to the pastor's sermon and looked out across the wide crowd of two hundred and some parishioners looking up either blankly or worshipfully at the pastor. The Important Man wondered what each and every one of those people would do to him if they knew.

The Gospel this week was Luke Chapter Sixteen. The verse was twenty-four. The parable of the rich man. The pastor's voice was a wealthy and resonant bass. It echoed across the audience saying, "And he said, 'Father Abraham have mercy on me and send Lazarus that he may dip the tip of his finger in water, and cool my tongue, for I am tormented in this flame.'"

The pastor continued reading. The Important Man repositioned the bible on his robe-covered lap. The robe was a rich maroon colored silk jobby. It made him sweat. The last phrase of the verse had struck him. He smiled slightly. In his ears he kept hearing the tormented screams of his first thirteen victims. The Memorex Moments were pleasing to him. He smiled slightly. The bible seemed to move of it's own accord. Then his face turned dark. The vision of a certain willful karaoke singer ruined his pleasure. The bible settled down. She was even getting to him in church!

The dissociative side of his brain whirred. The bibliography of his greatest fires flipped through his brain like a CD collection in a juke box display. His all-time greatest hit, the Lake Superior Trading Post fire in Grand Marais caught his attention. Surely that blaze would snuff out the impertinent singer's stubborn obstinacy. He smiled. Arson was the greatest. The perfect crime. Rarely an arrest. His bible boinged.

The other side of his cranium hummed along merrily. Thinking the owner was a respected deacon in the church, a dutiful husband and father who worked for the City of Duluth, the conscious side of said brain, reveled in his position as Church Council Member and Sunday School teacher.

Unfortunately for fourteen fire chiefs in small towns from Bena to Ball Club to Zim in Minnesota, to Irma, Maple, Booganville and Gile in Wisconsin, what passed for conscience resided solely in the church side of his bipolar skull. The great gulf between Abraham and Lazarus was a minute crack in the sidewalk compared to the split in The Important Man's personality. He knew he could burn any building in the world with virtual impunity. All he had to do was keep reffing high school hockey games and steadfastly deny the demon of fire had set up shop in his soul.

"Wretched man that I am. Who shall deliver me from this body of death? The very thing I hate, these I do," his deacon self heard the pastor preach.

The demon side thought about the Minnesota Block in Superior. Built in 1892, the massive building on the corner of Tower and Belknap was said to be, "Completely fire proof" by architect C.C. Haight. Built by the Land and River Improvement Company, an insurance underwriter said it was, "The best insurance risk I ever saw — it couldn't burn if it tried."

His demon side knew a challenge when he read about one. The fire fanatic knew the intimate details of all the

Burn Baby Burn

fires that made the non-lineal locus across time and Tower Avenue a real-time locus for pyromaniacs who have practiced their trade in Superior for the last one hundred years.

As a case in point, the Grand Opera House had been lit several times. It burned in 1909 and 1911 and survived. Back then there was some merit in disfigurement. *And, Important Demon Man thought, there was a certain art to only partially burning a building, only torching it enough to cause permanent scarring. Like damaging a child's psyche only partially so it would never quite be free from a healthy amount of self doubt.* The Grand Opera House burned to the ground in a spectacular blaze on 1939. Important Demon Man knew the Minnesota Block was thought to be unburnable, but he believed fervently that the building now known as The Board of Trade, didn't have such a reputation and that arson technology had come a long way in a hundred and seven years.

"Go eat peas. The mashed potatoes are ended," Demon heard.

"May the Love of God be with you always," Deacon heard. And the most successful, prolific and least likely candidate as the greatest arsonist in the history of the world packed his family into the Plymouth Voyager and headed to The Old Country Buffet at the Miller Hill Mall to beat the rest of the church rush to lunch.

Mike Savage

16

Sadly, as is the fashion with mankind, the outward is judged with far more importance than is wise. This is why we should take to heart the stirring words of Jesus speaking to the Pharisees, "Hypocrites! You polish the outside of the cup, but inside you are ravening wolves!"

— John Gemmill, misquoting the scriptures to his congregation at Lanark, Ontario, Canada in 1885. He was merging Matthew 7:15 and Matthew 23:25.

Burn Baby Burn

Bethany walked out of her apartment wearing a short black miniskirt (leather), three inch black vinyl platform shoes, a tight knit top of rough spun cotton (maroon with gold threads woven in a prominent vertical pattern), a mildly spiked dog collar and a purse the size of a credit card on steroids.

The shapely young journalist had heard the horn honk outside her apartment and dashed down to meet her father and this "sizzling" partner. What she hadn't done was look up. Platform shoes will cause caution when negotiating steep steps. What she saw <u>By the Time She Got to the Sidewalk</u> was a long black limousine about the size of Garrison Keillor's ego, or at least his jealousy at being upstaged by Governor Jesse.

Anyway, Bethany stopped dead full and looked at the car. Then she looked up the street. Then she looked down the street. No Caprice. No Alphonse "Dave" Davecki. No nothing, so she did what any good journalist in the same situation would do. She stood there with her mouth hanging open wearing a confused look on her cute round face.

The next thing that happened was logical. The rear window on the limo powered down and a disembodied man's voice echoed from the bowels of the behemoth. No, it wasn't a Pohlad lad on a pickup mission. It was a somewhat familiar sounding voice that said, "Hey beautiful. Want to have a good time?"

"Daaaaaddy!" Bethany screamed. "What on earth are you doing?"

Davecki's bushy haired head then poked out the window. His smiling face beamed at his daughter. "I told you

Mike Savage

we'd get in, didn't I? Besides, in addition to this lovely limo, I also will have two, count 'em two, drop dead gorgeous women on my arms when we roll up to The Hot Place." At that, Davecki flung the door open wide and fairly sprung from the car. He was adorned in the most god-awful suit he'd ever been in. Bubba had done her afternoon's work well. She'd dented Davecki's Visa Gold and had spent $2,200 dollars on a Ralph Lauren. It was the first time in twenty-three years that he'd looked even halfway decent. In addition to his sartorial pedigree, his coolness was assured by the three hundred dollar Specs sunglasses on his nose. What happened next was as close to unbelievable as Bethany the trained journalist could imagine.

A Venus, a Madonna, a Silkie, a thoroughbred through and through gracefully stepped from the door of the limo as if there were five hundred papparazzi gathered around.

Bethany clomped her mouth open and shut.

Davecki laughed. "I'm sure there are questions associated with that walleye swallow Honey, but you have to breathe and expel air to make words happen."

"Oh my GOD! DADDY!!"

"Get a life Bethany, this is work. I'd like you to meet Andrea "Bubba" Carlstrom. My TEMPORARY partner."

"Pleased," Bubba said, extending her hand toward Babbling Bethie.

"Ahem! Ahem....Same," Bethany choked out.

Bubba was wearing a beaded floor length fire red Gucci evening gown slit up to "there." There was no bra. Passion red stiletto heels with an open toe and thin straps that wound above the ankle. The hair was swept up and looked like the "do" Ivana wore when crashing the an-

Burn Baby Burn

nual Miss USA contest. In her left hand was a beaded tote ala Kate Winslet of the Titanic. The small fringe on it swayed gently as she reached out to shake Bethie's hand.

They shook. And then they both trembled. And then they looked at the man between them. That man was oblivious to everything. Everything that is, except the fact that the three of them were standing around looking dumbfounded. "Well let's get this done ladies!" he grinned and gestured toward the still open limousine door. Everyone laughed. Everyone piled into the limo and the stretch elongated itself down the street in search of I-94 and the quickest route to St. Paul.

The limo rounded the corner passing the Olde Irish Pub with its green awning. It rolled down the block and nosed into an open space behind a fire engine red Dodge Stealth with the license plate, TIHS HO.

"Oh shit," the driver said and cranked the limo's front end in a short arc away from the front of a tall brick building. There wasn't much room for disembarking passengers. A line of people stood in front of the building. They were encircled by a thick velvet theater rope strung between stubby upright stanchions of faux gold.

Every pair of eyes in the line ogled the limo. The car stopped and the driver appeared out of the front door like a Pop Tart sproinging from the toaster. Sprinting around the front of the car, the chauffeur, dressed in a spiffy black tux and natty hat, opened the rear door with a flourish. The driver stood motionless in the growing darkness. The sound of resonating bass speakers and booming rock lyrics oozed through the brick facia and made its muffled way around the scene like a homeless, former stock broker searching for goodies in dumpsters.

Mike Savage

From within the limo, laughter. And nothing more. Silence. Some giggling and then...nothing. The driver remained motionless. The crowd stared. A man standing next to a valet's podium looked at the scene over the top of black horn-rimmed half spectacles. This man was skinny to the supermodel point. His face seemed to be pouring off the skull like a big drop of water falling from the faucet. The nose, the lips, the cheekbones, the eyebrows all seemed to be converging at a focal point five inches off the end of the swooping nose. This face, being prominent enough, was not, however the most outstanding feature of the bouncer. He was over seven feet tall. The owner of said two faced-ness was now staring at the limo. The law of beautiful faces was not working here.

The driver coughed a mild little, "Ahem," and still...nothing.

Thirty-four seconds after the ahem, Davecki stepped from the limo. He was smiling and looking around. He looked up at the building. Halfway up the facade, large red letters illuminated from behind and trimmed in gold said, THE HOT PLACE. Yellow flames of plastic leapt from the tops of each letter. Hanging above the door in front of which perched the emaciated "bouncer" were the words, WELCOME TO THE HALL OF FLAME.

Davecki turned his gaze away without looking at the bouncer and announced back into the limo, "Ladies...we have arrived." He stretched his arm into the darkness of the limo exit and waited. Presently he withdrew said arm upon which was a dainty hand. Bethany emerged and there was a gasp from the onlookers. It was a woman's gasp, complete with the requisite coloration of jealousy, Davecki noted. He maneuvered Bethany to the side of

Burn Baby Burn

the door. Davecki's arm resubmerged itself into the pool of coolness and seemed to fish around a bit. Then it caught something and started pulling. A palpable sense of tension started to make itself known. It flowed from the crowd and the Maître d' and bounced off the chauffeur and echoed through Bethany and Davecki. After several reverberations around the Circuit City of the gathered sane and insane, the palpable tension metamorphosed into a true "moment unto itself" and joined the onlookers waiting to see what Davecki had hooked himself into.

When Bubba emerged the moment fairly shrieked and took a knee. It was ready to do the queen's bidding. It was ready to charge into battle and sacrifice itself for the goddess standing on the curb in downtown St. Paul, Minnesota.

Davecki made a nifty transition from helper-out-of-the-limo-man to coequal with the goddess by deftly crooking his arm into an escort pose. Bubba didn't miss a beat. She interwove her goddess-like arm and started gliding toward the head of the line. Davecki had simultaneously crooked his other arm and Bethany merged into Davecki's side like an address/merge command from a mailing label database.

The three of them advanced on the Maître d'. Behind them the limo door slammed shut. Not one of the forty-seven entres'de-hopeful uttered even the tiniest complaint. With each step toward the bouncer Davecki could see the man's resolute countenance changing. It was going from hard ass, you'll-never-ever-get-in to, how-may-I-serve-you-Master? Davecki kept smiling and kept striding forward with his arms burdened by the weight of glorious youth and beauty.

Mike Savage

The Maître d' remembered his caste and stopped staring. He looked down first. Then he looked away. He looked at the line-up of let-me-ins. Davecki followed the bouncer's look and, saw a Goth couple. The Goth Man had black lipstick with thick white powder on his face to improve the contrast. He also had black painted fingernails with spangles sprinkled into the lacquer. Goth Man's date was a large woman and squat. She had on an immense patent leather bra that held up several acres of densely tattooed skin. A leather miniskirt about twelve sizes bigger than Bethie's held up the bottom of the ensemble while, way up on top, an explosion of black spiked hair looked like the business end of a cat-o-nine-tails. Upon seeing the death couple and the rest of the line-up of spiffy and natty and trendy and yuppie and loser couples in the que Davecki muttered, "The future of our country." He thought, *reminds me of barn cats on the window ledge wanting to come in from the cold.*

"What?" Bethany said as they followed the world's most unlikely looking bouncer. He'd turned from his podium and was heading for the door.

"Nothing," Davecki replied.

"He said, 'The future of our country,'" Bubba said.

"You're so judgemental Daddy," Bethany said as the Maître d' reached for the silver door handle that resided in the center of a large field of blazing red. His hand was the size of a Hundai hubcap.

"Hey! No FAIR!" the Goth chick cried.

"Fair's not gettin' in EVER," Tree Man said laughing. His smile broadened and he said to the trio entering his domain, "Don't run the old guy too hard ladies. We don't like the amblance comin' here."

Burn Baby Burn

Bethany laughed hard. Her shoulders shook.

Bubba howled and shrieked, "HE wears US out!"

Davecki grinned and said, "I'm just afraid one of THOSE will be handling my Social Security claim some day." He nodded toward the offended and offending couple.

Bethany was about to answer, but the door swung open. They were instantly engulfed by the raw, unmuffled-by-brick-and-building, music. It barged across the trio like a cigar aficionado sharing his smoke across a table. The door closed behind them and Bethany yelled, "Cool."

"We're in," Bubba hooted.

Davecki looked across the small foyer they were standing in. Below them and stretching away to seeming infinity in the cigarette smoke were several hundred gyrating bodies.

Bethany cried above the cacophony, "Everyone knows there won't be any such thing as Social Security by the time you get old Daddy."

"Great news Honey," Davecki yelled.

Mike Savage

17

Valedmar Valinkovsky was a man, he was a big man. Not as big as Danial Boone, but as big as chaos and wide as non-local, lithium-enhanced intergalactic communication. "Vali" understood the need for chaos better than Maxwell Smart.

Burn Baby Burn

Very good clubs knock the socks off anyone walking in. The best make customers go numb and dumb in the first three seconds. Shocked patrons buy lots of booze. They think they're euphoric. That's good for the owners who make a lot of money. That's good for the customers. They medicate to their heart's content.

What's good for most people is bad for a cop. Shock is anti-cop. Shock is debilitating to reason. Of course there is the rare time when instinctual response is appropriate. Like when an officer's life is in danger. But mortal danger is uncommon, especially for a detective. Especially for a detective like Dave Davecki. He didn't like the clueless writers of TV shows and mystery novels who always made the detective more heroic and braver than the average muskrat. (Thank you HDT). Still, Davecki WAS in the big city of Minneapolis. He WAS in the rarefied atmosphere of a lunatic asylum that appeared to be a dance hall. And he WAS after some bad bad guys that wouldn't hesitate to end his life.

So, as he stood on the landing overlooking the mass of writhing bodies, he had to shake his head slightly. He needed to think clearly. Things can go awful bad awful fast sometimes. But, resisting the assaulting confusion was difficult. He was, after all, standing between two utterly beautiful creatures. Being with Bethany and Bubba was a rush in and of itself. And there was the onslaught of music. The mass of people being illuminated by strobe light looked surreal. And there were no familiar colors. No blue sky. No green. No brown houses. No white clouds. Everything was red or black or too dark to perceive in the millisecond bursts of steely blue light that illuminated the room. In effect, it was bizarre. More bizarre than the Star Wars bar where Obi Wan and Luke met Han Solo.

"This place reminds me of Phipp's," Bubba said.

"The place in Hayward?" Bethany asked.

"Well, actually Seeley," Bubba answered.

"What place in Hayward?" Davecki asked.

The girls looked at each other. Bubba raised her eyebrows. Bethany shook her head.

"What?" Davecki asked, looking forth and back at both of them.

Bethany looked at Bubba. She shook her head.

Bubba smiled and shrugged her shoulders. "There's a strip joint north of Hayward. Pretty raunchy. Animal acts. Sexual contact. Wild place I'm told," Bubba explained.

"You're told?" Davecki said frowning at Carlstrom. He looked at Bethany. Scowled. "And how do you know about this joint young lady?"

Bethany looked down. She raised her eyes but not her head. Looking at her father as though she was peering over a pair of glasses, she said, "You get all kinds of information in a newsroom. There were stories circulating that a certain well known quarterback for a popular pro football team punched out a fan there."

"Really? Who?" Davecki asked.

"I never repeat gossip," Bethany said. "Professional ethics," she added and looked away.

"Way down in Madison I heard he spent the night in jail," Bubba said.

"Who was it? Why wasn't it in all the papers?" Davecki asked.

Bethany looked at the ceiling. "Pro sports teams spend a lot of money, pump a ton of money into newspapers."

Burn Baby Burn

"So President's aren't the only ones above the law," Bubba said.

"What are you two talking about?" Dave asked.

The two girls rolled their eyes at each other again.

He knew when he was clueless. Davecki dropped his line of questioning. There were badder men than spoiled overpaid athletes to pursue. Besides, he also knew he was never a questioning type of detective. He was more of a go out there and snoop around and see what happens when you turn over a rock, open an unlocked door or poke a pile of garbage with a stick. Besides being shamed by the girls' looks, Davecki was being troubled by two other things.

One was a smell. The other was a sound. The smell was as impossible to distinguish in the smoky atmosphere as a snowflake in a blizzard. But the sound. There was a vague thread of recognition. A sliver of something familiar was trying to pierce his muddled brain. The convulsing gray matter that had once been Davecki's mind wanted to understand the sound. But the once proud and organized synapses had been reduced to a trembling puddle of gelatinous nerve endings. Davecki shook his head again as Bethany and Bubba tugged him down the steps toward the writhing mass of humanity between them and the bar. Davecki knew he had to jump-start his thinking. *Okay. What are the ABCs of Investigation?* A hint of reality rose up out of the quivering puddle.

Accept nothing. Believe no one. Confirm, confirm, confirm, rose up from the pool of his mind and saluted smartly. Then, right next to the saluting soldier, the words *Come on baby light my fire* jumped up out of the lake of consciousness. *JIM MORRISON REPORTING FOR*

Mike Savage

DUTY, the second soldier said. He realized the song blasting out of the mega-speakers hanging from the walls and ceiling was The Doors.

Davecki grinned. He'd recovered. The shock was gone. Back was his head. He gripped the arms of his two gorgeous ladies more tightly and, instead of being dragged into the foray, he plunged enthusiastically into the maelstrom. Just before hitting the crowd, Davecki remembered the smell. He sniffed. He smiled. It would be tough, but he knew he would figure it out now that his head was back. *Lilies?*

Diving into the dancers he recalled going to a dance in White Mountain, Alaska. It was June. It was midnight and broad daylight outside. Inside, the kids had completely covered the windows and blacked out the insistent reality of the <u>Midnight</u> <u>Sun</u>. He had walked from the serenity of the tundra village into the blackness of the hall. There too he had been engulfed by the overwhelming roar of blaring rock music. His eyes, which had been enjoying approximately round-the-clock sunlight for weeks could see nothing in the sudden and total darkness. The thread of sanity that saved him back then was a woman's voice yelling in his ear, "DANCE!" Confused by the shriek and blinded as he was, Davecki did as he was told and started dancing. After several minutes his vision returned. He saw he was dancing with a teenage girl whose beauty was all gathered up at the front of her round face like a plate painting. She was flailing the dusky air with wild arms and grinning madly. They would have danced until dawn if there had been a dawn. As it was, they danced themselves to exhaustion.

Recalling White Mountain in The Hot Place gave

Burn Baby Burn

Davecki confidence. He'd adjusted to Alaska. Talk about culture shock. He'd adjusted to round the clock sunlight. He'd adjusted to instant and total darkness. He'd adjusted to dancing with an Eskimo child. He would adjust to this AND his Jim Garner nose would figure out what aroma was bugging the hell out of him. *Church?*

The acquired confidence helped Davecki and his pals make the plunge through the dance floor. A pressure wave flowed before the trio. People who seemed to be writhing in mortal agony one second felt the trio's presence and moved aside. The men on the floor clutched their sanity at the sight of Bethany and Bubba. The women eyeballed Davecki with lust, pretending they were not in the least threatened by the awesome femininity at his sides.

As they cut through the crowd like the Coast Guard cutter Mackinaw opening a channel through January ice in Whitefish Bay, Davecki could see there were two dance floors in the building. The one they were on was sunken. The one they were heading for was raised, on the same level as the entry foyer. The place was colossal and it was jam packed with what seemed to Davecki to be at least a thousand people. All around the huge arena of dancers, at a height of twelve feet above the tallest head in the place, a balcony perched. All along the balcony, bodies leaned on the railing. Every pair of eyes on those leaning bodies were looking down on the arena floor. It reminded Davecki of the Colosseum. On the field below, gyrating bodies fighting for some sort of recognition. Above, peering down on the masses like an elite class of Roman demigods, the masters.

They docked at the thirty yard long bar that had seven bartenders behind it. He looked at the faces of Bubba and

Mike Savage

Bethany. They were smiling. Bubba's lips moved. He couldn't understand a word, but, with his best attempt at lip reading, he believed she'd just asked him what he wanted to drink. "Yukon Jack on the rocks," he bellowed. He could barely hear his own words.

Bubba smiled and turned toward the bar. People flowed past like smelt running up the Lester River. They bumped him. He bumped back. A hand grabbed his ass. He turned to see a painted face. It wasn't pretty. In fact, from what Davecki could discern beyond the make up, the mug was downright ugly. Butt ugly would be complimentary. It was the kind of face that fell all toward the bottom. Like a sagging water balloon, the eyes, nose, jowls and lips all indicated that their main point of interest was an inch or two just below the rounded chin that seemed to be holding every feature on the face from falling to the floor. It was the kind of face, that, had it been on a man, Davecki would have instantly wanted to punch. But this face was being carried around by a <u>Thirty Something</u> woman, so Davecki's desire to smash it like a rotting pumpkin faded into a vague sense of disease.

Another anti-punching influence on Davecki was that the face was interesting. It had flames painted on it like the hood and door of a souped up '57 Chevy. Yellow and orange flames streaked upward from the eyebrows that were fuzed out and had been colored a blaze orange. The eyebrows looked like they were orange-hot pokers that had rested in the blistering hot coals of a blacksmith's forge. There were dark rings painted thick around the eyes. Eyelashes and lids were powdered black. They looked like ashes from a dead campfire. Below the nose was the mouth. From the corners of the lips, flames leaped up the

Burn Baby Burn

floridcheeks that were bulbous to the point of looking like they should be hung on the pugnacious face of a bulldog. He was wondering if he should speak. The eyes of Flame Woman were blaze yellow. *Contacts* he thought. As was the case with Davecki, he often felt he had to say whatever came into his mind. He was about to comment on the eerie yellow eyes when there was a tug on his arm. He turned and saw Bubba brandishing a glass of amber fluid wrapped around the ice cubes contained therein. "Thanks," he said and noted that somehow he was able to hear himself.

He actually heard Bubba say, "You're welcome." A young guy who looked like <u>The</u> <u>Bell</u> <u>Prince</u> <u>of</u> <u>Fresh</u> <u>Air</u> walked up to Bubba and said something.

She slapped him hard.

He staggered backward and vanished the way a puppy runs behind the couch when it's swatted.

A young guy who looked like Ted Danson was talking to Bethany.

No slapping.

Another young guy walked up and stood next to Bubba. This one looked like Ralph Fiennes. He said something. She smiled. Davecki felt his guts jump and realized he was jealous. *Bad sign*. He shook his head. The realization was like noticing your little sister was getting breasts. An unwelcome awareness at best. He had to get away from the knowledge that had just knocked on the door of his awareness.

A convenient avoidance reaction sprang up in his mind. *Why does everyone look so young?* Davecki thought. With Bubba and Bethany occupied, he swirled the moonlight liquid around the ice cubes. He was impatient to

Mike Savage

temper the whiskey so he could sip it well. Staring into the alcohol pool the way he used to stare into the deep blue eyes of his high school girlfriend, Davecki felt pressure on his arm. He looked aside and saw a red haired woman. She was pressing her breasts into his arm. She held a cigarette that seemed to be three inches too long. "LIGHT ME," she said.

She doesn't look so young. He shrugged his shoulders and said, "No matches!"

She stared at him for half a second, said, "Loser!" and turned away into the sea of chaotic noise, bodies, flashing strobe lights and varying densities of smoke that looked for all the world like real live fog swirling around the Aerial Lift Bridge.

He sloshed his whiskey some more and raised his glass. He turned and saw that Flame Lady was still there.

"You're OLD!" she hollered.

"Thanks!" Davecki said.

"Ida Hoe," Flame Lady yelled. She stuck out her hand.

What in the world does Idaho have to do with the price of tea in China? he thought. "Pleased to meet you," he said. "I'm The Old Guy!" *You are one homely woman.*

They shook hands. Just as Davecki released Ida's beefy hand he was bumped from behind. The Yukon Jack in his other hand sloshed out of the glass and washed over the flames on Ida's face like some fireman was trying to quench the roaring blaze. "What the?" Davecki said.

Turning he saw Bethany was surrounded by two burly men. The Ted Danson look-a-like had been shoved into Davecki and was rubbing his cheek. The Burly Men were leading Bethany forcibly through the crowd. They cut a swath through the crowd that looked like a big Bayliner

Burn Baby Burn

planing out after leaving the dock at Barker's Island. Davecki grabbed Bubba by the elbow. Fiennes Man looked stricken. Davecki handed his glass to the startled actor-look-a-like and yanked Bubba into the wake of the departing trio.

The Bulky Men and Bethany headed up the stairs to the balcony. Davecki and Bubba, followed. "What's going on?" Bubba asked.

"I don't know what, but it's something and it doesn't look good for Bethie," Davecki answered. Ascending the wide stairway, he looked up. To the right, all along the railing were bodies jammed in like fishermen on opening day at a salmon spawning hole. To the left it was the same only, to Davecki, this crowd looked like vultures on the Serengetti leaning forward out of a baobab tree, watching lions devour a Dik Dik, waiting for the chance to swoop down and feed.

The left handed crowd was different. About twenty feet down the crowded railing of solid (in)humanity there was a vacancy in the crowd about twenty feet long. Directly in the middle of that odd spatial anomaly stood a human form. Beyond the unnerving gash the human salmon loaf started again.

Walking up the stairs automatically, Davecki focused on the human form. There was a certain blackness to the individual. It wasn't just that the clothing was dark, there seemed to be a discernible absence of light, a black hole surrounding the form.

Davecki shuddered.

It had to be a man. The form was tall, with wide shoulders. The taper to the waist was definitely male. The face showed white skin around dark sunglasses. But the skin itself wasn't Nordic white. It was sooty-white. Then the form turned its head toward Davecki. A brilliant flash of light beaconed from the man's face. It was like a strong flashlight beam had been turned on and pointed in Davecki's direction.

What the? Davecki thought. The Bulky Man/Bethany trio in front turned left at the top of the stairs. Davecki and Bubba swerved left also. They wound through the entirely male crowd. It reminded Davecki of a mass of maggots on a six day old deer carcass in August.

They came upon a velvet rope beyond which there were no people for twenty feet. The lone figure in the space turned further and smiled again. Davecki realized what the flashlight beam-thing was. The dark man's teeth were brilliant white. They gleamed out like a lone star against the velvet blackness of a moonless sky. Davecki felt his guts, from his groin to his belly button, seize in a puke reflex.

"Ouch! You're hurting me," Bubba said, trying to pull her hand from Davecki's death grip.

He said, "Sorry," and shook his head. He let go of her hand. They remained stopped behind Bethany and the body guards. Bethany glanced over her shoulder. He stared back trying to convey confidence. He wanted to say that it would all be fine. Didn't.

The figure beyond stood looking the ensemble over. *Inspection time*, Davecki guessed. While waiting, he thought of maggots. He'd heard about We Fest, The Country Music Jam, Sturgis, Laconia and Biketoberfest in Daytona. All maggot conventions. The Democratic National Convention, The Hague, The Politiburo...maggot love-ins. He shook his head. Tried to rid himself of the

Burn Baby Burn

unusual train of thought. It didn't help. A vision of Boris Yeltsin reaching between Bill Clinton's legs only to find a vodka bottle there alerted Davecki to the realization that he was getting into some pretty whacky territory mentally. He shuffled his feet ever so slightly. *This is fucking weird.*

He wanted to shake his head again. But he'd already done that. He didn't want to appear rattled. Then Boris Yeltsin at a press conference popped up on his mind screen. Yeltsin was on network TV explaining that his relationship with Clinton, while not technically sexual, WAS appropriate for HEADS of state.

Why am I thinking like this? Where the hell is this going? He was going to try and answer the question when the man in black nodded. Bulky Man Number One reached down and unfastened the velvet hooked rope. Bethany and Bulky Man Two moved through the opening.

Davecki followed.

Bulky Man One put up his hand. It was a big hand. It plunked down on to Davecki's chest like a car battery falling into place under the hood. Davecki looked at Bulky Man One. The behemoth looked stupid to Davecki. He had a pointy head that resembled the Governor's. *Bad sign.* Stupid guys didn't know when to stop, Davecki knew. In a battle they would just keep biting and kicking and chewing and spewing violence until they were either overpowered or dead. Davecki actually admired that kind of man. However he didn't ever want to wrestle with such a raw fighting demon. Davecki's entire body tensed when he realized he was evaluating the basics of hand to hand combat. He wanted desperately to reach behind his coat and feel for the Beretta there.

Mike Savage

He looked at Bubba, wished he'd left her downstairs. *She could handle pick up artists. But this?* He looked back at Man With Big Hand On My Chest and saw that the "Cretin" was looking across the "Hall" at Dark Loner.

Dark Loner wagged his head forth and back a couple of times. The hand stayed on Davecki's chest. Davecki glanced at Bulky Man Two with Bethany. They were standing to the side just inside the velvet rope. The bodyguard was looking at the Dark Loner. Then Bethany's captor glanced over to Davecki. He hadn't seen Bulky Man Two's face until now and he realized he looked like both Wesley Snipes AND Samuel Jackson. *Lando Calrisian.*

Davecki stole a glance at Bubba. Her face was steely. Her eyes were pinched slightly together. Davecki saw she was still clutching her minuscule purse and hoped there was a .380 therein.

Davecki looked back at Bethany. She was looking at Dark Loner. Davecki felt the hand on his chest fall away. Bulky Man Number One stepped aside and swept an arm towards Dark Loner as if he was allowing passage to the throne of royalty.

Stepping into the unpeopled section of the balcony, Davecki felt he suddenly knew what it was like to enter the eye of a hurricane. No bodies, no grab-ass, no shoving, no stinking hairdos, no spilled beer or gyrating assholes. It even seemed quieter. Davecki could even discern the lyrics. It was <u>Soul</u> <u>Asylum</u>. Grant Young's drumming accentuated the words. *I should have become a musician. Then, instead of being in this pit, I could be in Ely running a resort on the shores of Mitchell Lake.*

The Man With The Battery Hand lead the group to-

Burn Baby Burn

ward Dark Loner. As they got closer, Loner extended his hand to shake. Davecki thought he heard him say, "Mitch Crandal." The black arm extended a hand that sported a black leather glove pulled on tightly. *If it doesn't fit, you must acquit*, Davecki thought as he shook the man's hand. Davecki sniffed. *Incense? Lilies?*

"Nice to meet you Mitch," Davecki said.

The Man in Black rolled his eyes. "M<u>a</u>tch," he yelled.

"Sorry," Davecki said.

Looking at Bethany and then Bubba, Match yelled, "Great bitches for an old mutha like you."

Davecki felt a several megawatt jump in the already electric air. The jolt acted like a car accident. Time slowed down. His perception heightened. His brain went into hyper-vigilant mode. All things were knowable in this state. He watched as Crandal reached into the coat pocket of his black blazer. Crandal pulled out a roll of bills. The green was wrapped in a rubber band. Crandal pulled the binder off and let it constrict down his hand and snap to his wrist. Crandal fanned the flash roll. Davecki saw it was nothing but hundreds.

Thanks to Davecki's hyper-perception he had the leisure to think, *Probably counterfeit hundreds handcrafted by dutiful Iranians intent on destroying the Great Satan America with an inflation bomb. Better than fusion.*

In the meantime, Crandal tilted his head toward Bethany. "How much?" he asked, riffing the bills again.

Next to him Davecki felt Bubba's voltage jump again. This time exponentially. He saw her face go from steely to deadly.

"What?" Davecki heard his voice ask.

"You heard me jerk-off. How much for the prime

pussy?" Crandal said, indicating Bethany again. "Besides, she's young enough to be your daughter." Then Crandal eyed Bubba, "The flashy hooker wannabe is more your speed asshole. Me? I like the hot young grooves that get super wet and go fucking nuts when you Meth 'em. They ride you all night when they're hopped up."

Crandal's face went from speech to smiling in what seemed to Davecki to be half an hour. Davecki observed that he could see individual facial muscles pulling Crandal's lips into a curve pointing toward the Armani sunglasses. He observed that he was observing his observations and laughed inwardly at his ability to multi-task when in hyper-vigilance mode.

Crandal's gleaming teeth were perfectly aligned. Davecki analyzed the tone of voice, decided Crandal couldn't know Bethany was really his daughter, decided the insult was just an insult and decided that the professional thing would be to let the insult pass.

Davecki also felt his guts violently urging him to smash the bastard's perfect teeth in, crush his thousand dollar glasses and haul his ass to jail. He wanted to "murdurlize" the creep. He, of course, would do all this for the poor sap's own good. For Crandal was now in real danger of being passionately murdered by both Bethany and Bubba. He could call it protective custody. But then again, he wasn't in Superior. And, Davecki knew he wasn't in mortal danger. So, he couldn't just gun the fucker down. Then too, understandably, there would be active and insistent resistance from Crandal and his body guards, Bulky Men One and Two.

The accelerated brain kilohertz that allowed Davecki to make all these complicated observations and perform

Burn Baby Burn

all the impressive mental gymnastics that were going on inside his head, also made it possible for him to dispassionately observe as his guts vetoed "with extreme prejudice, all of his training and most of his common sense.

For, there in the middle of a sweeping left hook was a hand. That hand was attached to an arm and that arm was hooked to a shoulder. That shoulder was his own, his very own.

So, even had he been circumspect, it was too late, for as he watched the sweep of his left hand strike out like an angry rattlesnake and swat the flash roll from Crandal's hand, he wondered, *how can two such opposite things be going on inside me at the same time and be so detached from one another?*

Mike Savage

18

The love of money is the root of all evil.

— Jesus

The only thing stronger in this world than the love of a mother for her children is the love of a father for his daughter.

— Edwin P.T. Gemmill, 1883

Burn Baby Burn

Beautiful was the sight of the flash roll flying out of Crandal's hand. Elegant was its arc as it sailed through the hostility laden air. Inevitable was its destination. The crowd below. Thanks to the friendly time anomaly instituted by Crandal's pernicious hostility toward Davecki's daughter, the wad of money seemed to take its own good time looping over the balcony railing. The thick roll of Franklins started coming apart and spreading like anti-radar chaff flying from the butt of a locked-on F-16. The bills fluttered like fall leaves and drifted toward the unsuspecting crowd below.

Crandal was not amused. Fortunately he loved money and took the opportunity to watch his small fortune sail toward the crowd below. In that respite of time, Davecki did something he had to do. He didn't want to, but he shoved Bethany hard enough to hurt her. "RUN!" he bellowed.

Luckily Bethany didn't share her father's affinity to self endangerment. Using her Old Man's push, she turned and fled in the direction they'd just come.

Pushing off Bethany, Davecki lunged for Crandal's throat. Wrapping a large, rage motivated hand around Crandal's neck felt satisfying to Davecki. With his other hand, Davecki grabbed Crandal by the ass of his slick black pants. Before either of the Bulky Men present could earn the large sums of money they were being paid to protect him, Crandal and his smoky face were meeting up with the twelve-by-twelve white pine support timber that held the balcony up. On the rebound, Crandal's body felt significantly limper in Davecki's grip. The Superior cop marshalled his strength at the back of Crandal's re-

Mike Savage

bound from the pine wood, the better to throw the sleazy asshole over the railing in pursuit of his cash.

There was one thing wrong with Davecki's plan. Bulky Man One had engaged his itty bitty brain and was grasping Davecki around the neck with an arm that resembled a massive tree limb. Thus halted in his effort to toss Crandal to the wolves below, Davecki suddenly became very interested in breathing. The oak limb around his windpipe choked him. Being basically interested in self preservation, he dropped Crandal like a sack of potatoes to work on the problem of appropriating air for his suddenly starving lungs. As he wiggled around in the grasp of the strong man, Davecki heard an unusual sound.

It was a primal scream so penetrating, it overpowered the music. Bulky Man's hold on Davecki's neck loosened. Davecki gasped. Both men turned toward the sound of the screech. They saw Bubba. They saw Bubba standing over Bulky Man Two. Her dress was ripped even further up the side. But her dignity was intact. She was in the rather delicate act of pulling her spike heel from the crotch of Bulky Man Two, who was the source of the agonizing primal yowl.

At the sight of his buddy's disembowlment, Davecki's assailant reacted the way any good steroid freak would. His inordinate concern for the amazing shrinking testicles problem he and his kind faced made him convulse at the thought of his own family jewels being similarly abused. He released his grip.

Davecki instantly reached behind his coat and jerked out the Beretta. Shoving it in Bulky Man One's face made the monster back off. Bubba kicked her other heel from her foot and jumped over to Davecki. She took his gun

Burn Baby Burn

and nodded down to Crandal. Davecki grabbed the unconscious fool by the long hair on the back of his head and heaved him up. Crandal was a lump. A two hundred pound lump of limp human. Normally Davecki wouldn't have been able to lift that much dead weight. But he was still enraged. The flaccid Crandal looked to weigh about ten ounces as Davecki dragged him to the railing. He looked over and laughed.

Below, there were several hundred people fighting like gladiators for the bills, some of which were still floating downward. Davecki flung Crandal into the air and didn't even wait to watch what happened. He turned back to Bubba and said, "Let's get outta here."

"Couldn't agree more," She answered. She started walking around Bulky Man One. He stood still and pivoted, following her as she rotated. She kept the gun steadily trained on his nose. She glanced at the crowd of people by the velvet rope. Bethany had just vanished into that crowd. In that second, Bulky Man dove for Bubba. She would have shot him dead if Davecki hadn't anticipated the Hulking One's move and had already insinuated himself between Bubba and her attacker. The two men collided and crashed to the floor.

"Go!" Davecki yelled. "Find Bethany!" he yelled. Then he had a wrestling match on his hands. Bulky Man One was at least three times stronger than Davecki. He grabbed the cop around the waist and started squeezing. Davecki gasped. His vision went dark. When the lights came back on, it had to be only a second later, for, he could see Bubba's sweet ass diving through the crowd that parted for the gun wielding fem fatale.

Bubba's fate suddenly became secondary to Davecki.

Mike Savage

Bulky Man, or BM as Davecki had suddenly decided to nickname the shit-for-brains cocksucker, picked the Superior cop up and ran him toward the railing. *Poetic justice*, Davecki thought as he was launched into space in one fluid motion.

It reminded Davecki of sky diving. He looked down thinking he'd see Crandal's carcass below. Not. What he did see was a scrambling morass of maggots fighting like banshees for cold hard cash. Ben Franklins in large quantities just don't start raining down on degenerate mobs every night of the week.

As he floated downward, Davecki thought of The Short Happy Life of Frances Macomber. For one second there, ramming Crandal's face into the timber, Davecki knew he was pure. Pure animal. Pure killing machine. Purely deadly and utterly justified because of his love for his daughter. Davecki smiled. He could see that contact with the humans below was imminent and he didn't relish the idea of what that meant, but still, he smiled. It had been a great moment of simplicity, unity, serenity.

The impact was surprisingly soft. He crashed into the hedonist creeps scrambling for instant, nontaxable income. The sound of his "Ooof" was barely discernible amidst the yelling and the music. The blow knocked the wind out of his chest. He was incapacitated. Because the fools he was now intimate with were basically soulless, they didn't have much in the way of sympathy for a man who came thudding into them at high velocity from above. They did only what could be expected from heathens.

They kicked his ass. They stomped his carcass, hauled his ashes, mauled his mainframe, mashed his mandibles, crunched his clavicle and generally shredded the pitiable

Burn Baby Burn

amount of self esteem he'd gotten from crushing Crandal's nose flatter than piss on a platter.

Instead of curling up in a ball and dying, Davecki did the next best thing. He curled up in a ball and started trying to roll away from the abuse. In a few seconds the rain of bludgeoning lessened sufficiently to allow him to stand. On wobbly legs, Davecki staggered toward the exit. In the confusion, he could see someone standing on the elevated landing. It was Flame Woman. She was waving. She was signalling Davecki to, "come hither," as his mother used to say. Being basically without coherence, Davecki could come up with no good reason not to comply. He walked toward Flame Woman as quickly as he could.

Just as quickly his progress was halted. He was spun around. *GOD DAMN SADDAM!!* It was Match Crandal in the flesh. Well, it was Match Crandal in what little flesh there was left of him after being thrown bloody into the pool of piranhas behind them. Davecki could hardly believe his eyes. Crandal's face looked like the contents of a gut-shot whitetail's belly. But, more interesting to Davecki, was what else he saw. It was Crandal's balled up fist traveling at fifty or sixty miles an hour toward Davecki's nose.

The collision sounded like a twelve pound sledge whacking a watermelon. The sound of crunching bone seemed to please Crandal. After all, it was, at last, not his body being havocked. Apparently the pleasure of punching Davecki made Crandal happy, for, he repeated the punching process several times in rapid succession.

Davecki stood there observing his own pummeling. He could probably have stood by and watched this for quite some time. However, yet another interesting event was happening in the shallow background. *Ah the comfort of chaos.*

There behind Crandal's head and the sweeping right hooks that were bashing Davecki, was a three and a half foot long steel stool swinging on a wide arc around the radius of Bethany's arms.

"WHANG!!" the chair reverberated.

"THUNK!" Crandal's head resonated. The blow sounded like a Sammy Sosa swatted hard ball. Crandal's legs instantly lost all communications with the aforementioned head and buckled like a Monica Lewinski wannabe meeting the CEO of MedTronics.

It was getting difficult for Davecki to see. His mouth was filled with blood. His teeth felt like bobbers floating in melted ice cream. He was reeling around like a Weebles. He didn't fall down. Bethany grabbed him and said, "Let's get outta here!"

"Sluabble snuffle snop," Davecki said.

Bethany grabbed him and they plowed through the white trash standing around wondering what the hell was going on like they were a Vermilion County plow clearing roads after the traditional March blizzard. Unfortunately the blizzard brought more than snow. When they got to the door, the Minneapolis cops were storming in. In the melee, Davecki and Bethany were separated.

"Eeek," he heard her shriek and she was gone.

"Ugh," he said when a cop grabbed him by the neck between powerful fingers. *Like a lobster claw.*

"You're coming with me," the cop said. *This guy's got a tough job.*

The cop dragged Davecki out the door and hauled his

Burn Baby Burn

ass toward a big blue van sitting at the curb. *I wonder if that thing's run down any innocent bystanders lately?* There was no line of I-wanna-get-ins now. No skinny bouncer. There were just several squad cars, the paddy wagon and a TV van with a grip on the roof setting up the satellite dish. *Phone Home*, Davecki's brain contributed. He huffed a gurgling little laugh through the slime in his maw. The Minneapolis blue tightened his grip and asked, "What's so funny?"

Davecki wished he had the strength to pull out his badge, pull the "fellow cop" ploy. Get out of the pinch. Overcoming the shock of entering a strange nightclub is one thing. Overcoming the shock of someone trying to buy your daughter AND having your face bashed in is another. Davecki thought of the immortal words of the patron saint of all loyal Wisconsinites, Vince Lombardi, who said, "Fatigue makes cowards of us all." Plus, for some reason, he didn't want to reveal his identity to his arrestor. "Snorggle, slupe," was all he could manage.

The cop manhandled Davecki toward the rear of the paddy wagon, reefed on the handle and swung the door wide. He shoved Davecki up the steps and slammed the door soundly. Davecki collapsed on a bench seat along the nearest wall. He would have held his head in his hands but couldn't because, across from him, he saw a sight that, at best, was unwelcome and at most, deeply frightening.

Mike Savage

19

Some scars just have to be shown.

— Mathew B. Petrosky

Some revenges must never be known.

— Ryan K. Petrosky

Burn Baby Burn

Embedded on the bench across from him, sat the ugly hooker, Ida Hoe. The flame paintings on her face were smudged and smeary. The orange of her eyebrows was jagged now. Her entire face looked like stock market day-charts gone insane. Light brown eyebrow hairs, now denuded of their gaudy paint, reminded Davecki of eating home butchered chicken wings. The bristles stuck out like errant pin feathers, unplucked. She smiled and spread her legs a little. "Whew!" she said fanning up her legs with her left hand while the right hiked up the leather skirt wrapped tightly around her wide hips. "Hotter than blue blazes up there," she said.

Davecki groaned. *Where's Bethany? Bubba?* He could see fuchsia panties peeking at him beyond Ida's fanning.

"You're a sight," Ida said.

I could say the same for you. "Snugh," Davecki said. He swallowed blood.

"For a cop, you're pretty stupid," Ida said.

Davecki rested his head against the truck's side wall. The steel felt cool through his hair. He swallowed, licked the inside of his mouth, ran his tongue over the front of his teeth. "What makes you think I'm a cop?"

"I'm the ugly hooker Ida Hoe. I know these things."

Davecki chuckled. *No pretense here.* "That obvious?"

"Not until you started playing demolition ball with Crandal's head."

"You saw that?"

"Followed youse guys upstairs when I seen something was going on."

"Hmmmm," Davecki said. He smiled. The smile was cut short because it hurt. He reached for his face. Touched a finger gently to his tender nose. "Man. That was sweet. It was worth it. Just smashing him was worth this," he said prodding his skin lightly.

They listened to the hubbub outside. There were sirens and shouts and car engines racing. A voice shouted, "Come on Kenny we need an uplink NOW!" Davecki looked at Ida.

"Reporter," they both said at the same time.

Ida laughed.

Davecki snorted. "Ouch!" he cried.

"You're in a world of hurt."

"No shit."

The tumult went on outside. They both listened. After a minute or so Davecki asked, "How'd you get such a funny name."

Ida quit her crotch fanning. "Daddy had a wicked sense of humor. He was having fun with Ebonics way before it was popular. Said my younger sister was his L'Angel and I was De Hoe." Ida didn't look away.

"You don't look black."

"I'm Norwegian. Daddy was a Norsky. Ma was Swede. My last name's really Mattsen."

"Humph," Davecki said and closed his eyes. They were already half closed from the beating, so it wasn't that difficult a project.

"What makes me 'Stupid for a cop?'"

"You're in here ain't 'cha?" Ida tugged the tight white top out of the belt line of her skirt.

"You know...you just don't hear those good old names any more," Davecki said.

"Huh?" Ida asked.

"Ida. I like that name. It's old fashioned. Solid. Like

Burn Baby Burn

June. Those old names, you just don't get them much any more. It's like something from Thomas Hardy."

"What the hell you babbling about?" Ida said.

"Oh nothing. I just like your name."

"Well I like you too honey. Only I don't know your name."

Davecki pulled his head off the wall. He opened his eyes a bit. Smiled. "It's an old fashioned name too. You probably won't like it," he said.

"Try me."

"Alphonse."

"Wow! Even your name's old," Ida exclaimed.

"Thanks."

"You're welcome. You want a quick blow job? Only twenty bucks. Professional discount."

Davecki grinned, rested his head. "Thanks. Not now."

"Suit yerself." Ida flapped the bottom of her top. "God it's hot in here. Is it hot in here? You hot? I mean, Christ. I'm boiling. Is it hot?"

"Feels fine to me," Davecki answered.

Ida said, "I think I'm going into the change. One minute I'm normal. The next I'm sweating bullets." She fanned herself with her garment.

Huge tracts of land. Davecki said, "Yeah. I hear it's a bitch."

"You mean to tell me your parents actually named you Alphonse and wasn't joking around?" Ida said continuing her flapping.

"Yup. But everyone calls me Dave."

"Why's that?"

"Because my last name is Davecki. Dave stuck in third grade. It's been that way ever since."

Mike Savage

Ida was about to say something when the door clanged open again. Another cop, not the one who stuffed Davecki, was shoving a drunk into the van. Beyond the cop's head Davecki could see a reporter getting ready for a stand-up. Bathed in bright quartz-halogen lighting the reporter was nervous. She rocked forth and back on the balls of her red pump clad feet. Beyond the news broad, on the edge of the circle of light, Davecki saw Bethany and Bubba. They were talking to a man in a suit. *Minneapolis Dick.*

The cop pushed the drunk in far enough to get the door closed. The drunk could hardly navigate. He crawled to the bench beside Davecki and hooked an elbow. He got enough purchase to arranged himself into a sitting position on the floor. "Name's Gene," he announced looking at Davecki first. Gene's eyeballs fluttered left and fell on Ida. He stared. To Davecki the aging alcoholic looked like Young Frankenstein.

"What the hell you looking at?" Ida said.

"Nothing," Gene said. His face held a stupid smirk. He didn't look away.

"Get a good look asshole," Ida said hoisting her top.

This made Gene wilder. "Oh my god!" he groaned.

"Shut the fuck up," Ida said quickly lowering her top. "Smack him one for me will you officer?"

Gene looked at Davecki. "You a cop?"

"Yeah. I'm here to make sure everything stays calm and collected," Davecki answered.

"What happened to your face?"

"Got stomped in the fight. Now shut up and go to sleep or I'll up-charge you from drunk and disorderly to solicitation."

"Hey! That's not fair. I didn't do no such thing!"

Burn Baby Burn

Ida laughed. "You sure did. I can testify to that Mr. Green Gene."

"Awww," Wilder moaned. "I ain't got no luck." He rested the side of his head on the crook of his arm and continued staring at Ida.

"What you got against Crandal?" Ida asked.

"That's just the problem. Got nothing."

"What's that mean?"

"It means me and my partner came all the way down here because of a stupid match book and all I got was a brawl, a smashed face and a lot of explaining to do when we get to booking."

"What was you wanting to get?"

Davecki sighed. He realized Ida knew nothing of the arsons in Superior. Nobody in the Twin Cities would even care if the whole damn town burned down. It would make the news for a night or two and then there'd be some new disaster somewhere. "I'm not from here. I'm a cop in Superior, Wisconsin... Came down here to try and find out who's been setting fires to the old buildings in our town." Talking was difficult for Davecki. His face was beginning to stiffen up. The pain was beginning to throb.

His pain was eased somewhat by Ida's next words. "Well shit man. That's no frigging mystery. Everybody who's anybody down here...well, anybody who's anybody who hangs at The Hot Place would tell you Match Crandal's your man."

"How come you know so much about Crandal?"

Ida stared hard at Davecki. "You going to bust his ass?" She kept staring. He could see she was evaluating him. Then her face changed. He knew she'd made a decision. "No way. You'll never catch him. He's too smart for you. You could maybe shoot him a few times. But you'll never get a conviction. Shooting him. That would be easiest. It'd be best if you just filled him full of lead 'cause YOU ain't never going to catch him."

"I could never shoot him. Even if I wanted to, I could never shoot him unless he brandishes a weapon."

Ida laughed. "Brandishes a weapon. That's rich. What are you? Some kinda middle-aged rookie? Quoting the book? Come on. I ain't gonna say scratch to you about Match Crandal unless you put some suffering on him like he did me."

Davecki thought back to the balcony. Crandal had tried to buy his daughter. "I could have killed the bastard earlier..."

"Well that's great news. Now let me show you last year's news flash," Ida said. She reefed on the bottom of her shirt again.

"Awwwwk," Wilder squawked.

Do all hookers down here act this way? Davecki was about to say something about knocking it off, but was stopped short by Ida. She held up her left hand and said, "Don't say nothing!" She pulled the shirt way up with her right and held it back to the side of her face. She was looking down at herself.

Wilder gurgled, gasped and went silent.

Then Davecki saw.

Ida pointed to the area where her cleavage started. "See that?!? See that?" she said. Anger infused her words. The rage made her voice rich and resonant like the heavy hum of big truck tires on hot asphalt. Ida pointed to an ugly tangle of scar tissue on the skin of her chest. "That's how come I know so much about Match Crandal," She

Burn Baby Burn

said. Her voice sounded like it came from the depths of hell.

"What the????" Davecki said.

20

We didn't start the fire, it was always burning since the world was turning.

— Billy Joel

Burn Baby Burn

Remedial fortune always smiled on Dave Davecki. Many times he didn't know that *good* things were happening to him. Often the blessings were disguised, looked like curses. Like being thrown into a paddy wagon by a Minneapolis cop. That could look bad. Or, he could be locked inside a step van with a hooker and a drunk. That could be construed as less than a blessing.

Fortunately, Alphonse "Dave" Davecki had learned that some of God's best work is done down in the gutters. In the churches, sometimes the stained glass got in the way of real, honest-to-goodness Holy Spirit work. But, out in the world where the ass kickers and the dick lickers and the money grubbers fought and lied and connived, out in the blood and the guts and the beer, sometimes there was so damn much grace flowing unseen through the veins of every heroin addict and hooker, that even Davecki had to admit that a power greater than himself was hauling the freight in an almighty powerful way.

However, at this particular point in time, at this unique juncture of history, Davecki wasn't quite thinking Holy Spirit type thoughts. He was thinking about the ugliness on Ida's chest.

"See that?!? See that?!? That's why I know everything there is to know about Match Crandal. That's why I know someone like YOU ain't got a snowball's chance in hell to put the prick away."

Davecki grinned. "You're transferring Ida."

She pulled her shirt down. "I'll transfer your ass right into the drunk tank with ol' Gene there if you don't shut the fuck up. All's I gotta do is talk to sergeant when we get to the station and you'll be sitting in the corner pro-

Mike Savage

tecting your lily white ass hoping some big fucking fecal freak Indian doesn't wake up and fall in love with you."

Jesus, he thought and kept his yap shut.

Ida made a clucking sound. She glanced at Davecki and then fixed her eyes on the door to her right. "The bastard picked me up one night about two years ago. He'd passed on me a few times. I figured he wasn't interested because of my face. None of the other girls had anything bad to say about him. But of course, they were pretty. So, it was a bit of a surprise when the window of his Jag rolled down and he waved me over.

"When I leaned into the car, I didn't like the smell of him right away. Stunk like lilies. Yuk! Reminded me of Catholic Mass. Ick! But, one thing the girls HAD said was he tipped like hell. So I got in.

Right away he said he didn't want anything going on in his Jaguar so we went to an apartment. When we got there, he lit about thirty candles and snorted some lines. He was drinking too. Said he'd pay extra if he could cuff me to the bed. I didn't like the thought of it, but then he showed me his roll and peeled off five hundred.

"I said okay and he locked me down. But it wasn't working for him. He wasn't getting any buzz, any juice. He stayed limp as cooked spaghetti. He got real steamed. Went kind of nuts. He started throwing shit and tearing things apart. I got scared and started thrashing around and yelling for him to let me go.

"That was a mistake, yelling. It got his attention and he looked at me real funny. He just stared at me like he was dreaming and then, after about a minute or so, he took the box of big ol' farmer matches he'd used to light the candles with and built this little teepee of matches

Burn Baby Burn

between my tits. Then he took one of them butane lighters for grilling. You know the ones that look a little like a gun?"

Davecki nodded. He could barely move, but he nodded.

"The bastard lit it up and burned me bad. I screamed and tossed and he roasted me good with his fancy lighter on high. That made him hard but I was so wild, he never did do me. He just laughed and laughed and then did some sort of little dance before he took off."

"God," Davecki said.

"God's got nothing to do with it."

"Huh?"

"It's all from the Devil."

"What's that?"

Ida eyed him. She snorted a little derisive laugh. She scratched her thigh with long false fingernails, bright red. "I was there screaming for three days. Thought I was a goner but woke up in Fairview. Ever since, I been fucking all his friends for free to get enough information to pay him back."

"Jesus," Davecki said.

"That's why you got to shoot him for me."

Davecki rested his weary head on the side wall again. "That is not going to happen."

"Why the hell not?"

"Because it ain't right to repay evil for evil. There are laws."

Ida laughed. It was a startled laugh that was loud. It bounced off the steel walls adding layers of brittleness with each reverberation. "Evil's irrelevant man. It's the fucking Millennium! The fucking governor of the state is

Mike Savage

a former pathological killer for the Navy who packs iron for his own protection. The whole goddamned world is frigging crazy and you're sitting there telling me that Match Crandal doesn't deserve to be shot to death seven hundred fucking times."

"I can't take the law into my own hands. The law's all we got. If everyone started shooting everyone who deserved it, there'd be mayhem."

"They do it on the L.A. freeways all the fucking time man. You from the Dark Ages or something?"

"I'm from Superior where the bad guys get caught and the good guys get to live peaceably."

"Sounds like heaven or some frigging daydream," Ida snorted.

"It ain't heaven, but it's damn close. Now, if you want Match Crandal to pay for what he did to you, all you gotta do is help me get the evidence that he burned down the Tower Building in Superior, that he was the one who tied the karaoke singer to the chair in the basement and burned her alive."

"That shouldn't be too hard."

Davecki opened his eyes wide. "You serious?"

"You're fucking weird. You know that?"

"Thank you."

Beyond the thin metal walls the van's occupants could hear the trained voice of the TV reporter telling viewers what was happening in their fair city. "A brawl at The Hot Place on Hennypenny Avenue in Downtown Minneapolis got the attention of over twenty policemen this evening. At least three people have already been arrested. Police are still sorting out the details. The owner of The Hot Place, according to the research team back at the sta-

Burn Baby Burn

tion, is listed as Mrs. Albertina Crandal. I'm waiting to talk to Lieutenant Todd Larson of the Crime Division who is in charge here at the scene. I'll have more on this breaking story in a minute. Back to you at the studio Larry."

Davecki looked at Ida. "You ever think of ditching the life and leaving town?"

"That an offer?"

"No. Just wondering if you get tired of being pissed at Crandal."

The ugly hooker shifted around, leaned forward. Resting her elbows on her knees, she said, "Never. I'll never stop 'til he's dead."

Davecki coughed a little. "I don't mean to be stupid here Ida, but, hey. I mean, it didn't happen to me, but... Ummm. Wouldn't you settle for him being in jail for a long long time? I mean. It wasn't like he killed your sister or something."

Ida looked Davecki over. "You are one hooked up asshole. You know that?"

Davecki looked around. He shrugged his shoulders, "You talking to ME?" he said.

"He did kill my sister."

"Jesus."

"Myrna came to town to get me to straighten out. She moved in with me. We were going to start a business at home. Day care. We were going to make it go." Ida looked down for the first time. Her shoulders sagged.

"And," Davecki said.

"I made the big mistake of introducing her to Crandal. Cocksuckers fell in love. Or so Myrna said. 'Parently it was true, cause he wouldn't let her out of his sight. After all, SHE was the beautiful one."

Mike Savage

"What happened?"

"They moved in together. He wouldn't let her leave the condo. She was a prisoner for seven years. She'd go out for groceries and he'd spy on her. Said she was running around on him. One afternoon he and his brother stopped at the condo. Crandal bashed in the back of her head with a piece of firewood. He got away Scott free on some technicality. Just because he's hooked up with some heavy hitters in the criminal justice system doesn't mean he won't pay. Like I said, good and evil is irrelevant in this case. I am going to make the bastard pay."

"You got an awful fire of revenge burning in you Ida."

"I didn't start the fire. Seems like it's been burning ever since the world was turning."

"He's that well connected?"

"You bet your fucking ass he's connected. Can do any damn thing he wants. He and his fire worshipping buddies got cart blanche."

"Cart Blanche? That don't sound like a hooker."

"Some of my clients don't look like Johns either, but if they ain't university professors they sure as hell talk like 'em."

"I see."

"You don't see shit."

"A good friend recently told me that very same thing."

"Very perceptive friend."

"You'd like him. You two would make a nice couple."

"Maybe after I kill Crandal or get you to kill him for me. Maybe I'd just like to meet this guy. Get out of the life and stay out."

"We'll see," Davecki said. "You never know."

Just then the paddy wagon door opened again. A red

Burn Baby Burn

faced cop with a yuppie in his grip shoved the Armani suited dink into the van. A hundred dollar bill flew out of the cop's fist. It fluttered to the floor. "Thanks for the contribution Dumb Fuck," the cop said and picked the bill. "It'll make a great contribution to the Boys and Girls Club. Too bad it didn't keep you out of jail." He glared at Ida, Davecki, Gene the Wilder. "What's the matter with him?" the cop said poking his nose toward the drunk on the floor.

Everyone looked down. The drunk formerly known as Gene was staring blankly at Ida. "Ewww," Yuppie Dink said. "Take a shower will ya?" and he moved past Davecki and sat down. The door slammed shut. Davecki sat in silence. Two was company. Wilder hardly made three. But this new guy. It was definitely, three's a crowd. *It sure would be nice to be able to shoot Crandal in the nuts.* Davecki envisioned the smoky bastard writhing in pain. He would have mercy and plug the fucker in the forehead and go back to Superior. *I miss the Big Lake.* He wanted to smell the cold breeze that carried in from Silver Bay past Couple-a-Harbors and down Tower Avenue. He looked at Ida. Her head was leaned back against the van wall. Her eyes were closed. Her lips, he noticed for the first time, were thin. *Actually, she's kinda pretty. In an ugly sort of way.* He looked at Yuppie Man. The geek smiled a wan smile. Davecki thought of Lan's wonton soup at the Taste of Saigon in Canal Park. Someone's stomach growled.

"Mine or yours?" Ida asked.

"Mine," Davecki said. He chuckled. He looked at Wilder. The bulgy eyed man stared at Ida with a wide unblinking leer.

Mike Savage

"Knock it off," Davecki barked.

Wilder didn't even flinch.

Ida studied the drunk. "You okay man?" she asked.

Yuppie Guy stared at the drunk on the floor. "I got a bad feeling about this," he said.

Davecki reached over and waved his hand in front of Wilder's face.

Nothing.

"He breathing?" Ida asked. She looked at Yuppie Scum. "I am not touching that vermin. He might give me AIDS or something," the suit said.

Davecki sighed and picked up Wilder's wrist. Before Davecki could even get a good grip, Wilder tipped over. Ida screamed. Yuppie Guy gasped. Davecki bellowed, "HEY OUT THERE!! HEY!! WE GOT A PROBLEM IN HERE!!"

Ida started stomping her feet and escalated her shrieking. Yuppie Man stood up and started rocking the van.

"COME ON GOD DAMMIT! OPEN THE GOD DAMN DOOR!" Davecki yelled.

The door swung open. The Minneapolis Blue with the cash flow problem stuck his hand, armed with a can of pepper spray, into the opening.

"Put that fucking thing away and help me stretch this guy out," Davecki yelled. Old cop habits die hard. Davecki was assuming command as if he weren't under arrest in a strange city.

The cop blinked, another cop's face peered into the van around the confused looking bribe taker. "What happened?" the second cop asked.

"Died of fright," Davecki snorted. He hitched his head toward Ida.

Burn Baby Burn

"Asshole!" she said. She tried to kick Davecki.

He laughed and winced when the pain reached his super bruised face.

"Knock it off you two," Cop Two said. He shoved past Bribery Man and assisted Davecki in lowering the corpse. "Know CPR?" he asked, looking at Dave.

"No fucking way," Davecki said with a grimace.

"Get the EMTs in here Bill," Cop Two said. Bribery Man's face vanished from the doorway.

"You got to do something," Yuppie Scum pleaded.

"Knock yourself out buddy," Cop Two said. "I'll do the chest. You clear the airway and breathe for him."

"Gaaak!" the yuppie gagged. His face turned white. Both delicate hands covered the dainty mouth. From behind those clasped hands, vomit spurted.

"Shit," Ida said. She went down to her knees, tilted Gene's wilder head. She stuck her fingers into the dead guy's mouth and commented, "I don't get what the big deal is." She pinched the unbreathing nose and puffed air into the open passageway.

When she rocked back, Cop Two pushed on the chest, "One, two, three, four, five," he said, bouncing on the dead guy's sternum.

"Gaaaaaak!" Yuppie No Stomach contributed from the corner.

"Jesus, Mary and Joseph," Davecki said.

As Ida breathed, Cop Two said, "Name's Raymynd Copp-Brule. I spell Raymond with a "Y" so as to stand apart and get noticed."

"Dave Davecki," Alphonse said. He reached inside his ruined suit coat and pulled out his badge.

Copp boinged Wilder's chest. When he was resuscitating he said, "Badging won't help you here."

After Ida breathed for Wilder she said, "His real name's Alphonse."

"No shit?" Copp said.

"No shit," Davecki said.

Ida and Copp-Brule pumped Gene for all his genes were worth. This they did for three minutes until a voice behind Davecki said, "Outta the way!"

Davecki stepped aside and a big black paramedic type crawled into the van. Squeezing Davecki into the corner, the black man looked at Gene and then Ida and said, "God for ugly."

Ida slapped him hard across the face.

"Ouch! God Damn! I was talking about him!" the EMT said, pointing at Wilder.

Ida sat back on the bench. "Right," she said.

EMT Man got oxygen going on Wilder. "He looks pretty dead, man. I don't know. Maybe we shouldn't waste the oxy on him."

Another paramedic squeezed into the van and answered. "We got to try,"

The EMTs worked on Wilder. "We need more room!"

Yuppie Scum moved forward. Ida and Davecki moved back. "You two!" Copp-Brule barked, "Step outside but don't even think of taking off. Bill, watch these two, especially her!"

"Okay, we've got to transport him," EMT One said.

Bribery Bill ordered Davecki to help with the stretcher. Everyone pitched in and got Wilder loaded. How fitting that the drunk, even in death, was once again getting loaded. In order to get him out of the paddy wagon, everyone had to give the EMTs space. In the confusion and

Burn Baby Burn

movement, in everyone's effort to save a life, Davecki almost didn't carpe diem.

Not Ida. As Wilder was being extracted from the van she grasped Davecki by the wrist and pulled him into the crowd, away from Officer Raymynd Copp-Brule and Bribery Man forever.

Mike Savage

21

Thoug the mills of God grind slowly;
yet they grind exceeding small;
Though with patience He stands waiting,
with exactness grinds He all.

— Friedrich Von Logau, *Retribution, 1654*

It takes forever to get anything done around here.

— B.D. Callahan, Superior Police Chief

Burn Baby Burn

Negotiating the crowd beside Ida, Davecki found himself singing silently, *Oh where oh where has my little dog gone?* In his declining years, Davecki's most entertaining organ had become his brain. Every morning, if Carl Jung was correct, Davecki's psyche tossed a bone to his brain in the form of a song lyric. Sometimes it was rock. Sometimes country. Sometimes, as in this case, it was a tune from his youth.

Always the song played over and over in his head until it solved a problem or created a new and fascinating path in the jungle of Davecki's intertwining thoughts. In this instance, it was as if Davecki was just waking up from a little nap in the paddy wagon. So his psyche tossed out the song from his toddler days. He wasn't fully aware that the song had deeper meanings. It played in his head as Davecki and Ida escaped while the cops were tending to Gene and his wilder-ness. "What a break," he said.

"No shit," Ida answered. "It couldn't have been better if a debate about truck portages in the Hubert H. Humphrey Boundary Waters Canoe Area Wilderness had broke out."

"You're the weirdest hooker I've ever met, Ida."

"Thank you officer," she said as they stopped running and continued to walk away from the scene. "Now what?"

Davecki stopped. He scratched his head and sniffed. "You know, I didn't think ol' Gene smelled at all. What was the problem with Yuppie Guy?"

"Nose candy will do that to an organ," Ida said. She laughed.

"I shoulda known," Davecki said.

Mike Savage

He stood there.

She stood there.

The city was growing quiet. It was getting later, or earlier. The hubbub of the riot scene was two blocks and another world away. Davecki looked up. A few blocks in the distance, tall buildings. These he knew, he could not leap in a single bound, so he did what came naturally. He farted.

"God you're gross," Ida said.

"Thank you."

Thusly relieved of the pressure that was on him, Davecki could actually have a rational synapse or two. *Relax.* He breathed deeply. "Ugh," he said. Now that's gross," he said whiffing himself. "If that yuppie were here he would probably pass out."

"Let's walk," Ida suggested.

They took off toward downtown. As they walked Davecki relaxed more. The stereo in his head played on. *Oh where oh where has my little dog gone?* "We've got to find the girls," Davecki said.

"And the girls would be..."

"My daughter Bethany and my partner Bubba."

"Your partner Bubba? Bubba is a girl?"

"Sure. When you meet her, you'll understand right away."

"I'm assuming the cover girl from the club is the partner and the Midwestern wholesome type who whanged Crandal was the daughter."

Davecki looked at Ida. She was a sight. Her freakish makeup looked like a nineties version of some Van Gogh wannabe's palate. The day-glow colors and neon hues were smeared around and blended in such a way that the

Burn Baby Burn

combination would make just about anyone want to cut off their ear. Davecki stared.

Ida looked at him.

Muteness clamped his tongue like a C-clamp on a gluing table.

Ida sighed. "The bar stupid. You spilled your drink on me while your lady friends were being hit upon by every sexual adventurer in the joint."

"Oh yeah. That." Davecki sniffed. "Whew. I feel better now." The stereo in his head switched songs. Another from his youth played. *Oh I went down south to smell my self singing polly-wolly-doodle-all-the-dayyyyy.* He raised his arm, tucked his nose in and sniffed.

"What the hell are you doing?" Ida said, moving away from her Newfoundland friend.

"Ever see the movie Papillon?"

"What?" Ida said, stepping yet further away. "You freaking out on me or something?"

Davecki looked at her. Through the makeup he saw genuine fright on the lady's face. He realized it would be foolish to reveal the magnitude of his dissociative thinking. Why panic the only friend he had right now? "Forget it. I tend to digress sometimes."

"Stay on task Davy," Ida said.

He took a few steps and breathed deeply. "Okay. I've..."

She looked at him with a sharp, mean glance.

"Okay. We've got to find the girls. Maybe they went to Bethie's apartment. We can get a cab and get the car and go see if they're there."

"Where?"

"The Mall of America parking lot."

Mike Savage

"The girls are at the Mall of America parking lot?"

Davecki shook his head. "Nooooo. The car is at the Mall of America parking lot. The girls are probably at the apartment. We get the car and go to the apartment and then we..."

"What?"

Davecki stopped. "I don't know. I just realized I don't have a plan anymore. It all went to hell when Crandal offered me money for Beth and I overreacted."

"For real?"

"Well shit yes!" Davecki said too loud. "A fucking police officer just can't go around smashing in the faces of John Q. Public."

Ida, who had edged closer to Davecki stepped away again, "John Q. Public?"

"Oh come on Ida. Quit doing what Bubba always does."

"And that would beeee?"

"Bugging me because I talk funny."

"Well quit talking funny."

"Well quit being critical."

"Well excuse me all to hell."

"You're excused."

They stopped walking. They were on the corner of some dingy street and some lowly avenue in the middle of the Midwest's most unusual city. The Twin Cities was a glorified farmer's market. The largest privately held corporation in the world, Cargill, had made the city into its private sales center for the grains of the Dakota Plateaus. Some guys from Two Harbors, Minnesota made the Twin Towns famous for tape, the sticky kind, not the musical kind made by Artists Formerly Known As Tal-

Burn Baby Burn

ented but Self Involved. And there were those loopy Canadian brothers who had whimsically destroyed the finest outdoor baseball/football facility on the continent and replaced it with an oversized shopping cart. Minneapolis and St. Paul were unlike every other megalopolis in the world in that they still held dear the communal consciousness that the rich were not busy destroying the culture and aggrandizing themselves and their lucky sperm club children.

For all the desperate clinging illusions, *THE CITIES*, really, had very few good places to eat at four in the morning. Davecki looked around. "I'm hungry. Let's eat. I gotta get something to eat. Then you can tell me The Rest of the Story."

"Mikey's Grill is open," Ida said.

"How far?"

"Just a couple of blocks. We can walk it."

"Let's go. Which way?"

Ida started walking east. Davecki followed. "I wonder where the hell the girls are?" he said to Ida, the last remaining Dutch Elm tree in the metro area and no one in particular.

Mike Savage

22

It seems obvious to me by now that people got no respect for Superior. After all, I mean, geeze, the whole damn town is going up in smoke. It's a regular weenie roast here and it's all because some people can't control themselves and their infantile urges. What the hell do they think this is? Some kind of free-lance urban renewal project or something?

—Bubba Carlstrom, Fire Marshall

Burn Baby Burn

Inscrutable Dave Davecki fiddled in Murderapolis while Jerome burned...Sundquist Hall to the ground. Jerome Frankie Sutter was a wild card in the Superior arson investigation. Not nearly as tangential as the mystery Duluth videotaper, but, nonetheless, a wild card that screwed up the logical investigation in a way that gave anal retentive type-A personalities the psychic runs.

Sutter set fires that confused the investigation. He'd come to town from Texas, yanked forcibly from the bosom of his dysfunction by parents Edna and Edgar. Edgar was transferred to the City of Rust and Despair by the Burlington Northern Railroad. Edna hated Superior with the white hot fury of a spurned Texas beauty pageant queen. Luckily there were no Superior cheerleader moms worth murdering. Always the oedipal son, Jerome assimilated Mommy's emotional heat and turned it into actual flames by assigning various degrees of inflammability to items of Wisconsin real property.

Like, for instance, the neighbor's garbage can. Garbage in Superior is serious business. Former Mayor Bruce Hagin, besides selling out the bird sanctuary of Barker's Island to monied real estate interests, dramatically overhauled the Sanitation Department's everyday existence. Out were the ugly steel garbage cans and the three-man crews necessary for efficient waste removal. In were new high volume wheeled "units" that required only one man and one truck. Fortunately for Jerome, the new units were flammable.

Another stroke of good fortune blessed Jerome in that the neighbor across the alley had been a Jar Head in Vietnam. Definitely psycho. Right up there with being a door

Mike Savage

gunner in a Huey. One morning, between his hits of Zoloft and pulls from his ever present bottle of Jamisons sweetened with Nytol, Jar Head Norman insulted Edna Sutter.

She was placing her neatly tied Glad Bag in Mayor Hagen's brown vinyl bin as Mr. Rehash the Past pushed his container to the alley. "Nice ass," Norman the Former Grunt cat-called.

Edna stomped back to her kitchen. Safe behind the newly installed bay window from Andco Vinyl Windows she glared at the lecherous Vet's-Clinic-regular and said, "The NERVE of that SOB. Why I never! I have half a mind to report him to the Center Against Sexual and Domestic Abuse!" Edna raved.

Twelve-year-old Jerome barely looked up from his bowl of Fruit Loops.

The next Thursday evening Psycho Neighbor wheeled his garbage can to the alley's edge. Perhaps he was hoping to catch a glimpse of Edna in evening attire instead of the powder blue robe of the week before. Only Jerome noted the change in the evil neighbor's routine. Around midnight the boy siphoned a quart of gasoline from the tank of Edgar's brand new eight horsepower Toro snowblower. This he dumped into Norman's garbage can. Then the fire freak sat on his haunches and held a flaming Burlington Northern flare to the bottom of the garbage can. It was poetic justice. Jerome had seen pictures of the Viet Cong squatting the same way. It was a blow struck in the name of psychic warfare. The flame thrower, stolen from the store of Burlington Northern stock Edgar had stolen from the railroad, melted a hole in the bottom of Mayor Hagen's pride and joy.

Talk about your Molotov Cocktails! When the sixty

Burn Baby Burn

gallon can of high density air/fuel mixture blew, it not only knocked Jerome thirty feet and rendered him unconscious, it summoned over one hundred neighbors from a ten block radius. The explosion and fire that resulted had several additional salubrious effects. Jerome's state of relaxation enabled Fire Chief C.J. Swansong time to arrive on the scene, hose down the smouldering pile of melted petrochemicals AND detain the slowly awakening firebug for the police.

Additionally, the detonation drove Norman the Nut to the booby hatch for good. This, of course, after he'd dived for cover under a mattress in the basement muttering, "Come and get me ya Gooks!" It was four days before anyone missed Norman. It took crisis counselor Dr. Jay Jardyne eight hours to coax the PTSS case out of the basement.

By far the best thing that Jerome's act of maternal protection accomplished was to introduce the Sutter family to the Superior Police Department.

The Officer of the Watch was Gilbert Gronsby, the evil twin brother of the late eco-hero Thurber Gronsby. "Show's over folks," Gronsby said to the assembled neighbors. He waited at the back of the ambulance while Steve the First Responder swabbed blood from Jerome's ears and installed clean cotton balls the size of tampons in the boy's auditory canals. Gronsby lead the dazed Jerome from the back of the ambulance to the waiting squad car while Edna pleaded for mercy. "Maam, it'd be best if you called your husband and you both came down to the station to pick the boy up," Gronsby explained. On the way to the Station, Gronsby called Detective Johnny J. Johansen, newly of the Arson Squad.

Mike Savage

J.J.J. was at the station when Gronsby led the pyromaniac in. "Put him in Interview Two," Three Jay said.

"Huh?" Jerome said twisting his head from side to side trying to hear through the cotton in his ears. He looked like <u>Frankenstein's</u> <u>Muppet</u>.

"His mother's on her way," Gronsby said.

In Interview Two, after agreeing to have the meeting taped, Edna explained that her husband couldn't be present because he, "Had a coal train to Wyoming." She spoke clearly into the recorder explaining Jerome's problem. "We didn't think much of it when he started eating matches as a toddler. He would forage for them in ashtrays. One afternoon when he was six I found him pouring milk into his father's large souvenir Northern Pacific ash tray. He had a spoon...said he was making cereal."

Three Jay looked at Gronsby who looked bored. Looking at Frankie, he saw that the boy appeared to be asleep. Edna plunged on, "About the same time I found a cigar box full of used and unused farmer matches and old BIC lighters under his bed."

"It was a collection," Jerome said from behind closed eyes.

J.J.J. livened up at the future convict's utterance and said, "When we want to hear from you, **I'll** ask." To Mrs. Sutter he said, "Go on."

Edna smiled. It was the smile of a woman who'd just saved fifty percent on a Yanni CD. She looked at Jerome and raised her nose in victory. "Well I said to him, 'You're collecting matches?' And then I said to him VERY seriously, 'Jerome, matches are not to be played with.'" Edna sighed. She folded her dainty hands. The slender fingers of those hands intertwined themselves like grape vines

Burn Baby Burn

growing up an arbor. "And do you think he listened?" She scowled at her son. "No. Of course not."

Edna puked Jerome's entire life history onto that tape. The business of immolating a stray cat; roasting a baby robin alive over a fire made with crumpled up Playboy center fold pages from Edgar's "den." (It was a dented travel trailer parked at the back of the Texas property). She told about the lit matches stuck through a hole in the sheet rock in the garage; the tree house going up in flames. Jerome was the <u>Best</u> <u>Little</u> <u>Firebug</u> <u>in</u> <u>Texas</u>. He brought his passion with him to Superior and shortly after detonating the garbage can, expressed his displeasure at having to live in "Siberia" by announcing that he would no longer be called Jerome. That he was now and foreverafter, FRANKIE. His next self expression was to burn down the Sutter family home. The family lost all of its earthly possessions including Muffy the kitten, the newly purchased pet, bought to appease Edna's separation anxiety.

Frankie wasn't prosecuted despite admitting to the crime. The loving parents continued to feed and clothe the ingrate, operating as they were under the child psychology of Marty Brookston's diagnosis that Frankie was clinically dystemic.

Edgar was inclined to believe that the pathetic little runt was merely, "All fucked up in ta haid." But dad, being the quintessential white middle American male, obeyed the declarations of the womenfolk in his life and kissed ass at work to get the big money trips driving TacTrains to Hibbing in order to pay for Frankie's therapy.

Poor Frankie. He suffered mightily for his sins. Twice a week he had to sit through an hour in counselor Marty

Mike Savage

Brookston's office on the second floor of the Old City Hall on the corner of Broadway and Hammond. He had to make up lurid tales of childhood sexual abuse while simultaneously concealing with furtive hands the boner he got every time he thought of torching the grand old building he sat in. At first Frankie hated Marty Brookston. But, during six years of therapy, he grew to love her. For, from the unsuspecting shrink's "reflective listening," Frankie learned all the tools of the dysfunction trade.

While the Superior Fire Department's eight units were still fighting the blaze at Sundquist Hall, Gil Gronsby was rolling his squad to the second home of the Sutter's. He asked a sleepy looking Edgar if Frankie was in. The railroad engineer yelled up the stairs, "Jerry! Get your skinny faggot ass down here! The cops want you!" Edgar exited toward the rear of the house saying, "He'll be right down."

"How 'bout we go for a ride Jerry?" Gronsby said.

"Call me Frank. Everyone calls me Frank now. Ride? Sure. Where?" Frankie asked. He was closing the door behind him.

"To UWS," Gronsby said.

They got in the car and cruised to the blaze site. Gronsby's squad was waved past the blockade at 21st and Catlin. The two of them sat silently as the accumulated wisdom of the combined liberal arts faculty of the finest university in the country was reduced to ashes. From the smoke and mayhem emerged a yellow clad fireman who held a piece of paper in his hands. It was C.J. Swansong, Chief of Fire Hall Five. He walked up to Gronsby's car and held out the half burned sheet of note paper. "Definitely arson," was all he said. He hustled back to the task at hand, extinguishing Frankie's handiwork.

Burn Baby Burn

On the half sheet of paper the <u>Remains</u> <u>of</u> <u>the</u> <u>Day</u> note said, "...uk you." on the first line. The second line, equally as obliterated by fire as the first said something like, "...essor fuck off!" Line three said, "...ve Frankie."

Gronsby grinned, "You eighteen yet Frank?"

"Huh?" was all Frankie could manage as he absently massaged his groin, transfixed as he was by the sight of the burning building.

"Looks like we've got to make another little trip downtown," Gronsby answered. "So how old are you now?" he said putting the squad in gear.

Frankie, hypnosis broken by the departure, said "Uh, seventeen."

"I think not Frank," Gronsby said, grabbing the radio mike. "It's too bad Davecki's out of town." He spoke into the microphone, "Squad 54..."

"Go ahead fifty-four."

"One to transport. ETA HQ three minutes."

"Roger fifty-four. Any instructions?"

"Yeah. Call the parents...Jerome Frank Sutter, 221 Likeyawanta St. Inform them of custody."

"Roger fifty-four"

After six years, Frankie was back in Interview-2. Absolutely nothing had changed. Not even the dust. As before, Frankie formulated his future and fidgeted. Even the dust was bored for it knew the story that was about to unfold. It, and similar sanctimonious sojourns into the realm of creative nonfiction, had been repeated endless times in Interview-2.

Gronsby sat hunched over with his forearms on the edge of the vinyl topped table.

"The whole problem is that I'm a clinically dystemic

Mike Savage

victim of post traumatic stress who is unable to fully discern the true meaning of the cause and effect relationship between my choices and their consequences," Frankie explained.

"Right," Gronsby said. He eyed the shut door. He raised his eyes and moved not a large muscle group. His thin lips were white, "The whole problem is I can't pistol whip you to within an inch of your worthless life you useless little firebug.

Frankie smiled thinly, "It's really a matter of sufficiently exploring the appropriateness and inappropriateness of expressing long repressed trauma and anxiety."

Gronsby sighed. "It's really a matter of just cutting your nuts off."

Frankie started shaking like one of Gordon Lightfoot's maple leafs in a <u>Gale</u> <u>of</u> <u>November</u>.

The juvenile was remanded to the custody of his parents. By the time Gronsby and the Arson Investigation Department (the AIDs Gang) put the story together, Jerome Frank Sutter had vanished from the face of Superior. His parents repeatedly avowed they knew nothing of his whereabouts.

As Nero as anyone in the AIDs Gang could figure, the new "Frank" had recently outted himself and fallen in love with one of the college's esteemed faculty. The note was shown to the one person in Sundquist Hall who knew exactly what everyone was doing, when, where and how. Queenie Bea had been the Reigning Secretary of Sundquist for longer than dirt. She was the undisputed heavyweight champion of power politics on the entire staff of UW-Superior. Upon examining the evidentiary note, Queenie said, "I see the author has demonstrated the typi-

Burn Baby Burn

cal exhilarating command of the English language possessed by the majority of riff-raff we call students here." Queenie told the AIDs guys to talk to Professor Volvo, adding that the guy was, "Pretty much an art fag anyway."

Upon seeing the note, Professor Art Fag said, "Yeah. Frank. He wrote a story that had a lot of potential. I gave him an "A" at first, but then I found out he didn't even know when he was using bad grammar so I changed the grade to an F. I guess he didn't like that."

"Apparently not," John J. Johansen, who was heading the investigation in Davecki's absence, said.

At the UWS Snackbar in the J. Renee Dildo Student Center, a fag cook told the investigators that Jerry didn't like it when the Professor in question flirted with him after class. Everyone on the AIDs Squad agreed that it was pretty much The Wyoming Solution with a Superior twist. All the evidence was entered into the registry and stored in the evidence locker after which the entire staff of the Arson Investigation Department went to the Anchor Bar and prayed for the soon return from Murderapolis of their heroes, Detective Dave Davecki and State Fire Marshal Bubba Carlstrom.

Of course they had no idea that Detective Dave was incarcerated in the back booth of Mikey's Grill with the ugly hooker Ida "Mattsen" Hoe. This fact didn't bother Davecki because he was learning all about the lurid lusts of Match Crandal and his fire cult groupies.

Mike Savage

23

In taking revenge, a man is but even with his enemy; but in passing it over, he is superior.

— Francis Bacon, "Of Revenge," Essays (1625)

Burn Baby Burn

Every big city has at least one. A funky place to eat that is small and smokey and sensible. In the middle of the downtown skyscrapers a little diner squats. Not the same as the village smithy's famed establishment, but, Mikey's Grill is, nevertheless, a Twin Cities institution. It's an old Pullman Car that seems to have been left behind by railroad empire builder James J. Hill. It sits on the corner downtown and attracts the most diverse and interesting customers The Twin Cities has to offer.

It offered Davecki a chance to wash the blood off his face and clean up after a fashion. He'd bought a bottle of Ibuprofen and eaten eight caplets. The Montagues he left alone. Thanks to the pain killer, Davecki was able to eat french fries. Most people wouldn't eat with a smashed up face. Not Dave Davecki. He'd learned to disregard physical pain as a young boy and could do it if necessary now that he was an adult. Plus he had an instinct that he was going to need the extra fuel before Ida Hoe was done with him, before this Match Crandal thing was over.

As he stuck a long greasy fry into his mouth, he found it odd to be at the diner. Chewing with a stiff face, he felt he belonged in a small country tavern that served a delicious fish fry on Friday nights. Had he known Jerome Frank Sutter was burning down a building in Superior, he might have been less willing to sit with Ida and feel uncomfortable. Had he known that catching Match Crandal wouldn't put an end to the arsons in Superior once and for all, he might have just called a cab, got in the Caprice, fetched Bubba, kissed Bethany good-bye and returned to Superior. He might have retired from the police force and retreated to his ore dock home there, to open a one of a kind drag-strip-in-the-sky where the victors launched their speeding vehicles into Allouez Bay to the delight of ESPN viewers everywhere.

But, none of these endearing fantasies would come true for Alphonse "Dave" Davecki because he still felt he could make a difference in Superior, in the world and in the realm of justice. Therefore, he listened to Ida Mattsen's story. She told it well:

"Match Crandal's father made a bunch of money selling fire extinguishers to people whose buildings had recently burned down. He also made a big impression on his son by beating him regularly for masturbating," Ida said.

"How do you know all this Ida?" Davecki stuck a long greasy french fry in his mouth.

"I know everything there is to know about that pecker head," Ida answered. "I been stalking the bastard for four years, ever since he killed Myrna. I'm here to tell you, I know more about Match Crandal than his Momma did. God rest her soul."

"Alright. Alright. I believe you. You know everything I need to know," Davecki said. *Accept nothing. Believe no one*, Davecki reminded himself.

"Crandal is the Grand Visor or something like that. He's the high mucky-muck of a bunch of fire worshippers who have monthly orgies and meetings where they all talk about the fires they've set and the damage they've done. They get credit for this and that. The more damage they do, the more credit. Human life? Shit man. That don't mean nothing to them. They all get together and count up their burns and pat one another on the back. It's worse than a bunch of little boys comparing their dicks."

Burn Baby Burn

There were a man and a woman in the booth across the narrow aisle from Ida and Davecki. The woman glared at Ida with a cross expression. "Mind your own business bitch!" Ida growled.

The woman harumphed.

The man snickered.

Davecki smiled.

The woman got up and left.

The man watched her go and then shrugged his shoulders. He then slid out of the booth and tagged along after his departing date.

"Pussy," Ida bitched.

"Which one?" Davecki asked.

"Both of 'em," Ida replied.

"Okay. So, you know so much about Crandal's business, answer me this. Is there any hard evidence around that I can use to convict him of arson or murder. Anything that will put him in prison for the rest of his life?"

"Prison ain't good enough for him."

"Maybe it's the best place for him. Maybe he deserves to become some big mutha's wife."

"That'd be too good for him. He needs to die," Ida sneered.

"I've read somewhere that the worst punishment a man can suffer is to be put in a cell with nothing but mirrors for walls."

"That's crap. I want him dead."

"I get the picture. You've made it abundantly clear. The only trouble is, I'm not your man. I'm not going to help you. Are you willing to help me put him in jail? If you're not then this conversation is over. It's been nice getting to know you and I've gotta get going."

Mike Savage

Ida looked at Davecki. "Bastard."

"Thank you."

She looked down. Below her ungodly face, a plate of eggs, hash browns, green peppers and pancakes were all smashed together. Eggs O'Brien the menu called it. *Ida Hoe look-a-like*, Davecki thought. Ida sat for a long time. *Thinking* Davecki thought. Then he realized she was doing something else. He saw that there were colored drops of water splashing onto the mangled mess of food. "What the?" he said.

Ida looked up. She was crying.

Big tears flowed out of her eyes, gathered pigment from the fire make-up on her skin and charged down her cheeks inflamed with shame of being tainted, being changed from pure tear into something contaminated by the world of gaudy cosmetics. "Okay. I'll settle for putting the bastard behind bars forever. What do you want?"

Davecki smiled. He felt bad about smiling in the face of such a face.

"What you grinning at asshole?"

"I'm happy you're helping."

"Big help you are. You don't deserve it. If I didn't want to get him so bad, I'd be outta here."

"Thanks." Davecki ate another fry. "I need something that proves Crandal burned down the Tower Building and murdered an innocent karaoke singer.

"Would a videotape do?"

"Depends."

"On what?"

"On whether or not it shows Crandal directly setting the fire or confessing to the fire."

"They tape all their meetings. I've seen some. They're

Burn Baby Burn

always getting up and standing in the Circle of Flame and telling the details of their burns."

"Can we get one with Crandal on it? Can we get any of those tapes. If we could get those tapes we would probably be able to arrest the whole bunch of em and fry 'em all."

"Fry em? I thought there was no way we could kill Crandal."

"Figure of speech my dear."

"My dear?"

"Figure of speech Ida."

"Shit."

"Sorry."

"For a second there I was getting my hopes up."

"Sorry. But I'd be willing to introduce you to Hjelmer Hjarvis."

"Sounds like a weirdo."

"True. But you'd like him."

"We'll see."

"Now. About those tapes."

"I could probably have some by this afternoon, if my luck holds."

"I can hardly wait."

Mike Savage

24

Rome fiddled while Nero burned.

> **— Lucretius Luc Longley,
> dyslexic biographer of Emporer Nero and
> ancestral sire of many generations of
> Chicago basketball stars.**

Burn Baby Burn

Liking was what it was all about. Bubba liked Todd. Todd liked Bubba. Bethany didn't want to be where she was. Bethany, Bubba and Todd were in Todd's police cruiser. They were driving around downtown looking for Alphonse "Dave" Davecki and the ugly hooker Ida Hoe. Bethany was sick of listening to the two cops talk. It was like listening in on a junior high kid asking his dream girl out.

"So you're a Pisces huh?" Larson said.

"Oh yes. I'm very Picean." Giggle, giggle.

"Gag me with a spoon," Bethany said under her breath. She was sure they wouldn't hear her, ensconced as she was in the back seat, far away and out of sight. *Next thing she'll be asking if she can turn on the siren. YUK.*

"Me, I'm a Leo," Larson said.

"Excuse me," Bethany said. "But, could we be looking for my father here instead of all this flirting? Why don't you just make a date and then we can find my father."

Larson looked in the rear view mirror. The hair on his head was dusky blonde. His face was wide Swede as opposed to the narrow Norwegian that differentiated the two Nordic types that overpopulated Minnesota. "Uh. Sorry," he said. His blue eyes looked concerned. "He can't be that far away. We'll find him."

"Maybe he took the limo," Carlstrom said. Her voice was icy.

"Daddy wouldn't ditch us like that. Besides, he was hurt," Bethany said. She looked out the window.

Carlstrom's voice was softer when she said, "You're right about that. Dave wouldn't just ditch us. Maybe that beating he took knocked him senseless or something. I

Mike Savage

can tell you he sure wasn't lured away by that woman."

"Which woman?" Larson asked.

"She was a real weirdo. Face all painted up like flames," Bethany answered.

"Short and ugly as sin?" Larson asked.

Both Carlstrom and Bethany were silent for too long.

"I mean. Geeze. I mean, it's not as if I'm being insulting or anything. I was just thinking it might be Ida Mattsen. If it is, it isn't that big a deal because she calls herself The Ugly Hooker.

"That's probably her," Carlstrom said, breaking the womanly coalition.

"You know her?" Bethany asked.

"Ida's been around for at least ten years. She's been after Match Crandal ever since he killed her sister. It all happened shortly before I came on the force. But, she's sort of an institution down here."

"How's that?" Carlstrom asked.

Larson turned his royal blue Crown Victoria, blew, down Hennypenny Avenue, and drove past an old Stately Theatre. "Everybody on the force, at least I think just about everyone, wishes she would either get the goods on Crandal or wipe him out herself. Me? I don't think she could ever kill him or that she even wants to get him caught."

"Why's that?" Carlstrom asked.

"Well, I don't think she could kill him because it would make her the same as him. And, I don't think she could actually get him caught because then she'd have no more reason to live."

"And this person is with my father?"

"That's what Officer Copp said. Said he saw them

Burn Baby Burn

sneaking off into the crowd when Wino Wilder died."

"I don't like the feeling I'm having," Bethany said.

"Relax. Your dad can take care of himself," Carlstrom said.

The blue boat from Ford Motor Company cruised slowly along the most storied thoroughfare in the history of Minneapolis. Its occupants scanned the sidewalks that were, for the most part deserted. A lightening in the sky beyond St. Paul hinted at something they would all realize soon, they'd been up all night. Dawn was coming.

"What's so difficult about putting Crandal behind bars?" Carlstrom asked.

"His mother owns half the city. His father had enough money to pass on buying the North Stars, the Twins AND the Vikings. Reportedly she said professional sports were the ruination of the country. Anyway, Crandal's rich and has spent the last thirty-five years being a jet setter and all around bad boy to the point of aggravation. When he was a kid he burned down several barns on the family compound near Lake Nebagamon. Then, after flunking out of Macalaster College, he stole enough money from Mommie to open a night club. Called it The Ring of Fire. Started selling memberships. It didn't take long to figure out that he was the leader of an arsonists club. What's taken forever is getting real evidence, enough to convict him," Larson explained.

"What do you mean, real evidence?" Carlstrom asked.

"Well. Everyone who's anyone knows Crandal's a firebug. What we can never manage to prove is that he's committed crimes. We get a witness. Get someone who's been thrown out of the club or someone who has been abused too badly. Well, the whole case somehow manages to evaporate. The tape turns out to be too vague. The witness recants or vanishes. There's always plenty of information, but never enough solid fact to incontrovertibly connect Crandal to a serious crime," Larson said.

"What's this Ida Mattsen got to do with it?" Bethany chipped in from the back seat. She scooted forward and leaned over the back rest.

"Ida has basically infiltrated the cult and is a sort of pet. They seem to keep her around for their amusement. I guess she can do..." Larson stopped. "Ahem. Well. I guess there's apparently some value to having her around. She's brought us tapes and reports on the goings on at the cult meetings, but the video and the confessions have never been substantial enough to warrant even arresting Crandal.

"We hauled him for questioning a couple of times, but he's slippery. He's got great lawyers and lots of money and, truthfully, we've never been able to prove that his little group of friends is anything more than a bunch of weirdos who SEEM to be dangerous," Larson said as he turned the car around in a wide sweeping U-Turn and almost ran into a homeless man scurrying across the street. "God Damn!" he cursed and hit the power-down button on the armrest. "Sean! Stay the hell out of the middle of the street will ya!" he bellowed at the slight man dodging the fender of the Crown Vic.

"Maniac!" the homeless hobo hollered.

"That's Sean Penn. Keeps trying to get hit by tourists so he can collect on their insurance," Larson explained.

"So what do you think?" Carlstrom asked.

"About Sean?" Larson asked.

"Noooo. About Crandal. Is he a recreational arsonist or is he harmless?"

Burn Baby Burn

"He's hardly harmless. He's the penultimate dangerous rich kid who will do whatever comes to mind if he doesn't get what he wants or doesn't get his way."

"Sort of a Soup Nazi," Bethany contributed.

"Huh?" Carlstrom said.

"Huh?" Larson said.

"Well, like on <u>Seinfeld</u>. You know. The Soup Nazi? He'd throw out anyone who didn't act just the way he thought they should."

"Crandal's a lot more dangerous than that," Larson said.

"I never said he wasn't more dangerous. What I said was Crandal has the same mind set as the Soup Nazi and Adolph Hitler and these spoiled rich kids who throw hissy fits when they don't get their way."

"Hissy fits?" Carlstrom said.

"Jesus, are you two that dense?"

"You're talking just like your father. Or, worse yet, like his buddy Hjelmer," Carlstrom said.

"Hjelmer?" Larson said.

"Don't ask," Carlstrom said.

"The reason I'm talking like my father is because you're doing what he says everyone does."

"And what's that?" Larson asked.

"Listening so that you can talk instead of listening so you can hear."

"Jesus there's two of 'em," Carlstrom said.

"No. Go on. I'm interested," Larson said. He looked in the rear view mirror and smiled.

Bethany smiled back. She threw a snide glance at Carlstrom. "All I'm saying is that Crandal and Adolph Hitler are the same. They will hurt anyone and do anything no matter how atrocious if they don't get their way. You just wait and see. In thirty years all these spoiled little rich kids who got everything given to them by their stupid yuppie parents will be injecting their parents like Jack Kevorkian clones because the old folks have become an inconvenience."

"God Almighty it's just like hearing her Old Man talk!" Carlstrom said.

"Hey! I love my Dad!" Bethany said.

"Ladies," Larson lamented. "Let's drop it okay? I'm hungry. Either of you ever been to Mikey's Grill?"

Burn Baby Burn

Mike Savage

25

The laws of changeless justice bind
Oppressor and oppressed;
And, close as sin and suffering joined,
We march to Fate abreast.

— John Greenleaf Whittier, At Port Royal, 1862

Burn Baby Burn

Analysis never came easily to Davecki. Sure he'd solved hundreds of crimes. Sure he'd asked some reasonably good questions in his time. But, for the most part, he was really a bumbler. He bumbled along until the truth became so painfully self evident that he had to handcuff it before it jumped up and bit him in the ass.

Fortunately for Ida, Davecki was not firing on all cylinders thanks to the beating he'd taken. Fortunately for Ida, "Detective Dave" was really pretty much unable to figure out that he was being taken for a ride when she said, "I've got some meeting tapes back at my place you could look at. Would they be evidence enough?"

Davecki scrubbed the corners of his mouth with the brown recycled napkin. Stains of deep fat fryer grease polluted the paper. That's lubing up my colon I bet, Davecki thought. "Meeting tapes? What are those?"

"All the cult meetings are taped. From beginning to end. That way when anyone gets in the circle and tells about their fires, the certification committee can evaluate them later. See if they pass. If they can go up a level or not."

"Up a level?"

"Sure. That's what it's all about. The higher the ranking in the club, the better the sex. The better the drugs. The better business deals. How do you think The Met got torn down?"

"Huh?"

Ida looked at Davecki like he was a first grader. She looked down her nose at him. She scowled. The frown lines around her eyes compressed.

He felt ashamed.

Mike Savage

"You know, Hammering Harmon Kilebrew's home park?"

"Oh," Davecki said, faking it. THAT Met."

"You don't know shit Davecki."

"Thank you for that vote of confidence. We Superior Police always need votes of confidence to keep our morale up."

"Are you being a smart ass? Are you getting sassy with me?" Ida put her hands on the edge of the table as if to shove off and leave Davecki on his own in the big city. "Because if you are sassing me young man I'll just leave you alone now and you can figure out yourself how to capture the elusive Mr. Match Crandal."

Davecki laughed.

"You laughing at me now?" Ida said.

"Geeze Ida, lighten up. You sound like my sixth grade teacher Mrs. Beeksma."

Ida sighed. "Don't mess around with me. I'm tired. I been up all night. Just don't fool around with me."

"I've been up all night too. AND I've had my face punched in. I'm not messing with you. I'm not fooling with you and I'm not trying to be a smarty pants. I'm just interested in seeing those tapes.

"Well, I can show 'em to you but you can't ever tell where you got them," Ida said.

"Now you're sounding like the Ida I know. Now what's all this about levels and business perks?"

"We can talk about that on the way," Ida said. "Pay the bill. I'll get a cab." Ida scooted out of the booth and darted down the aisle toward the door.

Davecki shook his head. She's flaking out on me or something. Going Sybil on me or something. He stood up

Burn Baby Burn

and looked at the check. "Cheap," he muttered. He went to the cash register and paid. All along the counter in either direction, silent humans were hunched over cups of coffee, plates of eggs O'Brian O'Bustrak or the largest pancakes south of Louis' in Superior. The waitress took his money and said, "What the hell run into your face?"

"He didn't run into nothing," Ida answered for Davecki. He turned and saw she'd come in from the dawn and that a yellow taxi was standing by the curb with the door open.

"I prefer to answer for myself," Davecki said to Ida. He turned to the waitress. "I got this mug in the path of several dozen oncoming fists," he said and smiled. For the first time in hours, it wasn't that painful to grin.

"Come on Davecki. Quit flirting," Ida said, tugging him by the arm.

"Just being sociable," he defended as Ida dragged him away from the last friendly face he was going to see for a while.

Mike Savage

26

Jupiter is slow looking into his notebook, but he always looks.

— Zenobius, Sententiae (2nd Cen.)

Burn Baby Burn

Fully one minute separated the Crown Vic pulling into the parking lot at the side of Mikey's Grill and the yellow LTD cab driving away from the front door. "God I hope he's okay," Bethany said from the back seat of the police car.

In the LTD Davecki said, "You know? I think the girls are okay. I remember seeing them talking to a nice looking, young cop. Probably a detective. I should call them."

Ida said, "You got a cell phone? Most cops have cell phones these days."

"I used one all the time. But then I got these lumps on my neck and the Doc said it was radiation from the cell phone and I gave it up. I don't miss it that much. I can call from your place."

Ida wasn't listening. Staring out the window, she seemed to Davecki to be A Thousand Acres away. "Ahem. Can I call from your place?" Davecki asked.

"Huh? Oh sure. Call from my place sure."

"You all right? You okay?"

"Sure. Sure. I'm fine. I'm finer than frogs hair," Ida answered. The cab rolled onward in silence. It took them south. "Uh, I live in a kind of unusual place. I mean, when we get there. Uh, well, it ain't exactly. It don't exactly look like a condo or an apartment building or anything. It's the best I can do under the circumstances. I mean, being a hooker and all."

"I understand completely," Davecki said. "My last case? My last big case? I got some help from someone just like you. She wasn't living in the greatest place either. But it worked out."

Ida snapped a look at Davecki. "You two together? You linked up with a lady from the life?"

Mike Savage

"Naw. Nothing like that. She helped. Did the right thing is all. We're just friends."

"Huh. Uh huh," Ida said. "It figures."

"What figures?"

The cab slowed down. "It figures you wouldn't want to help her back after she helped you."

"I never knew that was the way help worked," Davecki said. He looked out the window. He was lost. One thing about the Twin Cities. The entire metro area was a maze of confused streets and avenues. *Probably laid out by some drunken Irishman*, Davecki thought as he looked up the road. All along the wide street were big buildings of brick or poured concrete or steel. Warehouses in all directions. The cab was stopped in front of a squat red-brick building.

"Eight dollars twenty cents," the cabbie said through the hole in the Lexan shield.

Bulletproof, Davecki thought. He fished his wallet from the rumpled two thousand dollar rags he was wearing and stuffed a Hamilton through the opening. "Keep it," he said and pulled the latch.

He looked around. There was not one hint of anything residential about the area. There was no traffic. About two blocks away, as best as Davecki could estimate, he heard the sounds of traffic on a freeway. *I-94?*

"Walk this way," Ida said, heading for the double doors in the building twenty yards away.

For some reason Davecki thought of Gene Wilder. "I wonder if Gene the Drunk made it?"

"Who cares? He was just a wino."

"You're acting weird Ida. You coming down or something? You seemed a lot nicer earlier."

Burn Baby Burn

Ida was pushing on a button beside the big oak double doors. "I'm just tired. I get cranky when I stay up all night. Usually I'm home asleep by now."

Davecki suddenly felt the hair on the back of his neck stand up. "I thought this WAS your home."

Ida tensed up. "It. It is," she stammered.

A buzzer hummed in the door frame and the lock on the door clicked open. "You don't have a key?" Davecki asked.

Ida grabbed the door and pulled it open. "I never carry keys," she said stepping inside.

Davecki didn't follow.

"What's the deal? You want to see the tapes or not?"

Davecki looked the building over. He stopped his roving look at Ida's face. Something in his stomach wrenched and he wanted to puke. Something in his soul reacted with shame to his revulsion. "I'm coming," he said.

Ida turned and opened a second door and walked through as Davecki stepped across the portal. He scrinched up his nose just as the big door behind him slammed shut. *Lilies!* "Shit," he said.

But it was too late. Ida was standing next to the second set of doors holding one of them wide open. Through that door, Bulky Men One and Two were squeezing.

SHIT, SHIT, SHIT. The Superior cop was silent as the two hulking-type-hogans grabbed him by the armpits and dragged him into the dungeon of fire inhabited by the dragon himself, Match Crandal.

Mike Savage

27

Flame thrower latest weapon for S. Africans

    JOHANNESBURG, South Africa — Carjackers in this crime-beleaguered country these days risk a hot reception — a driver-operated flame thrower.
    It's the latest device to join the armory of personal security weapons deployed by a nerve-wracked citizenry.

— Duluth News Tribune, Sunday, Feb 7, 1999

Burn Baby Burn

"Lucky for us your bitch took your piece," Bulky Man One said as he patted Davecki in the small of his back and all around. "Nice ass," BM One said, slapping the cop on the behind.

"Knock it off Franz," a muffled voice drifted to Davecki's ears. He was standing in a dimly lit room. Several hundred candles were burning all around the large room. The walls were lined with old theater type chairs. The backs were wooden. The seats were padded thickly with old looking embroidered cloth. All the candles were burning with large yellow flames. The walls were painted red or black. It reminded Davecki of The Hot Place. Davecki tried to place where the sound of the voice came from. The center of the room was dark. The candle light from the distant walls was too feeble to illuminate the middle of the room. The voice radiated from that darkness.

"Nice work Ida. Thanks. I owe you," the voice said.

Davecki thought, *It has to be Crandal.* He'd no more than completed his thinking when an overhead light began to glow. At first it was a dim yellow flicker. Then the wavering light solidified. It turned into a weak orb of malevolent looking amber. As the light grew in intensity, the area in front of Davecki began to lighten up. He began to see that Crandal's henchmen had brought him into a large auditorium type room the center of which held a raised dais. The stage he stood on was a foot and a half off the floor. In the center of the stage, a large mushroom shaped chair supported a man. This man's face was bandaged and puffy. The man's shoulders supported a flame red satin robe with black trim on the lapels. Curlicues of black twisted into the shapes of flames on each side of the garment. "You are going to die," the voice said. "Nobody smashes my face in and lives."

God I hope he keeps talking. He sounds like he's the talking type. God I hope so.

The light stopped growing in brightness and the man at center stage lifted his right hand.

The light switch is on the side of the chair. Maybe some sort of control panel.

The man rose from the chair and descended toward Davecki. "My dear sir. I have no idea who you are or why you tried to kill me in my own place of business. But I assure you, you will not be leaving this building until all the flesh on your bones has been roasted into itty bitty bits of charcoal."

Thank You LORD, we got a talker. Davecki felt hope. He hoped it didn't show on his face as a bit of light or lessening of stress. He hoped he could maintain his grim visage. As the man got close enough to see in the dim light Davecki saw that it was indeed Match Crandal.

"What do you have to say for yourself my good man?" Crandal asked.

"I'd say you and your buddies here," Davecki glared at Ida, "have about a minute before half the cops in Minneapolis drive one of their big vans through the front doors and take you all to prison for a very long time."

Crandal snuffed a laugh. "Ouch! God damn you!" he said wincing. He put his left hand to his face. Between the fingers a cigarette burned. Gingerly touching the big bandage over his nose, Crandal said, "I'm taking small consolation that your face looks bad as well. I'm taking greater consolation that you aren't above prevaricating to save your life. And I'm taking the greatest consolation

Burn Baby Burn

that your face and your lies are both going to become smoke."

Oh God keep talking. What am I going to do? Davecki looked at the big men beside him. They were sequoias. He was a sapling birch. Crandal hadn't stopped glaring at Davecki. Davecki hadn't flinched.

"What do you have to say for yourself?" Crandal asked.

Remember the first time you lied to your mother? She said, "Look me in the eye and tell me you didn't steal that liquor. If you do that I'll believe you," she said. Davecki looked into Crandal's puffy eyes and said, "The Lord is my shepherd. From whence cometh my help."

"GOOD GOD! He's quoting the Bible!" Crandal screeched.

That's gotta hurt, Davecki thought remembering how much pain his face had given him when he was yelling for the cops to open the paddy wagon door.

"FRANZ! HANS! Bring him!" Crandal yelled.

Sounds like he's done jawing.

Davecki felt a degree of relief. At least now he knew Bulky Men's names. Crandal pivoted with such flair that his satin robe swirled out in a graceful arc. He then proceeded to swish across the floor towards the back of the building. Franz and Hans directed Davecki after their boss. Ida followed. Davecki could hear her heels clicking on the linoleum floor. Speaking of the floor, Davecki looked down as they passed the throne. There on the floor was a circle of flame painted all around the dais. *This is the Circle of Flame Ida talked about.*

The entourage crossed the wide space between the Circle of Flame and the rear of the building. Crandal

Mike Savage

reached into a pocket on the side of his robe. Davecki saw him pull something shiny out. There was a <u>Reflection of Evil</u> on the object from the candle light along the wall. Crandal pointed the object at the wall. A click came from his hand. A whirring sound started and then a bunch of rattling. In front of Crandal, Davecki could see a garage door opening. Bright blue light flushed into the auditorium of fire cultists in stark contrast to the lurking yellow light behind them.

Davecki saw a Jaguar. *I've always wanted one of those. Looks like I'll never get one now.*

Crandal walked into the garage. Franz, Hans, Davecki and Ida followed. Crandal clicked the opener. The door started down behind them. The noise of the closing door bounced around for several seconds. In this time, Crandal repocketed the controller and stood with folded arms next to the right front fender of his Jag. When the noise stopped, he said, "I've just had the neatest gadget installed on my car. It's the new car flame thrower from South Africa." He smiled and swept his hand toward the car. It was the same motion Franz had used when inviting Davecki and Bethany from the crowd on the balcony into Crandal's open space.

Where's Bethany right now?

"You see," Crandal said, turning toward the passenger's door of the emerald green Jag. "In South Africa there are so many car jackings that people like me needed some additional protection. Guns didn't work. The thieves saw people going for their weapon and just shot the fool dead, stole the car and took it to the chop shop where the body was chopped as well."

Keep talking. Keep talking.

Burn Baby Burn

Crandal stooped to his haunches and pointed to the Jaguar emblem on the quarter panel between the door and the wheel well. "See that? Looks like the Jag emblem doesn't it. Well it is. But, if you look closely, you'll see a perfectly concealed high pressure nozzle. There's one on each side of the car."

Talk, talk, talk.

"In Johannesburg carjackers most often make their move when people are waiting for the gates to their compounds to open. They rush up and brandish a weapon..." *Ida thought that sounded infantile when I said it.* "...and either kill the driver or, in the event the driver has some sense, simply drive off with the goods."

What the hell am I going to do?

Crandal stood. "You see, this little device has a foot activated button that turns both sides of the car into <u>Fields of Fire</u> in the real sense. Under seven hundred pounds of pressure a mixture of acetylene and fuel oil is ignited which effectively engulfs any would-be carjackers in a ball of incinerating napalm. Isn't that simply wonderful!?!" Crandal said beaming widely. "Ouch!" he said. "Damn." He twirled around. "And it doesn't even hurt the paint. How about that? Isn't that something? Quite remarkable, wouldn't you say?"

Davecki wouldn't say anything.

"Oh well. Cat's got his tongue," Crandal said. He looked beyond the three men before him. "You're looking rather grim Ida. You must have figured out what we're about to witness. I have yet to see this little flame thrower in action. Wouldn't you say it's a bit of poetic justice to roast a big wienie with my new ten thousand dollar toy?"

"I gotta go," Ida said.

Mike Savage

"You're not going anywhere Ida. If you do, you'll end up like your sister," Crandal grinned.

He looked at Davecki. Then he looked at Franz. "Chain him to the engine arch and wheel it around to the side of the car. I'll get it started and," he paused, "Ida here can push the foot switch while I get to watch our friend go up in smoke. How delightful!"

"Awwww Match. I don't wanna," Ida said. "After all, he's a cop and all. I don't wanna."

Crandal's eyebrows raised. "A cop you say?"

The more he talks the longer I live. Davecki decided it was time to connect with his enemy. "I'm Detective Dave Davecki from the Superior Police. If you know what's good for you, you'll stop this now."

"Oh I know what's good for me Mr. Davecki. And I just HAVE to tell you, it is even so much better for me that you're a police officer!" Crandal looked at Franz. "Just think Franz. A cop! This should take me right to the top nationally! How grand! Now chain him and go get the video camera. I've got to submit this good natured roast to the Advancement Committee."

Say something dammit.

Franz and Hans dragged Davecki to a ten foot tall steel arch. A ten inch steel beam ran horizontally across the apex of two triangular legs made from four inch tubular steel. At the bottom of each triangle, a big six inch rubber caster allowed the device to be rolled around the shop. From the middle of the horizontal beam a chain fall hung. There was about forty feet of chain wrapped around the device all together.

"Here, use these," Crandal said, opening the door to the Jag. He bent in and came back out with four sets of

Burn Baby Burn

hand cuffs. He jangled the cuffs in his hand like a Salvation Army bell ringer. "Look familiar Ida?" Crandal said leering at the hooker.

Ida said nothing. To Davecki she looked like a deer in the headlights. *I thought she liked me*, he thought. He recalled Sparky Anderson from 314 John in Superior. *I guess not all hookers are true blue at heart.*

Crandal extended the cuffs to Franz. The Mastiff of a Man let go of Davecki and grabbed the cuffs.

NOW! Davecki thought. But the trouble was, he was thinking about it and not acting. So, instead of erupting in a fit of rage and saving himself, Davecki stood by while Franz took the manacles from Crandal and cuffed him to the uprights of the engine puller.

If you're not going to do something, at least SAY something asshole! Davecki said, "Aren't you afraid it's going to be awfully messy? I mean, roasting me to death, besides being really stupid and bringing half the cops in Wisconsin and all of the FBI down on your hide..."

God dammit, don't freeze up now.

"...well, it's going to be awfully messy isn't it?"

"You know Dave. It's sad when a pitiful loser tries to buy time for his already wretched life by talking cute. They only do that in books and movies. You're banter is really quite pathetic," Crandal said.

Franz and Hans rolled the makeshift gallows to the side of the Jaguar.

"Me on the other hand. I'm supposed to be loquacious. I'm quite capable of acquitting myself admirably in the Banter Before Death department, for, you see, my dear fellow...I'm not the one doing the dying. "As to your question about the messiness of your impending doom.

Mike Savage

Don't worry about the mess at all. It may come as a bit of a surprise to you that both Franz and Hans, before coming into my employ, used to be housekeepers for the East German Olympic swimming team. Prior to their mad dash to freedom in America one of their primary duties was cleaning up the unimaginable messes made by those back alley sex changes. Sheesh. Those silly East Germans. They'll do anything to win a swim meet."

At that, Crandal swished his hand at Davecki and walked around the front of the car. "Come along Ida." He went to the driver's door and opened it. He got inside and started the car. A low throaty rumble burbled from the back of the Jag.

Nice pipes, Davecki thought. *Funny what ya think before dying.*

Burn Baby Burn

Mike Savage

28

Revenge is a dish that should be eaten cold.

— **English Proverb**

Burn Baby Burn

As he listened to the throaty rumble of the Jaguar's exhaust, Davecki thought, *I always wanted to be governor too. I'd never insult Indians and the Irish. I'd'a made one Sunday a month no motor vehicle day. I'd'a planted sunflowers on all the highway medians. I'd'a fired one half the DNR staff. I'd'a built that personal magnetic monorail I dreamed about. I'd'a encouraged people to take one less shower a week and shared Lake Superior with our brethren in Arizona, for a price of course.*

"Ida," Davecki heard. He realized he was daydreaming his way to certain immolation. But, really —he looked at the handcuffs and chains— there was nothing he could do. *I'm in the hands of the living God.* "Ida," he heard again, "come here and let me show you the foot switch."

Davecki realized it was Crandal's voice calling to the ugly hooker. Ida walked around the front of the Jag while Franz and Hans adjusted the engine puller with him strung up like a deer hide being scraped down before tanning.

"Move it a little south," Franz said. "That way it'll cook his balls first."

For the first time since meeting him, Bulky Man Two, the mute Hans, spoke. "No it won't. It won't roast his nuggies at all. He's too tall. It'll just toast his kneecaps and his legs is all," Hans said.

Davecki was being swung around like a tether ball in a high wind. Hans ignored Franz and repositioned the Engine Puller of Death. "There," Hans said. "Now quit fucking around with it."

"Geeze. Okay. All right already," Franz said. They both stood back and looked Davecki over.

"You're toast," Hans said.

Mike Savage

They both laughed uproariously. Franz said, "I'll go get the rubber gloves and the aspirators. If there's one thing I can't stand is the smell of deep fried cop flesh. You run out to the Suburban and get the shovel so we can scoop what's left into the HazMat barrel."

Hans said, "I'm looking forward to another trip to Lake Superior. How many roasteds have we dumped up there now?"

The two steroid freaks exited the room talking. Davecki overheard Franz say, "I dunno. Forty or fifty I'd say." As they vanished through a door in the back wall of the garage area, Davecki's attention turned toward Crandal and Ida. Crandal was just standing up from giving instructions to Ida.

"My GOD you're ugly woman! Have you ever considered suicide? It would be a mercy to us all," Crandal said. He laughed like a meth crazed rock drummer from Ely who had managed to escape the hell of big time recording contracts and settle down to a life of log cabins and better chemistry through herbicide fracking. "How in god's name did the DNA in your genes ever produce someone as beautiful as Myrna is beyond me?"

Crandal laughed again and started walking around the front of the car. As he swished around the fender, a still small voice began <u>Ely</u> <u>Echoing</u> from the cabin of the luxury vehicle. With each step, the voice grew louder. By the time Crandal was midway across the front of the car, the loud voice had become a wail. It was a wail of rage. It was a wail of anger. It was a wail of decades of released hostility that seemed to be emitting itself from all the solid objects in the room. Davecki eyed the far wall behind Crandal. All across the wall were rows and rows of Snap

Burn Baby Burn

On hand tools neatly hung from shiny metal pegs. Were those tools singing? Were they the source of the wail?

Davecki knew it was Ida.

Crandal didn't know what the hell was going on. "What the hell????" he said. He stopped and cocked his head like a German Shorthair trying to get a fix on a pheasant dashing across a bramble choked ravine in Kansas.

Davecki hung around.

Crandal turned and tried to look through the tinted windshield. The wailing continued to ascend the audio scale. Soon only dogs would be able to hear it. It sounded like some <u>Soul</u> was seeking <u>Asylum</u>. As the screaming grew louder, so did the roar of the Jag's exhaust rumble. Ida was revving the engine.

Then Davecki smiled. He could feel time slowing down again. He was getting a chemical brain bath from the vision in his head. He knew what Ida was about to do. And he knew Crandal couldn't possibly see it.

Davecki was right.

Crandal stood there staring at the windshield of his car. He looked like he was a fifth grader standing at the chalk board trying to figure out what the figures two plus two on the board meant. *Just keep being mystified.*

Davecki himself had once stood in front of his fifth grade class unable to tell Mrs. Orberg that the answer was four. But he could figure out that he was no longer afraid of Crandal. That equation was solved. *What about Franz 'n' Hans*? went through his cranium.

All this thought happened as Ida punched the accelerator peddle of the Jaguar to the floorboards and pulled the exotic car's shifter into drive. Smoke erupted from the rear tires.

Mike Savage

Crandal figured it out.

Too late.

The car leapt forward like a big cat pouncing on a Dik Dik. Davecki envisioned the slender little antelope of the African plains.

Crandal put out both hands to fend off the charging tons of automotive engineering.

That's pretty stupid. But then Davecki felt sad for thinking that. He would have done the same. Just like he had been planning on twisting out of the flame thrower's way when Ida turned it on him. But, for some reason, when it was Crandal exercising futility, Davecki felt sad. *Poor fucker. His Old Man probably held his head under water when he was young*, Davecki thought as the Jaguar rammed Crandal backwards. The car pushed him about fifteen feet straight back into the wide wall of tools. There he was impaled by approximately one hundred tool hangers, some of which were long enough to stick out the front of Crandal. But they weren't long enough to rend the fabric of his fancy red robe. For the most part he looked like he had suddenly sprouted several rows of pouty little breasts with erect nipples.

The bandages flew off Crandal's face. His eyes bulged out and blood squirted from his nose. He didn't even scream.

The tires were screaming though. The car was swerving around, fishtailing like it was accelerating up Lake Avenue in Duluth during a March snowstorm. This swerving action served to grind Crandal into the wall like he was a spider being ground into the barn wall by an ancient Finnish farmer tired of being bitten. Crandal's face was twisted into a permanent contorted grimace.

Burn Baby Burn

Davecki started hollering. "IDA! IDA!! IDA!!!"

Then the car stopped roaring. It shuddered and shook like a dog shaking water off. Then it rolled lazily backwards a few feet and began to purr at idle again. Ida had shifted into neutral. There was no screaming coming from the tires or the interior.

Davecki yelled, "Ida! You've got to get me outta these cuffs before..."

Franz and Hans came running into the room. Hans had a big aluminum snow shovel in one hand. Franz held a fist full of rubber gloves in one hand and a couple of AirMatic respirators in the other. "What the!?!" Franz yelled.

"Boss!" Hans hooted.

"Son of a bitch!" Franz said, freaking out. He dropped the goods in his hands and started running toward Crandal who was still pinned to the tool wall like a Monarch under glass. Franz dashed to the right of the car. Hans took the left. The moment they got alongside the front quarter Jaguar emblems, huge billowing jets of superheated flames leapt from the sides of the car like the afterburner of an F-14 Tomcat was trying to belch the beast off the deck of the aircraft carrier Eisenhower.

Both Hans and Franz were toast now.

And all Davecki had to do was hang around waiting for the Last Judgement. Eat your heart out Franz Kafka. Al Camus never had it so good.

If I ever get to be Governor I promise not to change a thing, Davecki thought/prayed. *Except I'd return all those wolves that were "migrated" from Palo-Markham to Wisconsin in the back of those Minnesota DNR pickups in the late 1970s.*

Mike Savage

29

**If thou follow thy star,
thou canst not fail of glorious heaven**

— Dante, The Divine Comedy, (1300-21)

Burn Baby Burn

Making its way north on I-35 amongst the other fourteen million cars in the metro area, the Caprice carried a silent Davecki and Carlstrom.

Davecki was trying to remember what his favorite food was. As usual every vehicle on the slab was doing at least eighty five. A big Lincoln SUV screamed past doing at least a hundred. Billowing clouds of hydrocarbons, free from the oppressive regulatory hand of the EPA, escaped from the dual exhaust. The murky pollution nearly obscured the vanity plate. However, it could be seen. It spoke volumes saying, GOV JET SKI.

"God it feels good to be heading home. I thought this Twin Cities gig would never end," Davecki said.

State Fire Marshal Bubba Carlstrom sat in the rider's seat. She sighed. "I'd like to be heading home too. Unfortunately I have to go to Superior to get my stuff first." She sighed again. "Besides," she said, "it wasn't so bad down there."

"You like him that much?"

Carlstrom tensed visibly. "Who?"

"Don't give me that crap Bubba. Larson. You dig him don't you?"

Bubba laughed. "Yeah. He's neat. It's been a long time since I met anyone nice."

"Define nice."

"Well, I can define not nice."

"Knock yourself out," Davecki said, steering the car around the sweeping entrance ramp where 35-W met 35-E.

"Well. I've got a lot of experience meeting people through the personal ads."

"Really? I've never done that. Seems scary."

"It is. I met with a guy in Perkins once. Advertised himself as forty-ish." She chuckled lowly.

"And?"

"Turned out he was fifty-two and looking for a twenty-five year old."

"That's rich. Any others?"

"Plenty. There was the guy who advertised himself as Average Looking."

Davecki grinned. "So, how bad was it?"

"Let's just say he had UNUSUAL hair growth on his ears and nose with big tufts of black wiry hair sticking out the collar of his T-shirt."

"Wow. You get around Bubba."

"You ain't heard nothing. There was the guy that said he was fun. He was good with a remote and a six-pack of Hamms."

They laughed.

"There was the guy who said he was Good Looking."

"Yes?"

"Arrogant Bastard."

Davecki merged out of the lane for the Forest Lake Exit. "Any more?"

"Tons. But I won't bore you too badly. There was the guy who advertised himself as stable. Turned out he was an occasional stalker but never got charged."

"You're too much Bubba," Davecki said swerving to avoid a chunk of fender in the roadway.

"I once agreed to meet a guy who described himself as a poet. Turned out he once wrote on a bathroom stall."

Davecki pounded the wheel.

"Then there was the guy who said he was Emotion-

Burn Baby Burn

ally Secure. In the span of one forty-five minute lunch he popped more medication than a hopped up neurosurgeon heading into the O.R."

"You're killing me here Bubba," Davecki gasped.

Bubba looked thoughtful. She said, "Then there was that other poet. Three of his personalities were depressed. Two were paranoid. A couple were schizophrenic."

Davecki laughed and said, "Well that would make four schizos then, right?"

"I guess so," Bubba grinned. "One guy said he was open minded. All that meant was he was willing to sleep with my sister on the first date."

"You got a sister?" Davecki asked.

Bubba roared. "It's a joke Dave."

They were in a good mood. They'd come a long way from the antagonism of their early association. Bubba sat smiling. She didn't reach for her smokes. Davecki didn't feel the urge to talk just to have some sound coming out of his mouth. By Pine City, Davecki said, "Well, I guess that about solves the string of arson fires in Superior."

"Let's hope so," Bubba said.

"What's that mean?"

"It means there's no guarantee they're over. Just because Crandal's dead and eighteen fire cult members will be spending long periods of time in Club Fed, doesn't mean all the fires in Superior were set by these guys."

"Well, the videotapes show that a large majority of them were initiation rites. We can assume we didn't get all the tapes can't we? I mean, don't you think the fires are going to stop?"

Carlstrom looked at Davecki. "You really are the optimistic type aren't you?"

Mike Savage

"What's that mean?"

"What it means is I envy you," Carlstrom said. She sighed heavily again and looked out the window. A billboard advertising the Grand Casino went past on the right. "What it means is, arson is never done. It's not like you can stop the crime if you catch the arsonist. Someone will always need the insurance money. Someone will always want revenge. Someone will always sink into that certain depravity as exemplified by our friend Match Crandal and his buddies."

"That's depressing."

"Only if you let it."

"What's your cure?"

Bubba grinned. "I'm going to look for work in the Twin Cities."

"Good move."

"And you?" Bubba asked.

"Me? I never get depressed."

"Liar."

"Oh well. Maybe once in a <u>Blue</u> <u>Moon</u>."

"SOOOO?"

"So what?"

"What are you going to do when we get back?"

"Well after I give Hjelmer Ida's phone number..."

Bubba interrupted. "I think it was pretty cool of Todd to not charge her."

"Hey. She saved my life."

"So you're going to repay her by introducing her to a hermit. What are they going to do? Get married and live in a cardboard box in the Pokegema swamp?"

"There could be worse things."

"True. They could isolate themselves on the end of

Burn Baby Burn

some god awful ore dock thing. The could spend most of their time driving around and having a relationship with an outdated Mustang."

Ignoring the dig, Davecki answered, "Or they could start a new life doing something they've always wanted."

"No shit? Like what?" Carlstrom asked.

Davecki grinned. "That's for me to know and you to find out," he answered.

"You are such an infant."

"Thank you Officer Carlstrom."

And on the Caprice rolled. It sailed past old farms with fallow fields and an ever increasing number of trees. A dirty F-250 pickup truck with a diesel fuel tank in the box passed them. Glued to the inside of the rear window was a bumper sticker. It said HUG A LOGGER, YOU'LL NEVER GO BACK TO TREES.

Mike Savage

30

There's no need to hang about waiting for the Last Judgement — it takes place every day.

— Albert Camus, The Fall (1956)

Burn Baby Burn

Extremely angry was how pissed the God of Fire was. He knew what had to be done. Davecki had ruined his life. Not the open life of church and Duluth politics. The clandestine one. The one that mattered. Now that Match Crandal was dead and the fire worship services had ended, there was no place to send his video tapes. There was, in effect, no reason for living, no reason for visiting the sacramental apartment in Superior. No reason to call upon the Hades for help. There was one consolation however.

Davecki would pay.

The first moonless night in September was perfect. The heavens sealed themselves off and he could be himself. *Nobody fails when they're being themselves.*

It was easy to "borrow" his friend's boat Oscar. Oscar was an open scow with a four cylinder Gray Marine engine mounted amidships. So named because it had the same slovenly appearance as the garbage can inhabited by the Sesame Street character, Oscar was always loosely tied to a remote dock on Kilner Bay. The key was always in the ignition. Oscar was always ready for adventure or whatever came his way. Born to be Wild, Oscar was. And, on this inky night when the heavens were steely, and the moon was in it's seventh phase and Jupiter was aligned with Mars, navigating the channels could only be done by someone who was intimate with darkness.

And intimate He was. The prow of the boat nosed through the inky waters with ease. The chuga, chuga of the four cylinder Gray Marine seemed serene. He stood at the helm ramrod straight. If his face could have been seen in the total blackness, it would have been revealed that his eyes were closed. The guidance he was receiving came to his black soul from the filthy evil of the darkness below. Hell was his only comfort now.

Davecki had taken away his earthly solace. He was allowing the evil bowels of the earth to console him and lead him across the dark waters beneath the High Bridge, past Peavey elevator, beyond Barker's Island. Little Oscar motored along through the blackness, the perfect vessel for such a mission. Innocent and obedient. Docile and stable. Capable of conveying justice or injustice with equanimity.

The scow was also perfect for hauling the twelve five-gallon cans of fuel oil that rested on the oak decking. An evidence trail didn't matter now. All that mattered was pay-back. Subtlety mattered not. Gone was the rationale for stealth. Gone was the motivation for ingenuity.

All that mattered was burning Davecki's prize real estate to the ground.

Navigating up to the dock was easy. The immense structure loomed out of the water like an outsized science fiction artifact on <u>Dune</u>. He didn't even tie Oscar up. The stubby scow lounged comfortably beside the massive concrete piers the dock was built on. First, the God of Fire ran to the parking lot and threw down the "gauntlet." The plastic case rattled as it hit the blacktop. Then he ran back along the massive piers, jumped into Oscar's open hull. He leaned low and stuck his hand into the viscous bilge water. After a few seconds of sloshing around he found the seacock and opened it. Inky bay water started rising inside Oscar's hull. In a few minutes <u>The</u> <u>Little</u> <u>Boat</u> <u>that</u> <u>Could</u> would be on the bottom. He rushed to off load the cans.

Ah fuel oil. The nectar of the gods! He loved the smell

Burn Baby Burn

of it, the slippery feel of it. He recalled his beloved wife in heat. And the BTUs! Ooooh, his groin felt good.

Heaving the heavy cans around and hauling them up the many-stepped stairs, he was tireless. He grinned as he sloshed. He whistled while he worked. He recalled those happy moments in his youth while playing with fire. He chuckled with satisfaction recalling the time he was supposed to treat the dog's ears for mites. He used gasoline instead of the medicine. *Boy did that dog run! It looked cool tearing across the lawn with flames shooting out of its ears.*

He had all the time in the world. He knew Davecki was at the Belgian Club across the slough enjoying the Hjelmer Hjarvis/Ida Mattsen wedding dance. The God of Fire was happy as he trotted up and down the entire length of the dock sloshing the combustible liquid on all the main timbers. *Why Davecki never removed the access stairway at the bay end of the dock, I'll never know.* It took an hour to empty all the cans. In the end, the deck, the timbers, Davecki's trailer, his Harley in the storage shed...it was all primed for burning.

This is going to be the biggest blaze in the history of Superior. Bigger than Elevator M. It'll be more memorable than the Peshtigo fire. It will certainly be more spectacular than the piddly fizzle that Mrs. O'Leary's cow ignited. And the fires in San Francisco after the earthquake? PALTRY!

All that remained was the ignition. He got down on his knees. From his pocket he pulled the flame cloth with the late Match Crandal's likeness screened on in smoky black ink. He spread the cloth out evenly on the massive timbers that formed the upper deck of the ore dock. Fuel oil started soaking the cloth, darkening Crandal's image. He looked up. The door of Davecki's Holiday Rambler was a foot away. He looked further up and saw, not the stars as any normal person would see, but the canopy of steely heaven isolating God from his wretched soul.

And he opened his ugly mouth and the howl of a predatious lupus on the hunt thrust itself out of that maw like a black snake searching for the apex of heaven. It was a long tortured wail of bereavement that trailed from his throat as if wolf were on an isolated tundra island crying, crying, crying. Signaling for compatriots to come and join him.

He was howling for comfort that would never come.

After his agonizing wail ended, he bent forward and placed his hands on the rough timbers. He lowered his face to the Flame Cloth and kissed the now saturated image of Match Crandal. He pressed his lips hard against the rag and smeared the copious fuel oil around and around like he was devouring the returned kisses of a sensuous lover. His fervor grew. He licked the rag and inhaled the fumes. His back arched and his eyes bulged. He wanted Match Crandal to be alive. He wanted this to be recorded on video for the entire clan's pleasure.

But it was never to be. The clan was in jail. *CRANDAL IS DEAD!!* The pain of this realization was so great, it felt like a Mack truck was inside his chest roaring around, wanting to escape the confines of his beastly heart. The grisly agony surged up his throat. His bulging neck pulsated with the seismic shocks of withering despair. The back of his mouth expanded like a giant subterranean cavern as the black fire of hatred surged forward. He parted his lips. He bared his fangs like a striking snake.

Burn Baby Burn

The pure evil within him puked out of his mouth and nose like projectile vomiting.

"Arrrrrrrrrrrg!" he screamed. Flames surged out.

The Flame Cloth burst into red hot ignition instantly, Match Crandal's image immolated for all time. The God of Fire reared back on his haunches spewing flame from his mouth and nose like a fireman's hose sprays water. The insane flames of hatred and evil engulfed Davecki's Holiday Rambler like it was a paper toy. The aluminum sides of the travel trailer started melting instantly. The metal looked like rain water sheeting down a plate glass window in a thunderstorm.

The primal scream continued as the God of Fire reared backward. He twisted away from the pain in his thighs and rolled in contorted convulsions as the fire spewed from his eyes and ears. The flames ignited fuel oil in every direction. When the breath of fire subsided from his lips, INFERNO took over. It roared. It screeched. It shrieked. The flames were alive. Each became a separate demon released from the torrid chest of the evil monster from Duluth who'd come to Superior to destroy the serene lifestyle of his new arch enemy.

He'd considered killing Davecki outright. But that wouldn't do. Now that Crandal was gone, he had to have something to live for. Killing the cop would simply deny the evil guy the pleasure of having an emotional focus for his demented psyche.

That big, tough, evil monster grew weary. He curled into a fetal position as the blaze grew in strength. The conflagration around him didn't singe his hair. His clothes didn't burn. He sucked his thumb. His flesh didn't wither from the heat. That was one of the primary benefits of

Mike Savage

being God of Fire. He was unflammable. Being immune to the flames also had the salutary effect of making him serene in his insanity. Pretty decent accomplishments for a thumb sucker from Duluth.

After a few moments of nursing on his own digit, his eyes popped open. He came awake. He pulled the thumb from his charred mouth and spit out a spray of charcoal. He coughed and looked around. There were flames everywhere. He smiled. He stood up and swished at the front of his clothes like he was straightening out after an afternoon nap. He spread his arms and twirled around like Michelle Kwan at the Olympics. *Ah glorious fire! It's better than a good hot shower after a week in the Boundary Waters!*

He looked about him. Everything was burning. *This is MOST satisfactory.* He rubbed his nose. Bits of black coal-like material fell into his hand like sand being poured from a shoe. He turned and walked to the end of the ore dock. As he left the engulfment of the flames, he shivered. The September air felt like he'd walked from a comfy house in January into fifty below. Out of the flames now, he could hear sirens in the distance. He put his toes to the edge of the dock. He looked down. It was one hundred and sixty five feet to the surface of the water. He smiled. It didn't matter. He bent his knees and launched himself <u>Into</u> <u>Thin</u> <u>Air</u>.

It was a long languorous swan dive that looked like it belonged to a Mexican cliff diver in Aky Poo Poo. The water didn't splash so much as it opened up to receive him. There was no sound. There were no waves. It was like an envelope flap retracted, received him, and closed without disturbance.

Burn Baby Burn

He surfaced four minutes later. Purified by the cleansing waters of Lake Superior, he swam across the channel. He waded ashore and threaded his way through the tangled bushes and undergrowth that had gathered together to try and choke the remaining life from the old lighthouse there. He ascended the dunes beyond and turned to watch. He smiled as the fire trucks gathered in the parking lot of the boat ramp. They were powerless to stop his handiwork.

He continued smiling as he turned toward the big lake. He grinned even more as he waded into the surf and swam to the thirty-one foot Bertram tugging at the end of it's sea anchor two hundred yards off shore. By noon the next day he would be trolling for forty pound lake trout in the waters of Siskiwit Bay on the east side of Isle Royale. As good an alibi as any and a hell of a lot of fun.

Mike Savage

31

And we know that God causes all things to work together for good to those who love God, to those who are called according to His purpose.

— Romans 8:28, the Bible

Burn Baby Burn

Reading a magazine article about capturing eagles by baiting them with dead fish, Starr Woman looked up. The September sky was pale blue. A warm southerly wind of gentle demeanor danced the first few red and yellow leaves across the lawn beneath the majestic balm of Gilead trees standing sentinel to the east. Ivory clouds the size of department store parking lots moved elegantly across the heavens. At her side sat the medicine sack Davecki had delivered months earlier.

She placed her magazine on the bench, lifted the bag, hefted its potentcy with her spirit. For the first time since she had received it, she felt it had lightened sufficiently to be in balance with her own power. For the first time since receiving the artifact, she knew she could open it.

Plucking at the draw strings she sighed. She could tell it would be a good gift from her sometimes dangerous brother. A smile emerged from her soul and spread across her face. Fingering the opening wider, she saw the power rising, emanating, flowing upward and into her space. At first she thought it was the aroma of lilies. But then she corrected herself and knew it to be lilacs. Her slender fingers removed the figurine within. It was an intricately carved likeness of Wapiti rendered in antler.

Starr Woman smiled even more broadly and knew the strength of the elk would be with her.

* * * * *

Fortune led Dave Davecki the way a mama duck leads her ducklings across a pond. So it was, that, as Davecki generally lucked out when solving crimes, he also got

Mike Savage

lucky in a very strange way on the night of Hjelmer and Ida's wedding.

The wedding dance was going well on all fronts. Cory the D.J. executed his famed gyrations from the stage of the Belgian Club as he played music ranging from rap to schottisches. Such are the ambiguities of culture in Superior. Let it never be said there is a dearth of diversity in our fair city. The dance floor was full of happy partners swinging one another around in a glee of motion. Hjelmer and Ida were gliding around like two teenagers glued together. Bubba and Officer Larson boogied in the corner. B.D. Callahan and his cheerful wife of thirty years shook their butays like they were in Junior High.

To Davecki, everything seemed right with the world. He was seated at a table in the corner talking instead of dancing.

"You know," Davecki said, "everything seems to be pretty all right with the world these days. Where'd you get that nice elk necklace?" Davecki asked nodding toward the carved Wapiti pendant dangling from a leather thong around Starr Woman's neck.

Starr woman smiled. Sitting across the table from him she nodded politely and said, "I found it <u>In The Heart of the Forest</u>." She laughed lightly and deflected Davecki's obvious question by quickly adding, "The only thing that would make it righter is if you'd dance with me."

"I don't dance," Davecki said.

"You do word dances all the time."

"Okay. Okay! All right already. Let's dance."

"I don't wanna."

"Now what?" Davecki said pushing his fingers through his thinning hair.

Burn Baby Burn

"It's no fun if I have to prompt you."

Davecki sighed. He looked up at Cory. The guy's two foot long black hair shimmered in the diffused light as he danced like a leaf in the wind. "Man that guy's really got the moves."

"Okay," Starr woman said.

"Huh?" Davecki said.

"Okay. I'll dance."

"What? You just said..."

"I changed my mind. Let's dance," Starr woman said. She got up and extended her hand.

Davecki rose. He was about to clasp her hand across the table when the big brown door to the dance hall burst open. There standing in all his fire regalia was Capt. Bob Swansong of the Superior Fire Department. He looked around the hall. Intensity flared from his face. He spotted Davecki and waved. It was a traffic directing cop's wave. "Get over here!" the wave said.

Davecki looked at Starr's extended hand. He looked at Captain Bob's wave. He looked back at Starr. She was watching the fireman. In fact all one hundred and fifty people were watching that wave.

"Excuse me," Davecki said.

It took eight minutes for the entire crowd, except Tommy Jr. the bartender —who would never desert his post, even for an event of such magnitude— to get their jackets, flee the building and pile into limos, cars, trucks and motorcycles. Not one of them wanted to miss seeing the blaze of the century. Everyone wanted to see Davecki's pad go up in flames.

Traffic had been blocked off way back on 30th Avenue East and as far down as 22nd Ave. East. But Davecki

Mike Savage

and Starr Woman and Hjelmer and Ida and Bubba and Officer Larson and Callahan and the little woman were permitted to pass beyond the barricades. At his first full glimpse of the disaster, Davecki's stomach felt the same way it did when the pilot of a big jet airplane cuts back on the engines shortly after taking off. There's that split second of doubt that the plane is in trouble and it is going to crash that accompanies the lurching in the guts.

Everyone got out of the limo. Everyone craned their necks skyward. The better to see the tops of the flames. The tips of the tongues flickered several hundred feet into the night sky. "WOW!" everyone said. Everyone except Davecki. He of the unsettled stomach could look upward no longer. He touched his chin to his chest and rubbed his neck. Then he bent down and, unnoticed by anyone, picked up a CD case and stuffed it inside his beloved bomber jacket. He looked around, sniffed. "Do I smell lilies?" he muttered. Nobody paid any attention to him.

"Wow!" Starr woman said looking at the fire.

"Wow!" Hjelmer said.

"Wow," Ida said.

By morning there was nothing left but twisted metal and smouldering columns of antique concrete sticking out of the Allouez Bay. All the brave firemen wandered around wearily, putting their equipment away, sitting on the running boards of their now-sooty trucks, talking into their cell phones reassuring their families back home that they were fine just fine.

"I'm tired," Davecki announced.

"You can stay at my place," Hjelmer offered.

Davecki looked at him blankly. "I'm not interested in a night in the Cardboard Hotel."

Burn Baby Burn

"It's really quite nice," Ida said.

"No doubt," Davecki said. "But not on your honeymoon night."

"Not a problem. We're staying at Nanaboujou in Grand Marais tonight and heading for Churchill, Manitoba in the morning," Hjarvis said. "It wouldn't be a bother."

"Thanks. But, no thanks," Davecki said.

"You could stay at my place for a while," Starr woman said.

"Really?"

"Sure why not? You need a place to call home while you figure out who in the world would want to burn down your palace."

"I think it's some Gangers," B.D. Callahan offered.

"Nope," Carlstrom answered. "It's a fire cult revenge thing for sure."

"Well we know one thing for sure," Davecki said smiling from ear to ear. "It certainly wasn't done for the insurance money."

"What's that mean?" Ida asked.

Davecki continued his grin, "There was no way on earth I could ever get insurance for this mess. So, now besides being homeless, I'm penniless too."

"Wow!" Larson said.

"All the more reason to find out who did this to you," Bubba said.

"Not going to happen," Davecki said. His smile gone.

"What?" everyone said simultaneously.

"I'm going to quit the Force and take up elk ranching."

"What in God's name are you babbling about Davecki," Bubba asked.

Mike Savage

Davecki smiled widely. He opened up his arms like he was the Pope blessing the crowd from his window in the Vatican. "We're all going to Julie's. I'm buying breakfast. AND I'm going to tell you all about the hottest new investment opportunity in a long time. Elk ranching for fun and profit."

"Please don't say hottest," Hjarvis said.

"Oops. Sorry," Davecki grinned.

"And I'll bet we can get in on the ground floor. Right?" Callahan said.

"Ah but of course," Davecki answered like a Grey Poupon commercial.

They all started moving toward the limo parked on U.S. 2. They were being herded by a shushing Davecki. He looked like a pioneer woman herding chickens across the lawn.

"What's this all about Dave?" Starr asked.

"You can't believe the money there is to be made in elk ranching," Davecki said. He laughed. "Plus. It's a lot of fun!"

"It's more likely there's money to be lost. A LOT of money," Bubba contributed.

"You are one weird cop," Officer Larson said, bending himself into the limo.

"Amen," Bubba said.

"Amen," B.D. said.

"Amen," everyone except Starr said.

"Thank you, thank you all. I knew I could count on your unwavering support," Davecki said.

As the crowd filed into the longest stretch limo Superior/Duluth had ever seen, Starr said, "How in the world are you going to raise elk? You don't own acre number

Burn Baby Burn

one. It's gotta take a lot of land to raise even just a few elk."

Davecki looked her in the eye. He said, "Well, I was thinking a beautiful herd of elk might look awful nice in the Town of Cloverland." He lowered his gaze and shuffled his feet like he was a schoolboy asking for a smooch.

"You're going to owe me BIG TIME Davecki," Starr said, getting into the limo.

He followed her into the crowded car and seated himself in the middle of all his dearest friends in the world. He looked at each of their faces one by one. When he was done studying them, he smiled. Then he reached inside his jacket and pulled out the CD case. He handed it to the slender, black haired driver with pierced eyebrows and said, "Would you stick this in and play it?"

The driver raised her bejeweled eyebrows and smirked. She said nothing though and she put the disc in the player.

As the car drove off the gravelly voice of Johnny Cash ground out of the speakers, "I fell in to a burning ring of fire..."

Everyone in the car stopped talking. All looked at Davecki. He started laughing hard enough to heal his stomach and everyone joined in a great guffaw.

And the car drove off. And the ore dock smouldered. And everyone went to Julie's and sat at the round table between the sun room and the cash register. Sue the waitress took their orders and told a joke about former Mayor Herb Bergson. She brought their brimming plates and everyone ate heartily of eggs and ham and toast and pancakes and milk and coffee and tea and good friendship.

Mike Savage

And everyone lived happily ever after.

Except the important man from Duluth. He was pissed when Davecki's early retirement was announced in the <u>Up</u> <u>Your's</u> <u>Newspaper</u> <u>Network</u>. Really pissed. He started making evil, maniacal plans immediately. No way was Davecki going to vanish into blissful obscurity in the country to hide behind the false security of ten foot high fences and the thundering hooves of three hundred stampeding elk running down hysterical TV reporters. Now that Crandal was dead Davecki was the only man alive worthy of the important man's devoted affection.

It's so nice to be loved.

Burn Baby Burn

Yet Another Puzzle

Want to figure out the name of the Important Man from Duluth? It has to do with the drop caps at the chapter beginnings.

Don't take the first sixteen too seriously.

Your hint is: **BRAVE FIREMEN ALL**.

Here's a couple of some additional anagrams for your enjoyment.

Evangelist = Evils agent.
Desperation = A rope ends it.
The Morse code = Here come dots.
Mother-in-law = Woman Hitler.
Snooze alarms = Alas! No more Z's.
Eleven plus two = Twelve plus one.
Princess Diana = Ascend in Paris
President Clinton of the USA = To copulate he finds interns.

The answer to the mystery anagram above is on page 58.

To order additional copies of

Burn Baby Burn

or receive a copy of the complete Savage Press catalog,

contact us at:

Phone Orders: 1-800-732-3867

Voice and Fax: (715) 394-9513

e-mail: savpress@spacestar.com

Visit online at: savpress.com

Visa or MasterCard accepted

Savage Press

Box 115, Superior, WI 54880 (715) 394-9513

Other Savage Press Books Available

In the Heart of the Forest by Diana Randolph

Appalachian Mettle by Paul Bennett

Hometown Wisconsin by Marshall J. Cook

The Year of the Buffalo, a novel of love and minor league baseball by Marshall J. Cook

Jackpine Savages by Frank Larson

Treasures from the Beginning of the World by Jeff Lewis

Stop in the Name of the Law by Alex O'Kash

Something in the Water by Mike Savage

Widow of the Waves by Bev Jamison

Dare to Kiss the Frog by van Hauen, Kastberg & Soden

Voices from the North Edge by St. Croix Writers

Gleanings from the Hillsides by E.M. Johnson

Keeper of the Town by Don Cameron

Thicker Than Water by Hazel Sangster

Mystic Bread by Mike Savage

The Lost Locomotive of the Battle-Axe by Mike Savage

Moments Beautiful Moments Bright by Brett Bartholomaus

Beyond the Mine by Peter J. Benzoni

Some Things You Never Forget by Clem Miller

Superior Catholics by Cheney and Meronek

Pathways by Mary B. Wadzinski

SoundBites by Kathy Kerchner

Treasured Thoughts by Sierra

Sailboat Log Book by Don Handy, Illus. by Gordon Slotness

Canoe & Kayaker's Floating Log Book by Don Handy

The Duluth Tour Book by Jeff Cornelius

If you haven't read the first in the series of Dave Davecki "Superior" murder mysteries be sure to order your copy of :

Something in the Water
A Superior Murder Mystery

Available at all bookstores nationwide

or contact Savage Press at:

1-800-732-3867

Voice and Fax: (715) 394-9513

e-mail: savpress@spacestar.com

Visit online at: savpress.com

Visa or MasterCard accepted

About the Author

Mike Savage was born in Ashland, Wisconsin. He grew up in Iron River, and Cornucopia, Wisconsin. He has written numerous novels and several poetry chapbooks. Following his education at the South Shore School District in Port Wing, Wisconsin, he attended the University of Wisconsin at Superior. He has sold over 1,000 articles and many more photos to such publications as: Power for Living, the Superior Evening Telegram, St. Louis Post-Dispatch, the Milwaukee Sentinel, Milwaukee Journal, St. Paul Pioneer Press-Dispatch, Alaska Business Monthly, Farmer Magazine, and many others. He became a corresponding editor for Hatton-Brown Publications of Montgomery, Alabama. In 1989 he started Savage Press which published *The Northern Reader* and a small book, *Stop in the Name of the Law*. Since then, Savage Press has published 48 books, the most recent being: *In the Heart of the Forest*, poems and pastel paintings by Drummond, Wisconsin's Diana Randolph; *Dare to Kiss the Frog* by Duluthian Arlene Soden with co-authors Finn van Hauen and Bjarne Kastberg from Denmark and *Burn Baby Burn*.